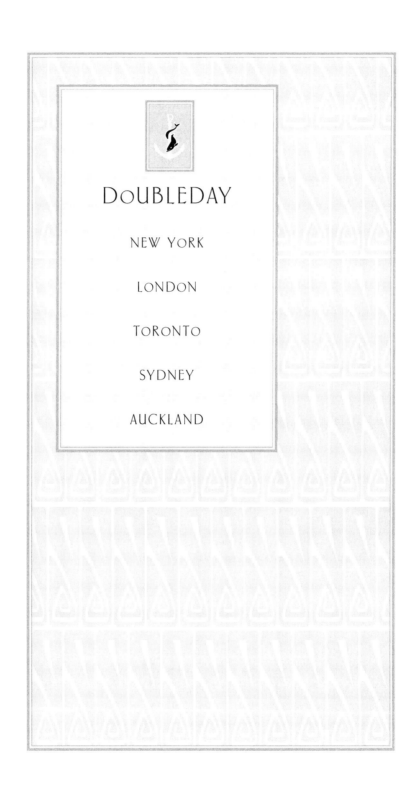

DoUBLEDAY

NEW YORK

LonDon

ToRoNTo

SYDNEY

AUCKLAND

MANoR HoUSE

PAIGE
RENSE

PUBLISHED BY DOUBLEDAY

a division of Bantam Doubleday Dell Publishing Group, Inc.
1540 Broadway, New York, New York 10036

DOUBLEDAY and the portrayal of an anchor with a dolphin
are trademarks of Doubleday, a division of
Bantam Doubleday Dell Publishing Group, Inc.

Book design by F. J. Levine

Library of Congress Cataloging-in-Publication Data
Rense, Paige.
     Manor house / Paige Rense. — 1st ed.
        p.   cm.
     I. Title.
   PS3568.E654M36   1997
813'.54—dc20   96-21174
                                            CIP

ISBN 0-385-48502-6

First Edition

To Kenneth Noland with love.

And, in loving memory,
Arthur Rense, without whom . . .

ACKNOWLEDGMENTS

Gratitude and thanks to . . .

Owen Laster, the most charming matchmaker.

Arlene Friedman, whose enthusiasm turned the light green.

Talented Bruce Tracy, this editor's editor.

Susan Dooley, whose skill made the last mile speed by.

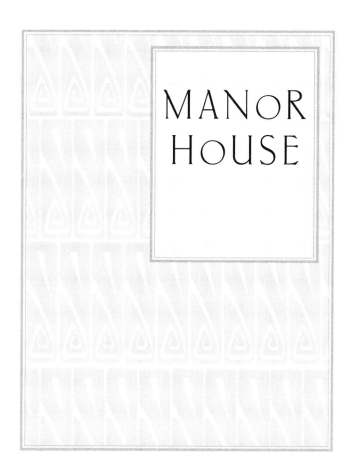

MANOR HOUSE

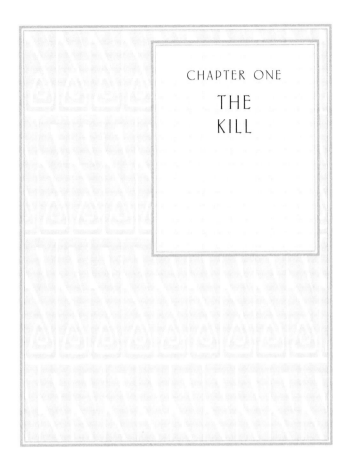

CHAPTER ONE

THE
KILL

Twenty minutes before his life ended, Beau Paxton, editor in chief of *Manor House* magazine, ordered another Gibson, straight up.

The police report later revealed that Paxton, walking a bit unsteadily, left Le Club in West Los Angeles in the heart of the decorating center at approximately 2:30 A.M. Paxton was accompanied by his friend, roommate and sometime uncle, Norton Birdwell. The two men were seen getting into a Mercedes convertible, top down, in the club's parking lot. As Paxton started the Mercedes, a man darted out from behind a neighboring car and jumped into the backseat. A witness described the man as "Black, wearing a leather motorcycle jacket. His hair was in dreadlocks and he had on sunglasses. At night. Like he thought he was famous or something!"

The same witness heard him say, "Who's the editor?" Paxton replied, "I am." The gunman shot him through the head, vaulted out of the convertible and ran to a dark sedan, idling at the curb on Melrose Avenue.

The witness was a waiter who had reluctantly agreed to take out the trash as a favor for his longtime lover, the club's chef. Because he was, of course, an actor between jobs, he gave a dramatic account of the event he had witnessed, richly embossed with layers of detail added with each telling. When it became known to him that the victim had been editor in chief of the prestigious magazine *Manor House*, his voice grew deeper in timbre, and his recital displayed dimensions hitherto unrevealed to casting directors. The dizzying thought of TV mobile units focusing their cameras on him brought forth freshets of inspiration.

In sharp contrast, Editor Paxton's "uncle," Norton Birdwell, could barely complete a sentence, so copious were his tears. His fragmented account spun into incoherence until he swore he could only remember the sound of a voice and then a shot.

It was soon learned that "Uncle Norton" was the sole beneficiary of a five-million-dollar policy insuring the life of Beau Paxton. The owners of *Manor House* had also taken out a five-million-dollar "key man" policy on the life of their editor.

Two motives. District Attorney Max Steiner looked up from the report on his desk and harrumphed to his secretary, "What the hell is this? Murder for hire in the land of chintz?"

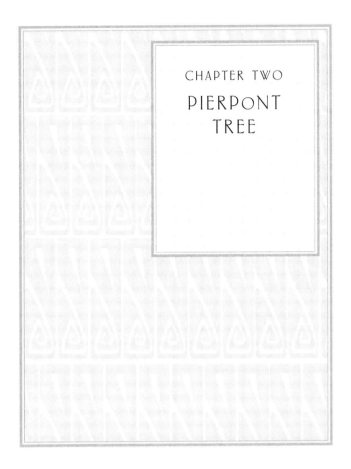

CHAPTER TWO

PIERPONT TREE

The rich may or may not be different from you and me, but they definitely have more choices. And they have historically chosen the best places for their first, second or twelfth home. They have chosen Seal Harbor in Maine, Hobe Sound in Florida, Pebble Beach in northern California.

In Southern California, some have chosen Santa Barbara. Among them were Mr. and Mrs. Pierpont Tree II, of Boston. Ponty and Helen were barely out of their teens when, on their honeymoon trip to the West Coast in the late 1920s, they fell in love with the foothills of the Santa Monica Mountains, overlooking the sea. Before leaving, they bought a thousand acres of ranch land and commissioned architect George Washington Smith to design and build a house. They had decided to make Santa Barbara their home.

George Washington Smith was the preeminent Santa Barbara architect of that era, and his assistant on the project was Lutah Maria Riggs, one of the few licensed female architects in the country. The two had just begun working out the plans for Casa Arbol when, in 1930, Smith died, and Lutah Maria Riggs became responsible for the house the Trees had commissioned.

America had moved into the Depression, and the Trees, third-generation heirs to a banking, utilities and railroad fortune, were urged to caution by the gray-faced Boston banker who handled the family money. They agreed to economize. They cut the number of bedrooms in the guest house from four to two.

Despite such restrictions, the creation of Casa Arbol was a joyous experience for Helen Tree and for Lutah Maria Riggs, who began to depart from Smith's design restraint. She enlarged windows, opening up views. She banked French doors, added closets vastly spacious for that period and, to expand the spectacular view of the ocean, built an enormous terrace paved with bricks in a herringbone pattern, partly sheltered by a roof covered with handmade pale, salmon-colored tile and, in time, by pink bougainvillea.

The terrace commanded a view of the Pacific, the afternoon glare softened by eucalyptus and sycamore trees. The lawn rolled several hundred feet down to a swimming pool, which was placed in lyrical symmetry to the house. The grounds contained Moorish arches, arbors, courtyards, secret gardens, patios, fireplaces, fountains and balconies, all the work of a man named Lockwood DeForest, who was the region's foremost landscaper.

The Trees lived happily at Casa Arbol, raising Thoroughbred horses and hosting an annual horse show at the end of the polo season in Santa Barbara. They gave a huge party after the last polo match, gathering owners of Thoroughbreds and polo ponies from East and West for a barbecue, followed by dancing in one of the barns which went on until first light.

Then, in 1941, the world changed. Pierpont Tree II went to war, serving with old classmates from Yale in the newly organized OSS.

When the war ended and he returned to Casa Arbol, he had become moody and secretive. Life at Casa Arbol might never have been the same if it hadn't been for an event that seemed miraculous to the middle-aged Trees. Long after they'd given up hope, they had a son, Pierpont Tree III.

When his parents died shortly after he'd finished college, Pier inherited it all. And it was Pier who sat now on the sheltered terrace, leaning on a table built from the sixteenth-century doors of a Spanish monastery, thinking about murder.

Several hours later he was still considering the TV news story about Beau Paxton's death and pondering the nature of those who kill when he heard Mattie's familiar footsteps coming from the direction of the kitchen. She placed a breakfast tray on the table and looked closely at Pier.

"You're having what Mama called a sinking spell."

Mattie placed a monogrammed heavy linen cloth and napkin in front of Pier, removed the silver-domed cover from the plate of scrambled eggs and crisp bacon, arranged the Georgian silver flatware, salt and pepper holders, toast rack and crystal jam pot.

"Mattie, why bother with all this? Just bring the food on a plate."

"You say that about once a month. And I always tell you the same thing. Your mother bothered. She always had my mama do breakfast this way for your father. That's the way she taught me to do it, and that's the way I'm always going to do it." Mattie sat down and poured herself a cup of coffee from the antique silver pot Mrs. Tree had purchased in London. She put her hand on Pier's. "Sure it's old-fashioned and nobody lives this way anymore, but your mother cared about traditions and she passed them on to us, so why not enjoy them? I do."

Pier looked at Mattie's round face, the color of his coffee, framed with short curly hair like that of her mother, Cecilia, who had taken care of the Tree family until she died. Now Mattie took care of Pier. "God, I hope you really do enjoy it, Mattie. I never want you to stick around because of a misguided notion that you owe it to me or the memory of our mothers."

"May I remind you, sonny, I've always lived here. This is my home, too. Your mama and your daddy each left me a potful and your money guy in Boston has been investing it for me ever since. Pier, I'm rich. Now, what's this about a guest for lunch? Who is it?"

"Not lunch, Mattie. Just drinks, later this afternoon. It's a man called Seth Rupert," said Pier. "He publishes a magazine about decorating, so he may drink spritzers or kirs or hummingbird nectar."

"Your grandmama was the onliest one to drink that."

"Getting into your Aunt Jemima role for the guests?" Pier asked, grinning at Mattie.

"Yassah. He never gonna notice me one bit, nosuh."

"Mattie, you're a damned racist. How did you get that way at UCSB? And what course are you taking now?"

"Renaissance Literature."

"Good one?"

"Professor's an asshole," said Mattie, "but he was born that way. What does this guy publish?"

"*Manor House.* Have you seen it?"

"Seen it? Racist. I might go into decorating next. I'm getting tired of the catering business."

"Thank God. Whenever someone dies around here, I'm afraid it's going to be one of your customers," said Pier, who had never been able to figure out how a cook as inept as Mattie had been able to con people into hiring her as a caterer. "That reminds me, what are we having for lunch?"

"New England boiled beef and potatoes. I'll set the small table under the trees." Mattie pushed her chair back and glared at Pier. "I know why you're out here mopin' around. You know I visited Hilary yesterday, but you haven't said a word."

Pier still said nothing, thinking of Hilary, the friend of his childhood, the one who'd written him once a week when other friends called him a traitor for interrupting college to serve in Vietnam, even though he was against the war. She was a woman who knew him as well as he knew himself.

Pier had been the center of his parents' universe and when they died, his mother first and his father less than a year later, he felt bereft. Managing the ranch, returning each evening to the emptiness of Casa Arbol, he had gravitated to Hilary for comfort and companionship. Eventually they married, a union of devoted friends, but never one of passion.

One afternoon, random violence changed their lives forever. They were driving back from a visit to a friend's horse ranch in the Santa Ynez valley, Hilary at the wheel of their convertible, Pier slumped down, napping in the passenger seat. Three drunks pulled up alongside the convertible, shouting obscenities at Hilary. One of the men threw an empty beer bottle at Pier, and then shot at the tires. He hit one. Hilary panicked, and before Pier could grab the steering wheel, their car ran into a huge rock outcropping and caught fire. The pickup truck sped past, the men laughing and waving. Hilary had been thrown from the car. Pier stumbled to her side just before the car exploded.

Hilary was in a coma and the best doctors in the country were unable to bring her out of it. The highway patrol, acting on Pier's description of the men and the truck, tried to find them and failed. Pier, with more time and more reason to care, succeeded.

Arrested and charged, the men claimed they were poor working men driving home when the "rich bitch," drunk, weaving across the road, endangered them. Pier hired a private investigator to provide the District Attorney with the evidence which convicted them.

Hilary did not come out of her coma. But Pier had found something to do with his life. He would help others find justice by any means available. Within the law, or not.

Pier put Hilary in a private hospital a few miles north of Santa Barbara, and for the first year he visited several times a week, hoping she might improve. Sometimes it seemed that she knew him. Most times not.

Pier pushed his thick, sandy hair away from his forehead and asked Mattie, "Any change?"

"No change. She never recognizes me. Stop feeling guilty. She doesn't know anyone. She's in her own little world, and she's never coming out."

"But that one doctor, Wiltz. He said there might be a chance."

"Doctors are assholes, too. There's no chance. Hilary's going to be like she is now until she dies. I'm taking care of her. You be happy with China, you hear?"

Pier turned toward the east side of the terrace. "I hear her onliest footsteps now."

Hilary had been in the hospital several years when, at a party given by an old friend, Pier met China Carlyle. He knew who she was, even though he'd never seen one of her movies. She had appeared in front of him, her titian hair swept up, her eyes a blue which changed to green as he looked down at her. Slim and tall in a strapless column of white silk pleats, she looked straight at him without the slightest hint of flirtation, took his hand and said, "You look so grim. Has the enemy stolen the Lost Ark?"

It wasn't just that China was beautiful. She was. She also had the power to effortlessly dominate a room, with a force that turned others toward her, focusing on her as a source of light.

It was no longer so effortless as it was when she had starred in movies for fifteen years, before she'd slipped herself in and out of two bad marriages and into alcohol to blur the memory of her baby daughter, who had died in infancy. When China drank enough she could convince herself it had never happened.

She could still capture a room, but now it took effort, a gathering up of energy that left her exhausted. The night she met Pier, she had felt sad and vulnerable.

The woman Pier fell in love with wasn't the one who could mesmerize a crowd. He would have walked away from that. Pier fell in love with a beautiful, intelligent woman who, like him, had been hurt.

That was ten years ago and they'd been together ever since. China retired from the screen and bought a few tree-covered acres adjoining Casa Arbol. She refused to live with Pier as long as his wife was still alive, and he did not protest. China built a clapboard cottage in the land of red tile roofs. "I grew up on Peck's Island, off the coast of Maine, and if I'm going to live in Brigadoon, it will be in a house that reminds me of my roots."

She never told Pier about the night they met. She had walked over to him because, blind without her glasses, she thought he was Harrison Ford.

China saw Pier and Mattie watching her. Pier's big frame slouched in his chair, hands clasped behind his head. She stopped, tapped a few steps and bowed. "Okay, gang. Who do I charm? To who do I do that voodoo that you know I do so well?"

"Seth Rupert, president of *Manor House* magazine. He and his twin brother own it. Their editor, Beau Paxton, was shot a couple of nights ago. An apparent robbery attempt, but the police aren't buying that. His boyfriend, one Norton Birdwell, older and a lot richer, is the suspect. He was with him at the time of the murder. The police think he hired a hit. Birdwell is the beneficiary of a five-million-dollar life insurance policy. The night before the murder, in the same bar, the two had a screaming fight. The police figure older guy thinks young fellow is going to leave him for someone else. Everyone in the bar heard Birdwell shout that he'd see Paxton dead before he'd let him go. You know that scene."

China looked at Mattie and shrugged. "Not me. When I was making movies, boy met girl and they lived happily ever after. Well, sometimes."

Mattie shrugged, too. "Now it's boy meets boy. Sometimes."

China dropped into one of the chairs and reached for the platter of Mattie's eggs and bacon. "Who'd be stupid enough to threaten to kill someone publicly, knowing they'd paid someone to do it?"

Pier shrugged. "Anger, booze."

"Just a silly, little impulse?"

A t five o'clock, China was sitting in the same chair, looking very different from the woman who had come to breakfast with her hair tied back with a piece of yarn, wearing faded blue jeans and a plaid linen shirt. For the visitor, she had become *the* China Carlyle, elegant in a pair of antique Chinese lounging pajamas, the blue silk trousers moving with her long legs, the embroidered jacket opening to reveal a chiffon camisole the color of old jade.

Pier nodded approvingly. "We'd better read him his rights. He'll take one look at you, China, and confess to anything. There's the bell." Pier turned toward Mattie, who had just placed a tray of smoked salmon on the big table. "Don't overdo your Mammy act," he called after her as she left the room.

Mattie returned, head slightly bowed, hands folded, eyes cast down. "Mr. Tree, sir, Mr. Rupert is here."

Pier crossed the terrace in a few easy strides and offered his hand. "Welcome. I'm Pierpont Tree and this is China Carlyle."

China directed a klieg light smile at Seth Rupert.

"Miss Carlyle . . ."

She interrupted with a shake of her head. "China, please. And Pier," she nodded toward the now silent man standing on her right. He watched the publisher intently.

"Before I bore you with business, let me tell you I'm your greatest fan, China. I would have *walked* up here from Los Angeles to meet you." He turned to Pier. "Several people suggested I call you about the, er, the matter at hand."

"I'm sure it's a difficult time for you," said Pier sympathetically. He paused and his tone of voice indicated a shift in subject. "Is Paxton's death going to hurt the magazine?"

"It might have once. Beau made it a point to attend every major party in the Western world and to know every society figure ever seen in the pages of *Town & Country* and *"W"*. Old rich or new rich, Beau knew them all. In the early days, it helped give us access to the editorial material we needed. Now people beg to be in *Manor House*, so Beau Paxton is little more than a figurehead, although people outside the magazine don't know that. The managing editor is the one who's really responsible for the magazine's success. It's Meg who makes the difference."

"Meg?"

"Meg Millar, the managing editor. It was her idea to jump right over the competition instead of fighting it out head-on. We charge a hundred dollars for a membership subscription, and prospective subscribers are invited to fill out an *application.* Advertisers apply."

"They *apply?*"

"Yes."

"And they go along with that?"

"Most do. They like their products showcased on sixteen-by-twenty-inch pages and eighty-pound, heavily enameled paper. And we don't let anyone, not even our own advertisers, rent our subscriber list. *Manor House* readers are not fair game for those who want to reach the rich with junk mail."

"Seth, come sit next to me and tell us more about magazines," said China. "I didn't realize I've been paying a hundred dollars a year for *Manor House.* Of course, it must be a very expensive magazine to produce."

"Very. But most of our subscribers renew year after year."

"How many subscribers are there?"

"One hundred and fifty thousand. We're not sold on newsstands at all but the magazine is in several hundred very upscale bookstores. We also do one *Manor House* book every other year with a special theme. The books sell for a hundred dollars each to subscribers who reserve a copy by paying in advance. We also place a limited number in the same bookstores which carry the magazine. Each book usually sells around fifty thousand copies. And our magazine advertising revenue is very substantial. My brother, Jonas, handles all of that. We're small publishers, but our net profit is very high. Almost unheard of. We don't have promotion and marketing departments and our circulation department is just three people, though our magazine is all over the world. We employ only about fifty full-time employees. My brother runs a tight ship. As he says, *zero slippage.*"

"Your brother, Jonas, runs the advertising end of things. And you?"

"In magazines there are two revenue streams, advertising and circulation. Jonas runs advertising, and I run circulation. We're listed as co-publishers on the masthead."

"Have you ever thought about going public, Seth? I'd certainly buy stock."

"Well now, China, you've touched a nerve. My brother wants to go public. But I say we've done fine so far, so why not continue? It's like the story about the camel that gets its nose under the tent and starts upsetting it. Seems to me it's best to just keep the camel away from the tent in the first place. I'm absolutely against it."

"But Jonas wants to?"

"Yes. Jonas is older by five minutes, and he's always had his way," said Seth, looking at China and smiling, "but not this time."

"I'm surprised no one has tried to buy the magazine outright," said China.

"They have," said Seth. "One offer was quite recent. Fred Hawkins, that somewhat shady New York investor, was determined to buy us out. We told him what we've told all the others who have made offers. Never."

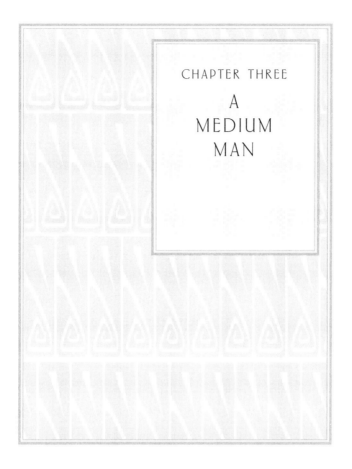

CHAPTER THREE

A
MEDIUM
MAN

China rose from the table, gave her hand to Seth Rupert and walked across the terrace and into the house. Rupert's eyes followed her, and Pier had a minute to study the man. Rupert looked like the hundreds of local TV anchors who announced the morning news in the motel rooms of America. Staring at the bland, familiar faces, travelers could feel they'd never left home. Light hair, not blond but not exactly brown, round glasses which gave

Rupert's face an owlish earnestness and hid eyes which might have been hazel or might have been gray, pale blue shirt, discreet tie, expensively tailored suit. Rupert was one of the "mediums" the police deplored. Medium height, medium weight, medium coloring.

When an eyewitness began, "He was just sort of medium . . ." even the toughest cop could be reduced to tears. Now, having coffee with Rupert under the century-old trees, Pier wondered if so medium a man might murder.

If he were guilty, why would he want to hire a private investigator? To camouflage his guilt? But that was a tricky business. Even the most inept sleuth might stumble onto something incriminating. Although, if the murder were, as the police believed, a professional hit, Rupert might feel absolute confidence that his guilt would never be discovered. Did Seth Rupert, and perhaps his twin brother, expect to pull off one of this year's perfect crimes? Murder among the rich is almost always about money. Only the poor murder for love.

"Seth, do you have any idea why anyone might want to kill your editor?"

"Not the slightest. It would be difficult to imagine anyone hating Beau. Not that he was loved by one and all, but he certainly wasn't hated enough for anyone to want him dead. You should also know we had a five-million-dollar key man life insurance policy on Beau's life. Not enough for us to do him in, if that thought occurs to anyone."

"It will occur to the police. What about Beau's personal life?"

"He was gay. Lived with Norton Birdwell, the man who was in the car the night Beau was killed. Birdwell is rich. His grandfather was a wildcatter. Drilled down in Texas with old man Hunt. Norton came to Hollywood a few years ago to produce movies with his own money. His movies flopped but he stayed on. As far as I know, he and Beau were pretty much like any married couple.

16

"Oh, there were rumors from time to time about Beau and young decorators who wanted to get their work in the magazine, but I figured they were started by people who were mad at Beau because he wouldn't publish their work."

Pier squinted up at the sun. "You mean Beau might have had his own casting couch? Be nice to me and I'll put you in the magazine?"

"It's possible." Rupert sighed and shook his head. "Several years ago there was a scandal when it came out that an editor of a society magazine had sold the cover."

"Sold the cover?" Pier looked at Seth Rupert with real curiosity. "How could that be?"

"They were doing a big feature on a city in South America and one of the leading families there wanted their daughter on the cover. They offered the editor fifty thousand dollars to make their dream come true. He did and was caught. Instead of firing him, the publishers just demoted him to contributing editor. They said his contacts were so valuable they couldn't let him go. Well, that's what Beau Paxton had in spades. Contacts."

"Your managing editor, Meg. Would she know if this talk about Beau Paxton and young decorators is true or not?"

"Probably," said Seth. "She knows everything that goes on at the magazine and in the decorating world, too. As you have probably gathered, I would like to retain you to investigate Beau Paxton's murder. Los Angeles is a big city. The police can't spare the manpower it may take, and someone should see that justice is done. We've had a lot of calls from advertisers—and some from subscribers—asking what's being done by the police, and what *we're* doing to find the killer."

"Your brother shares your views? Would my fee be paid by you two or by you or by the magazine?"

"By me. My brother believes the police can do the job. And they may," Seth conceded. "But if they can't, the trail will be cold. Do you agree?"

Pier nodded, wondering what else the brothers might disagree on. "Let me tell you about my fee. Twenty percent off the top goes to the police widows' fund. The balance, after expenses, is paid to the Hilary Tree Medical Research Foundation. I'll give you a letter of agreement, setting out the terms and fees. If you still want me to help, I'll begin right away."

"Let's not waste time. I'll read it and sign it now."

"Without your attorney looking it over?"

"I *am* an attorney. Never practiced but I handle the simple things myself."

Pier reached into the inner pocket of his blazer and placed a parchment envelope containing the agreement in front of Seth Rupert, who read it and signed with a signature surprisingly bold for a medium man.

"One more thing, Seth. This five-million-dollar life insurance policy on Beau Paxton. The police will consider that a pretty good motive. Is your company in need of funds?"

"To be succinct, no."

"Seth, you should know that if I discover that either you or your brother hired the hit on Paxton, I'll have to give the information to the D.A."

"Fair enough, Pier."

"Who inherits?"

"I don't know about Paxton's personal estate. He had *Manor House* stock, and he told me he was leaving that to Jonas and me—in equal shares. To anticipate your next question, between Jonas and myself, the surviving brother inherits. If we both die, the employees will own the magazine, with Meg Millar as the majority stockholder."

A few minutes later, as Rupert's BMW rolled down the eucalyptus-lined drive toward the great iron gates, Pier called out, without turning his head, "Alright, you two. He's gone. Let's hear it."

China's heels clicked sharply on the old bricks. Mattie came along from the direction of the kitchen. China, hair glowing golden red in the rays of the afternoon sun, began. "He's concealing something, Pier. I couldn't see his expression from where I was standing but I could hear him quite clearly. It was the tone of his voice. He didn't actually lie, but he didn't tell you everything he knows either."

Seth turned to Mattie. "How about you?"

"You said the guy who got shot is gay. So maybe this one is gay, too? Lovers' quarrel?"

China smiled as she poured herself a glass of mineral water.

"I like that, Mattie. Then Seth hires Pier, knowing a professional killer did the dirty, but no one will ever be able to track him down because he was on the next plane to Chicago while his gun was still smoking. Except, of course, he threw it in the ocean on his way to the airport. There. Case solved."

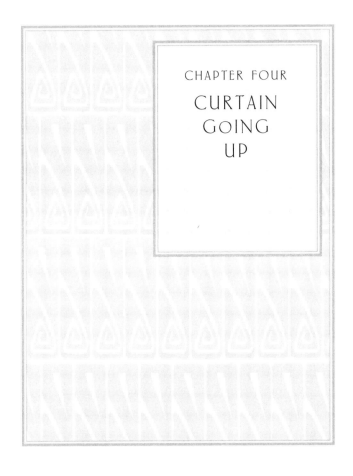

CHAPTER FOUR
CURTAIN GOING UP

Pierpont Tree punched the number for Eddie Navarro's beeper. It was Eddie who had saved Pier in the months after Hilary had been hospitalized. They had been roommates at Stanford, an unlikely pair, Pier elegant and privileged, Eddie on scholarship, scrambling up from near poverty. The campus protests against the Vietnam war infuriated Eddie, who raged at Pier that "Rich kids are wearing flowers in their hair and poor kids are dying."

The idea bothered Pier so much that he enlisted.

Eddie, embarrassed that Pier should do what he'd only talked about, followed suit. When the war was over, Pier went back to school. Eddie never did. He took a job with the Los Angeles police, married a woman from the old neighborhood and had a son. He had been working his way up through the hierarchy when his wife, Angela, had taken the boy and disappeared.

Eddie was obsessed with finding them. He was drinking heavily. Early retirement was suggested. He left the force and continued searching on his own. But no taxicab driver stepped forward to say, yeah, he remembered driving that lady to the airport. Airline ticket agents looked at the photo, taken just before Christmas, of three-year-old Joey, dressed in a red velour suit, sitting on his mother's lap, and shook their heads. Both of Angela's parents were dead and her only sister, ten years older, insisted that she had no idea where Angela and Joey might be. Eddie took to calling the sister, seven in the morning, eleven at night, hoping that Angela would answer. She never did. When the sister threatened to get a restraining order, Eddie stopped. He knew why Angela had left. He knew his family hadn't been vaporized in some unreported explosion or kidnapped by cultists. But knowing wasn't accepting, and every year, just before Joey's birthday, Eddie reached into the back of his bedroom closet and took out a few of the posters he'd had printed up all those years ago. The smiling toddler on his mother's lap would be a man now, the same age Eddie had been when Joey was born. Even a few years after he'd disappeared, Eddie knew his son would have changed beyond recognition. But there was Angela. Maybe someone would recognize Angela. The phone would ring and a voice would say, "Yeah, I know her." But now even Angela would have become someone else, and Eddie knew that when he reached into his dwindling pile of posters, he was not really searching. He was mourning.

Most of the time, Eddie lived in the present. You have to when you're a private detective. On one minor case, he called Pier to ask for information about a family in Santa Barbara, then followed up with a visit. Pier liked Eddie. Gradually they developed a working relationship.

There was no answer, but Pier knew Eddie often let the answering machine screen his calls. What was morning to Pier was the darkest night for Eddie, who often stayed out until dawn and slept until noon. Pier waited through the irritatingly long beep, and then left a message. While he waited for Eddie's return call, he looked at the silver-framed photographs of his parents on the eighteenth-century dining table he used as his desk. His mother had found the table at Partridge in London many years before, along with twenty-four chairs of the same period. His parents had entertained two presidents in this room, along with an assortment of senators, opera singers, newspaper publishers and visiting tycoons.

Pier had made the enormous high-ceilinged dining room his office. The chairs now lined the walls, each stoically accepting its new function, holding stacks of case folders. He couldn't tolerate the thought of file cabinets marking the huge Aubusson rug his parents had bought in Paris, so the chairs held the files, twelve on each side of the room, beginning with "A" at the far left. "W" and "X" shared a chair. So did "Y" and "Z."

Antique crystal chandeliers provided gentle light, which Pier had augmented with four Green and Green lamps standing at attention atop the table in a military row. He admitted to China that the arrangement looked more than a little like the main reading room in the New York Public library, but since that was one of his favorite rooms in the world, the effect pleased him mightily.

On one wall hung part of his parents' collection of early California *plein air* paintings. Most of the landscape artists had been friends of his mother and father.

On the wall opposite the French doors was a bulletin board only slightly smaller than the flight deck of an aircraft carrier. There, with white nine-by-twelve cards and multicolored marking pens, he boldly noted the most salient facts of his current case. Points large and small to be considered. Notebooks could be lost or stolen. A computer screen was too small. Pier was a big man and he was comfortable with things that were overscale for others. Often, when he seemed to have reached a dead end on a case, he would sit for hours staring at the cards, waiting for them to give up their secrets.

After he talked with Eddie, he would begin the Paxton case by placing blank cards on the bulletin board. Then he would make an appointment for lunch with Max Steiner, the Los Angeles District Attorney. Next, he would ask China who might give him a crash course on the world of interior decorating. Frances Adler, his mother's decorator, was the only name he knew and she was dead. He called China on one of the telephones banked on the table.

"China, I need to know everything I can about decorators and *Manor House* magazine. Who's who, what makes it go, why and how does it all happen? Got any ideas?"

China thought for a minute, then said, "Jack Banner, of course. You know he's an artist, but you may not know that he sells his paintings to decorators for their clients, the kind of people who subscribe to *Manor House.* And he's been doing it for thirty years."

"Perfect," said Pier. "I'll get Mattie to make up a picnic lunch, and we'll go calling."

While Mattie filled the picnic basket, Pier picked up the blue telephone and tapped out the number of Max Steiner's private line. Friends since their days in high school, Pier had supported

Steiner's political career from the beginning. After four rings, Steiner's secretary answered and told Pier the District Attorney was in the field.

Pier left a message just as the private line he always kept open for Eddie's calls began to ring. Pier answered, briefed Eddie quickly and gave him five names to check out. ". . . and, Eddie, check out Le Club, that society hangout where Beau Paxton was shot."

Pier started to give Eddie the address and was surprised when Eddie announced that he was a regular at Le Club.

"You?" asked Pier. "I hear it's mostly gay. Is there something you haven't told me, Eddie?

"It's a great sore? A sore? Oh, source." Eddie was explaining that his girlfriend, Marta, kept the books for the bar.

"Good. Listen, I'm going out now to learn all about interior decorators and, Eddie, if you don't come through on this, decorating is going to be the only career left for you. You'll be the only ex-cop in town doing drapes."

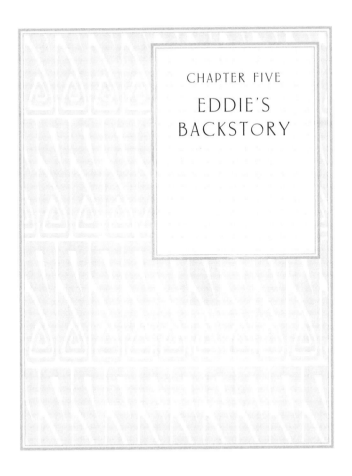

CHAPTER FIVE

EDDIE'S BACKSTORY

Eddie Navarro sat in his furnished Hollywood Hills apartment, receiver still in hand, wondering how he'd gotten himself tied to a partner who thought a sunrise worth seeing.

He walked into the kitchen and switched on the small TV set he kept on the local news channel. Then he cracked six eggs into a bowl, melted butter in a frying pan and spread strips of bacon in the micro-wave. A picture of a pro football player who sometimes showed up at Le Club came onto the TV screen. He was hanging his head, walking between two policemen. His suit coat looked too big for him. The voice-over was a woman's, cool, slightly scornful: "Patrick Coran was arrested last night after neighbors reported hearing screams coming from his apartment." The next picture on the screen was his wife's face, her eyes swollen shut with bruises, lips split, her hand pressed against her broken jaw. Eddie stared at the picture, then closed his eyes, unable to erase the image of Angela's face, eyes swollen closed, nose running blood. Like the face of the woman on the screen.

He'd been working overtime, putting aside the extra money for a down payment on a house. He might never have known things had gone wrong if one of the men on the night shift hadn't made a joke about Angela's boyfriend.

She hadn't denied it. "What do you expect? I'm alone all day, alone all night!" she had screamed. And the noise had set Joey crying, scrambling out of his bed to hang onto his mother's skirt, howling, as Eddie had hit Angela again, and again and again.

That was the last time he'd seen his son.

So now there was just Eddie and his guilt. And his girl, Marta, who, shortly after meeting him, had marched him to a shrink. She told him that if he kept on talking, one day he would stop feeling guilty.

Eddie had never been able to make Marta understand. It wasn't that he felt guilty. It's that he was guilty.

Marta had problems, too, but not as bad as his. Bad, though. She was the bookkeeper for a small, mob-connected chain of trendy bars. Eddie used to see her around the Cabaret Club. The bartender there was one of his best sources of information. One afternoon they talked and he learned about Marta's husband, Naldo. A new breed of con. A computer crook. He ran some kind of bank scam the Feds had tracked back to him. Before you could press Delete, the Family had hustled

Naldo across the border into Mexico and installed him in a high-rise apartment in Acapulco. The FBI came knocking on Marta's door, and there was a strange, clicking noise whenever she picked up her telephone, but for weeks she heard nothing about Naldo.

Then a man stopped her on the street and gave her a letter. Naldo was well. He would send for her when it was safe.

Naldo never sent for Marta. Why should he? He had never known such happiness, with the beach below his window, women when he wanted them and every technological gizmo and gadget, some even before they came on the market. He was ecstatic, wandering the Web, zooming down the Internet, but, mostly, devising money-moving schemes for the Family.

So no one really cared when Marta started seeing Eddie Navarro. Because she was only half Italian, the Family had never accepted her anyway. But she could be trusted to keep two sets of books, make cash deposits to the bank and off-the-books deposits to the street soldiers. They paid Marta well, but made it clear she could count on lifetime employment, like it or not. She made the best of it. It was easier after she met Eddie. Serving time wasn't quite so bad when you had company.

CHAPTER SIX

THE WONDERFUL WORLD OF DECORATING

Every city, every town, every village has its Source. Sometimes the Source is a journalist, sometimes not.

In Santa Barbara, Jack Banner is the Source. He's the one people call to find out what's going on, who's there, who isn't and why not. Visiting journalists doing the inevitable "real" Santa Barbara story check in with Jack. He'll know whatever and whoever they want to know. They hope he will tell. If he does, it will save them days, perhaps weeks, of research.

Banner is an artist whose work hangs on the walls of every major house in Santa Barbara. Many years ago, he was the court painter for Emperor Haile Selassie. He, his ex-wife and children got out when the shooting began. Banner is at home in Africa, India, Egypt, all of Europe. Even San Francisco.

He paints every morning in his small Carpinteria beach house, unique for its total lack of an ocean view. He has surrounded the house with an approximation of a tropical rain forest and that, in turn, is surrounded by a high wall of carved wood panels from an ancient Thai ceremonial house.

The interior reminds the visitor of an exotic jumble sale. Banner paintings cover the whitewashed walls, at least until the people dropping by for an afternoon drink buy them. They often try to buy the antique carved wood Burmese elephants or Thai ostriches festooned with necklaces of seashells and fresh flowers too. The length of a pine table is split dead center by a log holding a raggedy line of antique tin shorebirds. Flowers bloom singly and in masses on the Banner canvases, along with cockatoos, polar bears and, currently, cowboys on horseback.

Pier and China drove through the Thai-paneled gates into a clearing in the rain forest reserved for guest parking. Through the open doors of a flower-filled studio, they saw Banner, a wiry man, hair at cross-purposes, tails of his white button-down shirt half in and half out of his Levi's, painting at an easel with all the movement and energy of an orchestra conductor. "I hear you," he called out. "Almost finished. Come on in. I'll be right with you."

China led the way across the courtyard and had just set the picnic basket on the table when Banner came into the room, arms outstretched. He spotted the picnic basket. "My God, lunch! I never eat it, but that's probably because no one ever brings it to me. If people didn't invite me to parties, I'd starve. China, you're gorgeous, as always. Now, sit down. Pier, China said you're investigating Beau Paxton's murder and want to know about decorators. Ask away and I'll tell you whatever I can."

"First, what do you know about *Manor House?*" Pier asked.

"I know that getting published there is the ultimate for a decorator," Banner said. "Publicity is to a decorator what blood is to a vampire. Getting into *Manor House* means fame, and that means money. Those rich subscribers choose their decorators from the magazine."

Pier, who was always hungry, was considering the roast chicken sandwich Mattie had constructed. He took a bite, and then asked Jack, "How much would a decorator make on a job? Do they have fixed fees or what?"

"That I really don't know. But I do know a decorator in Los Angeles who latched onto a fellow with lots of bucks. Spent about ten million on a house in Palm Springs, fifteen on a house in Bel Air and twenty on his offices. I've heard decorators say they get about thirty percent of the total cost of furnishing your basic palace, so the decorator did alright. But you'd better check that out with someone who knows what they're talking about." Banner eyed a sandwich. "China, I'll just have a half. Mattie can't go wrong with sliced chicken. Can she?"

"You're safe, although you may not care for the peanut butter spread. But the bread is good."

"Maybe I'll just have a bread sandwich. What else do you want to know, Pier?"

"Anything you can tell me, Jack. Anything at all."

"Well, several decorators have told me it's dangerous to be too friendly with clients, because then they don't get paid. You know, the client says, 'Now we're such good friends, you're not going to actually send me a bill, are you?' One decorator in Palm Springs refuses to call his clients by their first name until the final bill is paid."

Banner warmed to the subject. "You know, Pier, in spite of the money, the relationship between the decorator and the client is usually very close. After all, the decorator gradually learns everything about the clients' private lives, and often the wife confides a little too much . . . or a lot too much. Either way, it's up close and personal."

Gesturing toward China, Banner said, "You'll know who this is, China. The wealthy widow of an L.A. tycoon was doing up a big house in Montecito when her decorator died. Well, they had just finished landscaping the huge pool and patio area, so she converted the barbecue pit into an Eternal Memorial Flame for the decorator. Every Sunday morning, her butler puts on a record of taps being played and puts a flag at half mast."

Pier lowered his head and groaned. "China, did you know about this?"

"Of course. But it's just another story from the wonderful world of decorating. And the eccentrics in Montecito. Like the woman, you know her, Jack, who cuts off the camellia blossoms because she only likes the leaves."

"And to think I've lived here all my life and didn't know about this rampant nuttiness." Pier groaned again and took a deep breath. "Let's get back to the magazine. Would it be an exaggeration to say that some decorators would do just about anything to have their work shown in *Manor House?*"

"It would be an understatement. When my house was in a few years ago, I heard from people all over the world. Some were acquaintances who just wanted to talk about old times. But others were absolute strangers who wanted to buy my paintings. I can imagine what being in *Manor House* means to a decorator. They *would* murder to be in the magazine."

Pier considered the chore of interviewing an endless stream of homicidal decorators. He squirmed in his chair, remembering the way his mother and Frances Adler used to go on about cabriole legs and piecrust tables. There was a pleading note in his voice when he said, "I need you on this one, China. The decorators are your assignment. They'll talk to you."

Then he turned to Jack. "Let me ask you another question. Have you ever heard rumors about Beau Paxton publishing a decorator's work in return for what they once called *favors?*"

Banner nodded. "It's been a rumor for years that if a decorator is young, male, gay and very, very attractive, chances are Beau Paxton will publish his work, even if he has to push the furniture around himself until the room looks good enough to photograph. In fact, I heard recently that he was sponsoring the career of a young decorator just out from New York. Got a job for him in Los Angeles so he would stay. It was a Scandinavian name. Lars, I think. But here in Santa Barbara, the locals say Beau Paxton was engaged to Dilly Dillingham. You know her, Pier?"

"Sure do. Haven't seen her for years. So Beau was bisexual?"

"Dilly's family is so rich, a social climber like Beau would go any way at all."

"Any rumors about payoffs? Would envelopes of cash placed discreetly in Beau Paxton's hand get a decorator's work published?"

"I don't think so. He owned part of the magazine, you know."

Pier nodded. Seth Rupert had mentioned that Beau held stock in the company.

"Also," Banner continued, "he lived with Norton Birdwell of the Texas oil Birdwells. Beau had plenty of money, though I suppose the fact that he was courting Dilly means he wanted more."

"If he didn't really need money, what do you think he *did* need?" asked Pier.

Jack Banner paused in mid-flight, reflecting as he looked into the garden. "I don't know. Maybe a spine. He was so passive. Charming in a pallid sort of way. Unfocused. I've heard the mother was formidable. Maybe she gutted him. There didn't seem to be anybody at home in that Dunhill suit. Supposedly the magazine is really run by a woman."

China held up her hand to stop Pier's questions. "Jack, do you want some of Mattie's bread pudding?"

"God, yes. An all-bread lunch is just what I need. And it's the one thing she knows how to make. I don't know how you two survive."

China spooned pudding into Jack Banner's kitchen Ming dishes. "Everyone want coffee?"

"Made a fresh pot just before you came. Sugar and milk on the tray." Banner began pacing. "What else, Pier?"

"What do you know about the woman behind the scenes at *Manor House?*"

"Nothing. Can't even remember her name. But I've heard that Beau Paxton could never have run it alone. Can't remember who told me. My memory dims by the hour."

"Jack, who would you talk to if you were in my place?"

"And wanted to know about decorators and *Manor House?*"

"Right."

"Let's see. Maybe Laddy Laramy. If he were a perfume, they'd call him Essence of Sleaze."

"Then why do people hire him?" asked Pier.

"He flatters them into submission. Pursues them and woos them relentlessly with sugar-coated words. Tells movie stars he's always idolized them. Money is not important. He'll work for a fraction of his usual fee. To decorate for them is his life's ambition. He lives only for their happiness."

"And they believe all that? China, would you believe that garbage?"

China, who had been sliding down in her chair while Jack talked, sighed and straightened up. "I *did* until I found out he said the same things to everyone. And, gentlemen, in my own defense, let me say that I was really busy, doing two pictures back-to-back. Later I found out he was getting kickbacks from everyone. And he had phony invoices sent to me. Oh, I hope he turns out to be the murderer, because I want to drop the gas pellets and watch the rat die."

"China!" said Jack. "That was just like your speech in *The Devil's Own*. What fire! What rage! What . . ."

"Careful, Jack," warned Pier. "She killed the dirty rat in that movie. In fact, she hit him on the head with a heavy object, very much like the coffeepot she's just picked up. What else do you know about decorators, China? Who did you hire after you fired the King of Sleaze?"

"Minnie Houston. You know her, Pier. She has a shop on Robertson near the Design Center. She did the house I was living in when we met. We're good friends."

"Never knew what the house looked like. I only saw you. But what about those phony invoices? Did you want to kill the rat for cheating you out of your life's savings?"

"My accountant could have killed him when he found out."

Banner considered the rest of his bread pudding. "Explain that, China. In detail. I sell a lot of paintings but I'm lousy at business. Maybe I can pick up a few pointers."

"This is making me mad all over again," said China. "Well, this is how it worked. Laddy would tell the antiques dealer he wanted to buy a desk for me. But he would only buy it if the dealer would give him an invoice for ten thousand dollars above the actual price. If the dealer wanted to make the sale enough to agree, then Laddy would pocket the extra ten thousand dollars on top of his usual commission on the desk."

"Why would the dealer do that?" asked Pier. "And how did your accountant find out?"

"Elementary, my dear Pierpont. Decorators buy tons of antiques and a few dealers want the business enough to do phony invoices for a good customer. Anyway, my accountant found out about it when he hired an appraiser to put a value on everything for insurance. The guy thought I'd paid too much for a lot of things, so he leaned on a couple of dealers, who finally confessed they had given Laddy inflated invoices. Cute, huh?"

"And this is the guy who's going to tell us about decorating?" asked Pier.

"Oh, Pier, please give Laddy your Clint Eastwood squint. He still owes me a few thousand dollars. Tell him you'll crush him like velvet if he doesn't pay up."

"I'll give it my best shot."

"I like that," said China happily. "Already you're thinking in terms of weapons."

"Why would he agree to talk to me?" asked Pier.

"Money. Offer him lunch and a fat consultation fee. He'll tell you everything."

"On second thought, I'll pass," said Pier. "Remember, decorators are your job. Now, Jack, how about letting me buy a painting? Maybe the landscape over there with the cowboy in the distance?"

"Sorry. Sold. It's being shipped off tomorrow to Texas—"

"Well then, the tropical scene with all the birds."

"Those birds fly away to Bermuda next week. Pier, I'm sorry, but all these paintings are sold."

"Here's a better idea," said Pier. "I'd like to commission a full-length portrait of China. Will you do that?"

"Now that would be a pleasure. Absolutely. When can we get started, China?"

"Not until we find out who murdered Beau Paxton. Until then, I'm a working girl again."

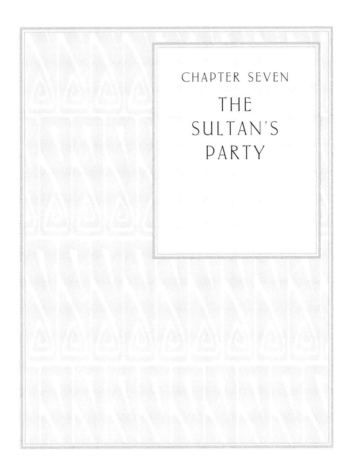

CHAPTER SEVEN

THE SULTAN'S PARTY

No one lives in Beverly Hills. There's no place left for living. In the eighties, it became one big board game for speculators, who would parlay an undistinguished house from two million to six million in eighteen months. They razed houses and built pseudo-swell structures on every square inch of property. Lawns were vanquished as the S&L's moved forward, armed with their Ugly House Kits, until real estate slumped down.

Although the real estate market dived down, determinedly seeking the bottom, traffic picked up. The light is harsh, the air curiously yellow, crime prevails and everyone coughs a lot.

Pier knew that China, sitting next to him in the passenger seat of his father's old Bentley, was nervous about the evening. He knew she was wondering if she could get through a big Hollywood party without drinking. She held her chin high, as if going into battle, that heartbreaking profile backlit by the streetlights. Pier turned left just before the Beverly Hills Hotel, then slowed north of Sunset to join the line of limousines and foreign motorcars moving slowly up the narrow street, lacquered metal gleaming, lubricated precision engines growling richly. "If we were in the old Range Rover," Pier pointed out, "we could drive right over all those cars ahead."

"I always feel we should be looking for watering holes," said China.

Pier turned and looked down at her. "You are the most gorgeous woman God ever created. They'll all want you to do another movie."

"Never again." China reached for Pier's hand. "I keep taking a deep breath but it doesn't help. I'm nervous. There'll be a lot of industry people at the party; as many as the Sultan can pack into his humble forty-million-dollar Gothic castle. He wants to buy a studio. Or so I hear. So they'll all turn out for the new player."

"Which studio?"

"Any with soundstages. He loves soundstages. He'd probably like to have his own lion, too."

"China, I know we're here to give moral support to Lulu. She's your friend and they're paying her a lot of money to sing for her supper, but what about all the other people?"

"You mean, why are they here when they could have stayed at home watching *Jeopardy?* Well, they all want everyone to know they're on the A list and they want to see who else is on the list. Or, more important, who isn't. This is the place to be tonight. Furthermore, the ladies need something to talk about when they meet for lunch tomorrow. You want to move to Beverly Hills so we can do this a lot?"

"I'd answer that but we've actually arrived."

A young parking attendant in black tie gave Pier a ticket for his car. "Sir, one of the Rolls will take you and the lady to the house."

"Can't we just walk?"

"The Sultan wants his guests to ride. He had seven Rolls shipped here from his own collection in Paris just for this party."

"Then by all means, we will Rolls up the hill."

China grimaced as another attendant in black tie opened the door and helped her into the Rolls.

"Excuse me, ma'am, aren't you China Carlyle?"

"Yes, I am." China blinded him with a full-voltage smile.

"You're my mother's favorite movie star."

"Oh, thank you so much. You may close the car door on your hand."

"He didn't hear you. It could have been worse. What if he hadn't recognized you at all?"

China didn't seem to hear.

"If only I could have a drink to get me through this. Don't worry, Pier, I won't, but sometimes it just hits me. All dressed up, going to a big party, lots of industry people, buzz, juice, electricity. It all goes with champagne. At least, it used to. Before. Thank goodness, I met you early in the evening. Any later and I might have slurred a word here and there and you would have passed me by."

The Rolls glided to a stop at the entrance to the Gothic monolith. Another black-tied attendant opened the car door for China. Pier took her arm and they entered through an allée of magnolia trees created by society's favorite florist, Doug Jones. A tuxedoed young man took their drink orders while another checked their names against the list on his clipboard. He directed them to a table nearby, where a young woman, also wearing a tuxedo, smiled at China and handed Pier two small envelopes with their seat assignments. China watched as he opened them.

"We're both at the *Gone With the Wind* table."

"Ah-hah. No one can tell which table is Number One. Of course, it will be the table with the Sultan and anyone who might sell him a movie studio. Well, we might as well mingle. Oh, Pier, there's Julie Warren. Over there. The brunette with the glasses. She writes a column for the *L.A. Tribune.* Knows everything that's going on. I'm sure she knew Beau Paxton. Come on, let's find out."

China led the way and Pier marveled once again as people stepped back to make way for her. Some knew her and spoke. Some smiled. Some stared. Some pretended they weren't looking. She acknowledged a greeting with a word or two to this one and that one but never stopped moving. China seemed to radiate an electrically charged field, a magnetic force that cleared a path for her. She seemed unconscious of her effect but Pier knew she wasn't. It was her uncanny ability to command attention by switching to an inner channel at will.

Julie Warren saw China, beamed and moved toward her, honing in on the heat generated by her fame. "China, you look more gorgeous than ever. Oh, I wish the Sultan had allowed my photographer to come. No press tonight, except yours truly. No paparazzi allowed outside either. And you," she turned her attention to Pier, "must be China's mystery man from Santa Barbara. My God, China, you didn't tell me he looks like Harrison Ford!"

She held out her hand to Pier. "I'm Julie Warren, *L.A. Tribune.* You are Pierpont Tree, aren't you?" Pier nodded assent. "Well, I'm delighted to meet you at last. Now, tell me, are you two married or not?"

"Not and no further comment," China replied, moving on with "Julie, we're the country bumpkins in the big city. You're the one who knows it all. What's this party all about? And how come they're serving alcohol? I thought it was forbidden."

"Oh, they're not Muslims," said Julie. "Or at least I don't think they are. But China, you haven't given Pier a chance to say a word and I want to hear *whatever* he has to say. Pier," Julie continued at a pace allowing no interruption, "you look rugged enough to do Marlboro commercials." A waiter appeared with their drinks. Pier handed China her water with lime and asked Julie if she would like another. She declined as Pier took his Scotch and looked down at her heart-shaped face. Bangs brushed the tops of her tortoise-rimmed glasses, her skin was layered with white powder and lipstick outlined the kind of Cupid's bow mouth not seen since silent films. Mascara beaded her lashes. Around fifty, Pier guessed. Less than five feet tall. He bent down to speak to her. "Julie, China tells me you know everything so I want to hear it all. I don't leave the high country much."

Julie's eyes squinted as she looked up at Pier doubtfully. "But what about those oh-so-private investigations of yours? Are you here tonight to investigate something?"

"Sorry. Lulu asked China to lend moral support and China asked me to come along."

"Mmmm. Lulu just got out of Betty Ford's recently, didn't she? *Again,*" Julie added pointedly, then turned her attention back to China. A star is a star. Pier, relieved, straightened up and looked around the room. The stem of Julie's glasses pressed her chin, making a dimple. "Look around, China. All the women of a certain age have read that collagen knocks out your immune system. They've stopped having the shots and their faces are collapsing. Absolutely *collapsing* right before our eyes!" Julie turned away as if the awful spectacle were too painful to behold, then changed the subject abruptly while studying China's face for signs of surgery. "This could be a big chance for Lulu to show everyone she still has it. Do you think she does, China?"

"Julie, when you have talent like hers, you never lose it. But she's fighting laryngitis."

"That's what Cisco Milan said when he canceled that big concert last month. Poor man. At his age he shouldn't be running around the country doing one-night stands. He has Alzheimer's, you know." China shot Julie a warning look, hoping to stop her, but Julie rattled on. ". . . he can't remember lyrics without a Teleprompter anymore. Bonnie," she looked up at Pier conspiratorially and added, "that's his wife, is spending his money as fast as she can so his kids by all his previous wives can't get it. And that's not all . . ."

China interjected firmly, "Julie, tell me about this house. Who's the Sultan's decorator? Count Dracula?"

"It is a little dark, isn't it? But just look at all the antiques. They must be worth a fortune."

"Why would he have antiques if they weren't worth a fortune? Ormolu by the ton, gold leaf, velvet, silk. Miles of brocade. Acres of tapestry. Black marble floors. Swags, valances, and bad period paintings on every wall." China continued until Julie was refocused on the decor.

Julie, always first to know, always first to tell, interrupted with a recital of the Sultan's riches. "He has a fleet of airplanes. Big ones, small ones. When he flies a group to Europe, there are seven hostesses to serve you. They change uniforms three times when you fly from California. Every meal has completely different china and silver. And each one has a printed menu. Actually *printed.*"

China could barely hear Pier mumbling, "All the food that's fit to print."

Julie, enraptured with her accounting, continued, "The Sultan has a full-time decorator who does all his houses. There are sixteen. This is the latest."

China asked, casually, "Do you think it will be in *Manor House?*"

Julie's eyes opened wider. "Oh, what a good question, China! I'll ask the Sultan's aide. The Sultan doesn't speak much English. When you're oh so rich, people speak *your* language. Maybe I could write the story if Beau Paxton could get the Sultan to agree—" Julie caught herself. "Oh, dear, it just hasn't sunk in yet that Beau isn't here anymore. That he's, you know . . ."

Pier leaned down again. "Dead?"

"Yes, Pier, since you put it so . . . so *definitely* . . . dead."

Pier, still inclined downward, spoke into Julie's ear. "Dead *is* definite."

She waved a hand tipped with pink nails. "Of course it is. Definite, I mean. Well, he was the most darling boy. I'm going to miss him. Have they found the murderer yet? Oh, I suppose they never will. It happened in a parking lot, didn't it, Pier? Outside Le Club? You must know."

"Only what I read in your newspaper. Beau Paxton doesn't sound like the kind of person who would have enemies."

"You must be joking. He made an enemy every time he rejected somebody's house. Powerful enemies. And all the decorators who couldn't get their work published in his magazine hated him. Then there was Norton Birdwell. He was so jealous of Beau he couldn't see straight. No pun intended. And I heard recently that Beau was absolutely bonkers about Lars Eklund, a hot young decorator from New York. He used to work for Mark Hampton. Or was it Mario Buatta? Anyway, I also heard that Beau was going to switch and marry a girl from Santa Barbara. Maybe you'd know her . . . but I can't remember her name . . ."

Pier, now interested, asked, "Dilly Dillingham?"

"Exactly!" Julie brightened as another thought seemed to occur. "Good heavens, who will replace Beau at *Manor House?* To get his job I would have killed—" Julie broke off and looked nervously at Pier. "Just a figure of speech. Still, Jonas Rupert is here tonight. I'll go find him this minute." The columnist turned away abruptly and plunged into the crowd.

"Were we dropped, China?"

"Not really. By Hollywood party standards that was a long and oh-so-deep conversation. And now we know your client's twin brother Jonas is here. Let's see if we can find him first. By the way, do you think Julie killed Beau Paxton? Great motive. Wanted his job."

Pier put his arm around China. "You're feeling better, aren't you, redhead?"

"Fine. Go ahead and swill your Scotch. But I warn you, I'm going to need a cigarette soon."

"Anytime you say. Tell me, does your friend Julie always babble that way?"

"No. She usually isn't so restrained. Probably trying to impress you. There, that must be Jonas Rupert over by the fireplace. He looks like Seth gone wrong. Quickly, maybe we can reach him before Julie spots him."

The crowd parted for China and she reached Jonas Rupert while Pier was still trying to catch up. If Seth Rupert was a hard-to-describe, medium man, no one would miss Jonas. His hair, darker than Seth's, was long, shaggy but expensively scissored. Even his tan looked expensive, too even, too perfect for the actual sun to have darkened the skin. Definitely machine-made. What in hell was China going to say to the man?

"Mr. Rupert." China's smile this time was low wattage but intense. Suitable for someone who has suffered a recent loss. "I'm so sorry about Beau Paxton. He was such a nice man and will be very much missed. Oh, excuse me. I'm China Carlyle. Darling, this is Mr. Rupert of *Manor House*." Pier noticed she had avoided mentioning his name.

"China's favorite, Mr. Rupert. And it's certainly the most beautiful magazine in the country."

"In the world," Jonas Rupert corrected with just a hint of a huff. Interesting, Pier mused, while China chatted with the publisher. Identical twins but Jonas' arrogant stance was very different from Seth. Tuning in, he heard Jonas ask China, "Did you know Beau well?"

"Not well at all. He called on me to discuss the possibility of publishing my house. I declined but I did enjoy our talk. He seemed quite likable. Was he, Mr. Rupert?"

"Call me Jonas, please. And may I call you China?"

"Certainly. And Mr. Tree is Pier."

"Pier? Oh. Of course. Pierpont Tree. My brother hired you to look into Beau's death. Frankly, I disagreed. The police are doing all that can be done. We must bury the past. Sad, of course. Very sad."

"Mr. Rupert, your brother Seth did ask me to look into Beau Paxton's murder and I'd like to talk to you later this week for some background information."

"Call my office for an appointment. Now, if you'll excuse me," Jonas replied curtly and moved swiftly to a group of men nearby. He began talking intensely to the nearest Forbes Four Hundred listee while glancing from time to time toward his next target, the biggest of the California billionaires, who was carefully stalking Fred Hawkins, the even bigger billionaire from New York.

"Now would you say we've been dropped?"

"Definitely. And look at him working his way around those King B's."

"King Bee? Not Queen Bee, China?"

"Remember 'B' movies? They were always the second half of the double feature. One producer made so many he was called King of the B's. That's the way I think about all these new billionaires. King B's. And there's poor old Andy Melton, who's worth only three or four hundred million. Don't you think he looks kind of shamefaced? You will notice there are no women in the King B's circle. Their real conversation is only with each other."

"Why doesn't the guy with three or four hundred million just charge right into the huddle?" Pier handed a passing waiter his empty glass and ordered another Scotch. "China?" She shook her head.

"He can't. He knows the King B's have that territory staked out. They've pissed in a circle and it's theirs. Rupert can join the huddle because he's in media. Media has a pass to go anywhere. Look, he's talking to Fred Hawkins. Did you know that Hawkins bought an estate in Far Hills just for his cars? It was in *People* magazine right after he'd gotten a 1913 Silver Ghost at auction. Hawkins said it wasn't extravagant because, and I quote, 'It's hard to park sixty cars in New York City.' "

Pier smiled to himself, imagining the scene when, twice a day, sixty minions would burst out of the door of Hawkins' high-rise and move sixty cars from one side of the street to the other in keeping with New York City's odd parking regulations. "That's not the only thing I've heard about Fred Hawkins," he said, watching as the billionaire gave Jonas Rupert the cold shoulder. "No one's ever proved it, but there are nasty rumors about the company Hawkins keeps. But tell me more about these King B's. Do they kill?" asked Pier.

"Every chance they get. That's their business. Of course, the first to go is the wife. She is promptly replaced by a stunning young woman, a more appropriate reflection of his new wealth. Often a former call girl. The senior versions were from Madam Claude's in

Paris. At least two were on call to the Shah of Iran. Now, Salina Covington, the New York writer who did my last interview, has a very interesting theory about all of that. Want to hear?"

Pier accepted a fresh Scotch from the waiter. "Just in time. I think I'm going to need this. What is Salina's theory?"

"Remember, you asked. She wanted to do an article on the role of the blow job in contemporary society. She . . ."

"She *what?* Goddamn it, China, I spilled my drink."

"That's alright. This rug's probably not worth a penny more than two hundred and fifty thousand dollars. Anyway, Salina's theory is that these men all married very young to nice, boring wives and the missionary position is all they've ever known and not much of that. But they didn't care. Early on they devoted their lives to making money. Later, after they're filthy rich, gorgeous young predators hunt them down and introduce them to the wonders of, well, variety. I don't want you to spill your drink again," China added sweetly. "They usually divorce their first wives within the year. Salina said she researched her theory thoroughly. For her books."

"She writes books?"

"Not by herself. Remember, Salina is also the second wife of a very rich man. She would never do anything so boring as sit in a room and write all day. And she certainly isn't the only one. Remember when Irwin asked me to write a Hollywood book? The first thing he said was 'Don't worry, I'll get someone to write it for you.' "

"Why *don't* you write a book, China?"

"Maybe that's what I do after you leave my bed at dawn. You think I go back to sleep, but maybe I'm writing my true confessions."

A very short, very bald young man suddenly appeared. "China! I'm Jeff Brittany. Remember me?"

China looked down and smiled with enormous insincerity. "No, but I have a feeling you're now the head of a studio, right?"

"Almost. Head of production at Magnetic."

"I'm so pleased. This is Mr. Tree. He's a civilian. Now tell me, have we met before?"

The young man looked about furtively for a moment, then, in lowered tones, answered, "I was in your agent's office. Harris & Harris. Remember?"

"I know you weren't Harris *or* Harris."

"No way. But at that time I was, well, sort of a trainee."

"You were in the mailroom?"

"Yes. I always brought your mail when you came to see Mr. Harris. You knew my aunt. She was Doris Harris' sister, Ruth. My name was Jeff Goldenwirtz."

"And now it's Brittany? It doesn't even begin with a 'G.' But I do remember. Of course. Your grandfather was a major stockholder at Magnetic. I'm so glad to know that some traditions remain."

Pier began to lead China away. "Excuse us, please. We're going to find our table."

China nodded a vague dismissal as she moved toward the terrace.

"*China.* Just a minute!" Brittany hurried after them. "I came over to make you an offer. I'm starting a new picture. Megabucks. And there's a great part for you. A real comeback role. And, you won't have to test for it," he paused for effect, "on *my* say-so."

China stopped.

One beat. Two beats. Half turn. Grew ten inches taller. Then she spoke. "Mr. Whatever-your-name-is, you're one of the reasons I *choose*, repeat, I *choose* never to do another picture." China took Pier's arm and turned away.

They followed a path carpeted with yellow bricks, flanked by rows of actors costumed as characters from *The Wizard of Oz*, the Scarecrow, the Cowardly Lion, the Tin Man and Dorothy with Toto. At the entrance to a Barnum and Bailey–size tent, a spotlighted pedestal on each side of the portico displayed two pairs of Judy Garland's red sequined slippers. A Cowardly Lion growled, "The slippers are originals. The Sultan bought them just for tonight's party."

China stopped again. Looked at the Cowardly Lion. Opened her mouth. Looked at Pier. Took a deep breath and exhaled slowly. "Never mind. I won't say a word. But if I get through tonight without drinking the place dry, you come to my AA meeting tomorrow and give testimony to my resolve."

"It's a deal. Now, let's find our table . . . My God, I don't believe it. Is it . . . ?" Pier stared. China stared. They both stared at the facade of a Southern plantation on the far side of the huge tent. "It's *Tara*. It's an exact reproduction of Tara! Pier, there are people on the veranda. In costume. Tell me they're not supposed to be Scarlett and Rhett. Please tell me they're not Melanie and Ashley and Bonnie Blue and . . ."

"China, don't miss the pony. The little girl's pony is there. And right now it's . . . oh, no . . ."

"And before dinner, too. Let's find our table before ah swoon."

A hoopskirted Southern belle materialized, speaking in a very bad accent. "Miss Carlyle, if yo'all will allow me, ah'll lead yo'all to the Sultan's table. Miss Carlyle, ah've wanted to play the kind of roles you played ever since ah was a li'l girl. Mama took me to every one of your movies. They jes do-an make 'em like that no moh."

China clutched Pier's arm. "Get her away from me before I strangle her." Suddenly, drums rolled, announcing a marching band that took the field in front of Tara playing "Camptown Races."

"Pier, they wouldn't."

"China, they would. And there they are."

One hundred "darkies" pranced out onto Tara's lawn dancing, shaking tambourines as they sang. "Pier, do you think he bought them just for tonight's party?"

49

CHAPTER EIGHT

THE
PARTY
BEGINS

"Here's our table," China announced brightly. Too brightly, Pier thought. Her smile was fixed, tense. He put his arm around her waist, but she pulled away to reach for a place card. "We're the first ones here, so let's find out who's at our table while I have my last cigarette. God, that sounds like I'm about to be shot, and that's just how I feel. Why did we ever leave Santa Barbara? Did I ever tell you that Mike Nichols calls it Santa Babs?"

Pier knew no response was expected. He stayed

close to China as she read each place card and thumbnailed each person. "Ah-hah! Elizabeth of the violet eyes is on the Sultan's left. I'm told she's slim again, by the way. And on the Sultan's right is a man with a name that sounds Arabic. Probably his interpreter. He'll provide English subtitles. Then I'm next on his right. You're next to me, thank heavens. And then . . . ah-hah, Julie Warren is on your left. Maybe you can get some more information about Beau Paxton and *Manor House.*" China didn't notice Pier's silence as her words tumbled out.

"Next to Julie we have Barry Dalton. Good. Julie can pitch movie ideas to him in case he buys another studio. You know, after he bought Cougar, he took it private, then sold it a couple of years later for a huge profit." China plucked another place card from the table. "Well, here's a surprise! Madonna. Maybe the Sultan really *is* going to buy a studio. Let's see who's next to Madonna." China studied the next place card. "Hmm, Gene Harris. He bought the old Gigantic lot a year ago. So he does have soundstages. And a film library. But he financed the deal with other people's money, most of which he's lost or inhaled." China moved to the next place card. "Oh, Pier, a mystery woman. Just one word on her card, Shareena. And she's seated with Roland Kendig, the British tycoon who bought Cougar from Barry Dalton! This table could be a Movie-of-the-Week. Maybe I'll just have one more cigarette." China opened her gold minaudière and took out an English Silk Cut. Her hand trembled. She knew Pier had noticed. China looked up at him, stricken. "I need a drink, Pier. I do. Please don't try to talk me out of it. We shouldn't have come. I thought I could handle it, but I was wrong. This is still a company town, and to them, I'm a has-been. It makes me feel like making one more movie just to show them I can still act anyone right off the screen. That's childish and self-destructive, but right now I want it so much it tastes like champagne. And I want that, too."

China looked around for a waiter but Pier turned her face toward his. "You're a *legend* to them. You can do a movie on your terms anytime. If you want a drink, that's your call. But, redhead, let me give you just one warning." China took Pier's hand and held it tightly, braced for what was to come. He spoke softly but his tone was threatening. "I'm going to tell Mattie on you and she won't let you have bread pudding ever again."

China looked startled for a moment, then slowly began to laugh. She held on to Pier and laughed until tears filled her eyes. By the time most of the table was seated, her mood had turned joyful. She knew she would be just fine and silently toasted Pier, sipping water from a French crystal goblet. Still smiling, China introduced herself to the Sultan's aide, who explained that His Serene Majesty would come to the table later. Roland Kendig didn't seem to mind Elizabeth Taylor's absence, so absorbed was he in the exotic Shareena, who was gazing at Kendig with huge, kohl-lined dark eyes. The Sultan's aide drew in his breath sharply as Kendig, pretending to make a point, traced his finger around the smooth, olive-skinned oval of Shareena's face. China asked the Sultan's aide about her.

"She is the Sultan's executive assistant."

"I don't suppose that involves a lot of typing, does it?"

"No, Miss Carlyle. Shareena has a secretary to do that."

"And is the Sultan's wife here tonight? Or is he married?"

"He is married, Miss Carlyle."

"Oh. Does he have, er, one wife or . . ."

"The Sultan has several wives. They do not appear in public. It is our custom."

"Oh. Elizabeth would never stand for that. But I assume the Sultan's interest in Miss Taylor is professional. People say he may buy a movie studio."

"You are so direct, Miss Carlyle." The Sultan's aide sighed deeply. "It is difficult for us to accustom ourselves to the candor of American women. But what you have heard is correct. The Sultan would like very much to buy a movie studio. He is very partial to the cinema and would like to have a film library in his palace. He has already built a theater. The Sultan will take the films back to his palace, so he can watch his movies at any time. Projectionists have already been hired."

"That's why he wants to buy a studio? So he can take all the movies back to his palace?"

"But yes, that is why he wants to buy a studio. Of course, he would also like to be on a soundstage while his own movie is being made."

"His movie? Singular? One movie?"

"That is correct. He would not need to buy a studio if he only wanted other people's movies. He thinks making one movie would be amusing. But no more."

"You know, I don't think Elizabeth is going to have the time of her life tonight. Tell me, after the Sultan has watched his movie being made and taken the studio's entire film library back to his palace, what will he do with the actual studio?"

"He might sell it to someone like Mr. Dalton. They have done much oil business. The Sultan likes Mr. Dalton."

"This is fascinating. Would the Sultan be interested in buying Gene Harris' studio, by any chance?"

"Oh, that I couldn't say, Miss Carlyle. But his studio does have many movies in its library. I do believe some of your movies are in that very library, if memory serves. You and Miss Taylor are the Sultan's favorite movie stars. In fact, I will confide that he prefers you, Miss Carlyle."

"Oh? Really? Call me China. And what about Madonna? Is she a favorite of the Sultan's too?"

"That was Shareena's idea. She thought the Sultan should meet a young star of the musical world, although he does not yet know who she is."

"Madonna may not have the time of her life tonight either. She seems to be making a late entrance. She did confirm that she would be here?"

"Confirm? I don't understand."

"Well, did someone call her people to confirm that she will be here tonight? Her schedule is . . ."

"But Miss Carlyle, the Sultan invited her. Shareena made the invitation."

"And Madonna accepted?"

"When the invitation is from the Sultan, acceptance is assumed."

"There may be a tiny problem if she didn't actually accept the invitation. A secretarial error, I'm sure. What I'm trying to say is, I don't think Madonna is going to show up tonight."

"Miss Carlyle, again I say to you that this was an invitation from the *Sultan.* Such invitations are automatically accepted and the guests *always* appear. Your Dr. Kissinger appears. Surely your Miss Madonna is not as important as Dr. Kissinger?"

"Well, umm, was Miss Taylor invited the same way Madonna was invited?"

"Of course."

"I'm afraid you're not going to have the time of your life tonight either." China patted the hand of the Sultan's aide, looked to her left and discovered Pier looking at her.

"Welcome back," he said. "I surveyed the table and Julie has been talking nonstop to Barry Dalton, so I've just been watching Shareena enchant Roland Kendig on one side and Gene Harris on the other. Have you found out what her role is in tonight's drama?"

"I'm not sure, my darling, but if neither Elizabeth Taylor nor Madonna shows up, it may be her last appearance anywhere on earth."

At that moment, China felt hands on her shoulders. Eyes narrowed, she turned to confront the offender and found herself eyeing the toupee of a man trying to kiss her cheek. She drew back. The toupee tilted upward, revealing the ashen face of Collin Greene, New York gossip columnist extraordinaire. It was said he would write up your party for a fee of from one to five thousand dollars. His middle name was not thought to be Integrity. To China's dismay, the Sultan's aide excused himself and Collin Greene slithered into the vacant chair, leaning so close to China she could smell his sour wine breath. She pulled back again. "I was told the Sultan had only allowed the *L.A. Tribune* here tonight. How did you manage it, Collie?"

"Easy. I came with Melba Gerson, everybody's agent. She owes me. The Sultan's people don't know who I am. Not a clue. China, I'm going to dish the hell out of this hoedown-by-the-oasis. Have you ever seen such vulgarity? But of course you have. God help you, you live here. How can you bear it? Los Angeles is absolutely what T. S. Eliot had in mind when he wrote *The Waste Land.* Dear girl, you must be lonely beyond belief."

China smiled her sweetest smile. "Not at all. My friends from New York call me almost daily to tell me how dreadful it is here. Most have lived here five to ten years and they're still complaining. If they do leave Los Angeles, they usually come back in a year or so. Then, at long last, they stop boring us with all that shit."

"Oh-ho! Forsaking the silver screen doesn't seem to have mellowed you, China. And is this the man who took you away from all that?"

China reluctantly introduced Pier, who nodded acknowledgment but didn't smile. Collin Greene looked closely at Pier, then continued, "I was just asking China what there is about California to like. The pace here is so slow. The only thing that moves is the traffic, if you call that moving. I met with an executive in his high-rise office and it was so quiet you could hear the clock tick tock, tick tock, tick tock," he whispered, his head moving from side to side.

Pier spoke for the first time. "You brought up an interesting point. Think of yourself back in that high-rise office, then imagine the sounds of New York traffic and construction. That's what you missed. You're equating noise with activity."

China turned even further away from Collie. "Pier, you're right. But if Woody Allen lived in California, his movies would never be made."

Collin's expression changed from arrogance to sneer. "What a blessing that would be! All that unsavory yearning for pussy. But, more important," he leaned toward China, "let me bring you up-to-date on some New York dish. Absolutely the *entrée*. Poor baby, out here you don't have the least notion of what's going on." Collin studiously ignored Pier and spoke directly to China in a stage whisper. "You know the rich young man who shot himself only a couple of weeks ago? You know who. It's absolutely top secret. For your ears only. No one, but no one, knows about this. He was sleeping with his mother. It started when she'd come home dead drunk and he'd help her undress. Somehow, it happened, on and off.

"Oops, that's a pun. Anyway, he was madly jealous of her new husband. All very complicated, but he just couldn't handle the whole . . ."

China said something clipped and decisive to Collin before turning her back on him, rather expressively, Pier thought. He took

56

China's hand. "We don't have to stay, redhead. You made the effort for Lulu. She'll understand. This dinner may go on for hours. It doesn't look as though they're going to serve until the Sultan appears, and God knows when that may be. His aide is coming back and the Sultan is *not* with him. You go. I'll say you're not feeling well and catch up with you."

Walking slowly, China let her feet follow the yellow brick road through the garden and back to the house. A young man, blond and suntanned, spotted her.

"Miss Carlyle, I am your greatest fan and I just had to tell you how much I admire you and that I hope you'll make another movie."

China kept moving, but asked politely, "And what is your name?"

"Lars Eklund. I've just moved out here from New York and . . ."

China halted. Pier caught up with them just as China turned. "Darling, what a wonderful coincidence. This is the decorator we've heard so much about." She turned back to Lars Eklund. "Why don't we find a quiet place to chat, just the three of us. Come along, Lars."

She took the young decorator's hand and led him past the Scarecrow, who was taking delicate puffs on his cigarette and then thrusting his arm straight out to keep the glowing tip away from his costume, and the Tin Man, who seemed to be putting something up his nose.

Pier followed them back to the house, smiling.

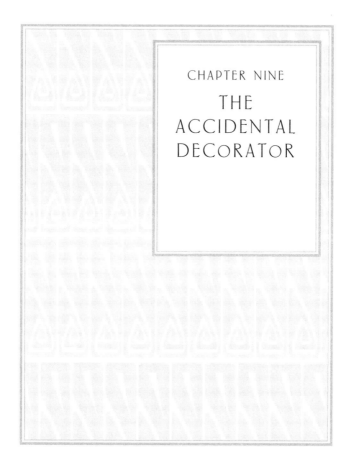

CHAPTER NINE

THE ACCIDENTAL DECORATOR

The fireplace in the library was large enough for human sacrifices. Virgins could be immolated vertically. The trunk of a small oak tree blazed in the hearth. Its crackling seemed to applaud China when she entered the enormous, book-lined room. Gliding toward a sofa the size of a small town, she sank gracefully into a sea of down-filled cushions.

"Lars, come sit next to me. Pier, pull that chair a little closer." China whispered, "You really want me to interview the decorators?" Pier nodded. "Good. I'll start, then you take over."

China smiled at the young decorator, who looked confused but eager to please the legendary China Carlyle. He tried not to fidget. Pier sat silently watching Lars, whose eyes were fixed on China.

She began. "Lars, since you're a decorator, you know *Manor House* magazine?"

"Of course! They're going to publish my work! Can you imagine, starting at the top like that? It's just heaven. You know, earlier this evening Julie Warren asked me about *Manor House* too. I was talking to Candice Bergen and she . . . Oh, my God, China Carlyle and Candice Bergen in one evening. It's just to die!"

"That's what I wanted to talk to you about . . ."

"Julie Warren—or Candice Bergen?"

"No. The 'to die' part. Death."

"Oh, ugh."

"Specifically, the death of Mr. Paxton."

"Beau? Beau Paxton? Is that who you mean?"

China looked at Lars and gave him the smile Pier had long ago cataloged as dangerous.

"Unless you know another Beau Paxton who was murdered."

Lars Eklund looked ingratiatingly at Pier, pleadingly at China, then began hyperventilating as he tried to speak each word simultaneously. "What I mean is, actually, I do know other *people* who were murdered. There was Renzo whose head was bashed in by a rough number he picked up. Morgan van Wrot's friend poisoned his paella. It was hard to notice with all the saffron . . ."

China interrupted. "Lars, try to focus on just one murder. Beau Paxton's. Pier is looking into it, unofficially. He just wants to ask you a few questions. Over to you, Mr. Tree."

The decorator's hazel eyes widened as he stared at Pier, then gasped, "Oh, my God, you're a . . . oh, my, a private eye? Oh, are you *the* Pierpont Tree? You live in that famous house in Santa Barbara? You're one of the Trees?"

Pier paused for a moment. "Lars, have the police contacted you?"

"The police? No! I'll tell you whatever you want to know. Oooh, this is just like a movie."

"Right. Like a movie," said Pier, as Lars Eklund shifted nervously. "Now, when was the last time you saw Beau?"

"Let me think. It happened on Tuesday night, didn't it? Or was it Monday? It was all so horrid. Oh, I know. It was Tuesday, because I was doing an installation until all hours right here in Beverly Hills."

"I'm not sure I want to ask this question, but what is an installation?"

"When a decorator buys absolutely everything down to the very last accessory, we put it all in storage until everything is moved into the house. *Installed,* all at once. Then the clients walk in. They see how wonderful it looks and they don't mind that you've spent their last cent. Ha, ha."

"That still doesn't answer the question of when you last saw Beau," Pier said.

Lars picked up a crystal ashtray from the table, looked at the bottom for a signature, then juggled it dismissively from one hand to the other. "Saturday," he said finally. "It was Saturday night. We had a drink together at Le Club. Just to talk about my work."

"Nothing suspicious, no one hanging around making Beau nervous?"

"No, it was just the usual crowd. And Beau wasn't nervous, just excited about my work. He kept saying how far I'd go. In the business, I mean."

"You didn't see him after that?" Pier scowled and Lars gave a mock shiver.

"You look so fierce!" said Lars. "No, I told you. I shouldn't even have taken time off on Saturday night. This was a really important job for me. But Beau . . . well, he was important too."

"So you were doing an installation the night of the murder. Where and for whom?"

"Barbara Meyers and her husband Stanley. Whittier Drive. North of Sunset, of course. Beau Paxton got the job for me and it's heaven if I do say so. Monochromatic. All in tones of khaki and . . ." Pier's scowl deepened. "Sorry. I know. Just questions and answers."

"Until what time were you there that evening?"

"Oh, good heavens, it must have been three in the morning. The newspaper said Paxton was murdered at about two so I'm in the clear."

"Except that where you were doesn't matter. You could have hired a hit man to do the job."

"Me? I didn't have any reason to kill Beau!"

"Do you know anyone who might have had reason to kill him?"

"My personal theory is, well, I know I shouldn't say this, but it might have been a girl up in Santa Barbara, Dilly Dillingham. I mean, I don't think she actually *did* it. She comes from a very good family. But she has all the money in the world so she certainly could afford the very best hit man. She thought Beau was going to marry her. Beau did girls sometimes. He still had this thing about denying he was gay. He told me all about it, but he was trying to be really tactful and break it off without hurting her. Also, her family is rich and influential so Beau was being very careful, because of the magazine, you know."

"He believed people in Santa Barbara might not let him publish their homes in *Manor House* if he offended the Dillinghams?"

"That's right. Dealing with all those rich people is not easy, but

Beau, because he was rich himself, knew just how far to go without getting killed. Oh, sorry. Anyway, Beau was trying to ease out of the Dilly thing. He told her he needed more time because he'd been a bachelor for so long and all that. She suspected he was trying to back out so she said he'd better not even think about it. She told Beau she'd see him dead first."

"In those words?"

"That's what Beau told me. We were going to live together so he wanted to start fresh. That's all I know. Honestly." He looked toward the door with an expression of naked longing.

Then Lars looked at China, begging permission to leave the room. She studied the ashtray. Lars stood warily, edging away from Pier. He was visibly relieved when China, glancing first at Pier, told the decorator he could return to the party. "Go ahead, Lars. I'm the good cop. But don't leave town without checking with me. Got it?"

"Oh, China, yes. Absolutely. Maybe we could have lunch sometime and . . ." Lars Eklund fled the room.

Pier laughed. "Maybe a guilty conscience accounts for his haste. Julie Warren told me earlier that she met Lars Eklund at the Hippodrome the night of the murder. Julie's hairdresser was there and he introduced them."

"Julie isn't known for accuracy."

"She remembers because she heard news of the murder on her car radio the next morning, which was the anniversary of her second divorce."

Pier led China through the house to one of the Rolls waiting in the motor court. "China, it's heaven, as Lars Eklund would say. He told us he had been doing an installation until three in the morning. It seems he took time out. Maybe he disguised himself and, as the line in an old movie would go, maybe he took time out for murder?"

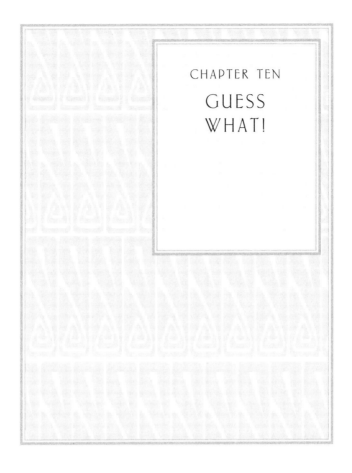

CHAPTER TEN

GUESS WHAT!

The next morning China Carlyle was in her kitchen, a pot of coffee at hand, a pack of cigarettes on the table next to the typewriter. Hair pulled back, fastened with tortoise combs, she wore freshly pressed jeans, a blue turtleneck sweater and a frown. It was almost nine o'clock. She had written only two hundred words since seven. Damn. It was impossible to remember what happened and who-said-what-when after she starred in her first movie and began to drink because she was so scared. She had felt pulled to pieces. Publicity releases proclaimed that she had hair like the setting sun and eyes as aqua as a summer sea. And, according to the director who had cast her in her first summer theater production in Maine, a voice so throaty and sensual that he'd had to keep the young men in the audience from climbing up on the stage. The next year he had signed China for summer stock in Connecticut.

There the writer William Stratton and his houseguest saw China in a small role. Stratton's guest was a motion picture director who flew her to Hollywood for a screen test that became legendary. China was an overnight sensation, even before she appeared in a movie. Her test rated more comparisons than any ever made. "As luminous as Garbo . . . as sensual as Monroe . . . vulnerable as Judy . . . earthy as Sophia . . . classy as Grace . . . *as . . . as . . . as.*" But an old-time producer who saw the test made the comparison most quoted. "As natural as Lassie . . ."

At first they wanted to change her name. Her own was "too theatrical," they said. She told a reporter from *Vanity Fair* why she had refused: "My mother's name was China. She died giving birth to me and my dad went off on a two-week binge. So my grandparents named me China too. When Dad sobered up, there I was with my mother's name and her red-blond hair. I grew up wanting to be the captain of a fishing boat off the coast of Maine like my dad. Acting never entered my head until after he died and I went to live with Mother's sister in Portland. Aunt Asia was the high school drama teacher. She gave me roles in her productions and then helped me get the summer stock job in Connecticut where I was discovered. Anyway, my name means a lot to me and I wouldn't let anyone change it. Not even for a movie career. After all, Dad left me his house on Peck's Island and his boat. I figured if I didn't make it in Hollywood, I'd go back to Maine and fish."

That's where China began her book. On Peck's Island, where her parents and grandparents were buried. Aunt Asia was still alive to help her with letters and memories. She had retired to the house on the island a few years ago. China had finally given the boat to the son of a fisherman friend of her father's because she knew he would want her alive and working, not dry-docked in a Portland shipyard. Every morning long before dawn, the boat still put out into the heavy seas around Maine with the word *China* painted in scarlet on the starboard bow.

Her book would be titled just *China*. She wanted to talk to Pier about it. But not yet. She had to write it alone, on her own. People would expect another tell-all but it wasn't and the underlying story was about her search for the mother she never knew. China looked once again at her mother's picture in an old seashell frame. The original China was seated on the porch steps of the Peck's Island house. What were you like? Were you happy? We look alike. Is my voice like yours? Aunt Asia says it is. If only I could hear you speak.

China heard the distant ring of the telephone in her study. It was the public line. Everyone had that number and the number had its own answering machine. She didn't have to answer but she was stuck on page 119 so she pushed her reading glasses down on her nose and paced swiftly through the house to answer on the fifth ring.

"China, I was just going to hang up."

"Who is this?"

"Must you always be so abrupt? It's Julie. Julie Warren. *L.A. Tribune* columnist and friend of some twenty years. Are you awake yet, China?"

"Yes, but isn't it early for you, Julie, after a late-night party?"

"Actually, yes. I'm still in bed, but if you can believe it, I was reading the early edition of my own newspaper and *guess what?*"

China paused for a moment, deciding. "Julie, do you remember Rina Marine? The former call girl who married John Wattles? Old-time producer worth millions? She was always typecast as a call girl. Well, they had a live-in Chinese couple. Rina always spoke Chinese to them. Her version. *Missee have bigee partee. You cookee for partee.* She insisted they call her *Missee.* Do you remember how it all ended?"

"No, but I think I'm going to regret calling you."

"One day, Rina called the couple into the living room, although I'm sure she would have called it a drawing room. She told them she had sad news. *Guessee whatee?* she asked. *Master and Missee have to make stop so much monee every month. So you go. Here one weekee salary.* The fellow, whatever his name was, said, *After ten years we fired with one week's salary, Missee?* She should have known by the way he hissed *Missee* that she was in trouble. Anyway, the next thing he said was *Guessee whatee, Missee? Surprise for you in kitchen. You come.* Like the dope she is, she followed him into the kitchen, where he stabbed her twice with a paring knife and ran. She almost bled to death before John heard her screams and came downstairs. She lived but she *never, never* said *Guess what* again. Now, Julie, you were saying?"

"Oh, my God. I'd forgotten how you can *be.* Now, what *was* I going to say? Oh, yes. There's a three-paragraph story in the second section of the paper this morning about that young decorator at the Sultan's party, Lars Eklund. He was a victim of a hit-and-run. I saw you and Pier talking to him. China, I'm trying to handle this like an investigative reporter and come up with all kinds of juicy facts."

China paused for an instant, then replied smoothly, "Julie, I don't know him at all. He was a fan. I agreed to tell him about one of my old movies . . ."

"China, that doesn't sound like you. You never want to talk about the past. It all seems like too much of a coincidence. You and Pierpont Tree, who is, after all, a kind of private investigator, sneak off with Lars and then Lars gets run over. Are you holding out on me?"

"Don't be silly, Julie. Frankly I was bored and feeling a little out of it. I needed an attention fix. Lars didn't mention how he happened to be there. Do you know?"

"Yes, of course I do. I called the Sultan's aide. He checked the list. This Lars Eklund fellow was the escort of Chooey Harrington. You know who she is, don't you, China? The socialite who was born without a brain. Anyway, I haven't been able to reach her. Listen, if you think of anything at all, call me."

"Sure. Now I'm going out to get the paper and read the story. Talk to you soon, Julie."

China hung up and sprinted to the front door. There, directly under a sprinkler, was the *Tribune.* She scooped it up, ran through the gate and on to Casa Arbol. She found Pier on the terrace, head bowed and pencil poised over a crossword puzzle.

"Pier, have you seen this? Here. Read that. Never mind, it doesn't say anything anyway except that he is twenty-six and from New York. May I have a sip of your coffee? Maybe a kiss?"

"In what order?" Pier kissed her before she could reply. "And who is twenty-six and from New York?"

"Lars Eklund. That young man you terrified at the Sultan's house. Beau Paxton's boyfriend. He was injured in a hit-and-run accident late last night. Near the Design Center."

"Near the Design Center? He would have wanted it that way."

"Pier, for shame. Seriously, does that close the case? Lars Eklund did it? The perfect crime but fate stepped in and punished him. God, I made a movie with the same plot. *Love for Sale.* I wore a platinum blond wig and was killed by an evil midget. But I deserved it. I was evil too."

"China, do you really think Lars Eklund killed Beau Paxton? What does your legendary intuition tell you?"

"It tells me no one killed Beau Paxton. He's still alive. Ran away with Elvis."

"Want coffee? I'll make a fresh pot."

"Thanks, I'd rather sip yours. Julie called this morning about the story. She wanted information about Lars. Told her he was just a fan. You don't think Lars had Beau Paxton killed?"

"China, do you really believe that rather silly boy could actually find a hit man, professional or otherwise, and order up a murder?"

China smiled thoughtfully. "Maybe Lars did some decorating for a big-time mafioso. They offered him a free hit in lieu of a fee and he chose Beau Paxton?"

"Why?"

"Maybe Beau was going to leave Lars for Dilly Dillingham and her money. After all, we don't know what his intentions really were. It's hearsay, isn't it? Couldn't Lars have been the killer?"

"If Lars killed Beau Paxton, who tried to kill Lars? Assuming it was no accident."

"Well, Peerless Detective, give me another sip of your coffee, and you tell me," said China.

"This seems to be the classic moment to call my favorite D.A. I'll ask Max Steiner to come up for lunch. His reelection campaign has begun, so he might oblige a major contributor."

"After the way you got Max off the hook when you solved the Anderson murder for him," said China, "he'll be glad to help with or without a campaign contribution."

"Sure. But he'll be even gladder to take a chopper up here if I ante up. I'd like to talk to him today or tomorrow so I can cross-check Eddie's findings."

China lit a cigarette and then waved a hand to clear away the smoke. "Sorry. I know you especially dislike this in the morning. What has Eddie found?"

"He's confirmed the gossip on Norton Birdwell. Birdwell inherited a bundle. Oil and oil-drilling equipment were the family business.

He took care of his widowed mother until she died, then headed for Hollywood. Bought a house on three acres in Bel Air, started financing movies. He liked hungry young actors. Lots of them. Then he met Beau Paxton. He was smitten. They lived together for years. Norton was the original big spender until his movie ventures flopped. Then the collapse of oil prices played hell with his cash flow. He's lost almost everything except his house and that's heavily mortgaged. Eddie thinks Beau knew about this and told Birdwell he was leaving him for someone else. Maybe Lars. Maybe Dilly Dillingham. Either way, Norton Birdwell had a strong motive for murder."

"Where did Eddie get all this?" China asked.

"Some from a lawyer down in Texas. Some he got from a gay bartender," said Pier.

"You're not going to tell me Eddie's gay?"

"No, he's a chameleon. He takes on the coloration of any scene. Whenever Marta has to work late at one of those bars she keeps the books for, Eddie picks her up. You know Eddie. He picks up information, too. The bars Marta works for are all mob-owned and some of them are gay."

"Okay, but doesn't it follow that Dilly Dillingham would have the same motive? If she knew Beau Paxton was leaving her for Lars Eklund, wouldn't she be inclined to have Beau shot? By the way, was it definitely murder for hire?"

"Another film title, China?"

"You're thinking of *This Gun for Hire*. Pier, be patient with me and tell me again why you're so sure it was a hired hit. Was it something the witness saw?"

"Something he heard. Just before the shot, the gunman said, *Who's the editor?* Beau Paxton said, *I am.* If it weren't for that question, overheard by the waiter, the police would have had no reason to think the murder was anything other than one more killing during a random robbery attempt."

"Ah-ha. Listen to this. What if the killer was so rattled he shot the wrong man? Maybe he wanted to know who the editor was so he could shoot the *other* one. What if Norton Birdwell was the real target? How's that for deductive reasoning?"

"High marks. And it's possible."

"But Birdwell is the one the police suspect?"

"Top of the charts."

"On your hit parade too?"

"Birdwell could have hired the hit man and told him to be damn sure he shot the right guy—"

"I just don't see Birdwell having a screaming match with Beau when he's got a hit man stationed outside in the parking lot. And how would Birdwell know enough about the underworld to hire a killer?" China looked puzzled for a moment. "Is 'underworld' a dated term? Anyway, how would he find someone?"

"How would you go about it, China Carlyle?"

"I forgot to bring an ashtray. Don't look, I'm going to use my saucer. Just remember, it's less icky than a fried egg."

"*North by Northwest?*"

"*To Catch a Thief.* Pier, if Max does come for lunch, am I invited?"

"Definitely not. Your beauty distracts him. The man can't even think when you're around. But think about this question.

"Was Beau Paxton going to go straight and marry the wealthy heiress Dilly Dillingham, or stay as sweet as he was and live happily ever after with the recently almost-late decorator Lars Eklund?"

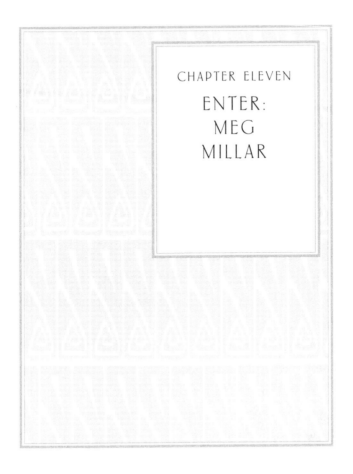

CHAPTER ELEVEN

ENTER: MEG MILLAR

Driving east on Sunset Boulevard, Pier counted another Range Rover. Twelve since Santa Barbara. He would bet the farm not one had ever been off-road.

Besides counting Rovers, he had been reviewing Beau Paxton's murder. A witness heard the shooter ask which one was the editor before pulling the trigger. That ruled out a random robbery attempt. If the accidental witness had not appeared, would Birdwell have reported the killer's question? No way to know. The murder of Beau Paxton was definitely deliberate, unless China was right and the target was really Norton Birdwell. But who would want to kill practically penniless Birdwell? No answer came to mind, so Pier considered motives. No shortage there.

Everyone seemed to have a good reason to want Beau dead. The client, Seth Rupert, stood to gain half of Beau's stock if *Manor House* went public as his brother Jonas wanted. Seth seemed to have more reason to kill brother Jonas than he did to kill Beau, although half of Beau's stock plus five million dollars from the insurance payoff could be more than enough motive. Eddie was already researching the value of *Manor House.* Then they could approximate the value of Beau Paxton's shares.

With Beau dead, Jonas, too, would receive half of Beau's stock. And, of course, half of the insurance on his life. Maybe Beau was on Seth's side against *Manor House* going public. Hiring someone to murder Beau would remove one obstruction in Jonas' path. If that were true, Seth's life might be in danger. Would Jonas hire a killer to do in his own brother?

Lars Eklund's "accident" would seem to eliminate him as a suspect, although it was remotely possible that the hit-and-run actually was an accident. Never eliminate the possibility of coincidence. Life supplies a load of them. Yes, Lars could have been just another accidental statistic. Not bloody likely.

Had Lars found out that Norton Birdwell had hired Beau Paxton's murderer? Then Birdwell paid to have Lars hit too? Kill them both. One hit, one hit-and-run? It seemed amateurish. Mafia movies to the contrary, death by hit-and-run was no sure thing.

Pier was about to meet another suspect with a strong motive. Meg Millar. She wanted Beau Paxton's job. And there was another twist. If both Seth and Jonas Rupert died, Meg would become the majority owner of *Manor House.* If Meg had paid a killer to murder Beau Paxton, might she not just continue on her merry way and have the Rupert brothers offed too? Then everything would be hers.

Pier remembered the Sultan's party. Julie Warren was the second or third person to say that Beau Paxton was engaged to Dilly Dillingham. Pier hadn't seen Dilly for three or four years, but she had always been a spoiled brat. Now she was a suspect. So was Meg. Obvious motive. Probably smart enough to think she could get away with it.

The Hotel Bel-Air sign was barely visible, but Pier spotted Stone Canyon Road just in time. The trees on either side of the narrow street leaned toward each other, branches meeting above and obscuring the sun. The mansions that lined the street were hidden too, protected by huge iron gates. It was obvious even to someone driving by that here landscaping alone cost more than the average house in Beverly Hills.

After a few blocks, Pier saw the tile roofs of the pink cottages clustered on the hotel grounds. The Bel-Air was a unique haven. Pier thought it the finest hotel in the world. He turned left off Stone Canyon into the entrance and drove up to the canopy, where Bob, the parking captain, opened the car door. "Haven't seen you for a long time, Mr. Tree. We've missed you."

Pier walked under the canvas canopy that sheltered the long, arched stone bridge. The bridge spanned a wide creek and a waterfall which spilled down quietly, as discreet as old money. In the upper pond, three swans, as ill mannered as all their kind, swam in stately fashion, carefully avoiding the waterfall. At the end of the bridge, Pier looked at his watch. He had a few minutes. He turned toward the glass-enclosed office of his friend Frank Bowling, who managed the hotel in the best European tradition. But the office was empty.

Pier continued through the passageway, banked year-round with flowers, and turned right on the path to the dining room. The maître d' greeted him and led the way to where Meg was waiting in the booth Pier had reserved. She was almost hidden by the large menu, but he could see the highlights in her dark blond hair, cut chin length and worn straight. A quick, shampoo-in-the-shower hairstyle. She had fair skin, dark brows, long lashes. Good posture. Shoulders back. White sweater, necklace of gold circles. Small hands, no rings. Gold watch with a large face. A woman conscious of time, which she probably had little of, but she had not kept him waiting.

As Pier neared the table, she looked up. Gray eyes. Lashes so thick they looked like smudged makeup.

"Mr. Tree?" Her voice was soft, unaccented.

Pier seated himself in the large booth, keeping enough distance between them to observe her without turning. "And you are the talented Miss Millar." At that moment, a waiter appeared with a menu for Pier, ready for drink orders. Pier asked Meg Millar, "Will you have wine or a Bloody Mary?"

"Thank you, but I think some tea would be nice."

"Iced?" the waiter asked, pencil poised.

"Hot, please."

"Herb or regular?"

"Regular."

"And you, sir?"

"Coffee."

"Iced?"

"No. Just hot coffee."

"Regular or decaffeinated?"

"Regular."

Pier smiled at Meg Millar and shrugged his shoulders. "Life today. Too many choices. Thank you for meeting me here. As I mentioned on the telephone, Seth Rupert asked me to look into Beau Paxton's murder. I'd appreciate some background on the magazine. Several people, including Seth, told me you're the one who really runs *Manor House*. Why didn't they make you editor? Were Paxton's contacts really that valuable?"

She looked at him directly. The intensity surprised him. "At first, yes, they probably were. However, *Manor House* is so well established now, the magazine itself has the strength. But both Ruperts probably still believe that without Beau's contacts the magazine will collapse."

"You don't think that will happen?"

Meg stared at Pier, evaluating him. "Maybe it's stupid of me to say this, but the magazine won't be hurt at all. I know all of Beau's contacts, and I do the work." Meg leaned forward and spoke with quiet intensity. "Mr. Tree, Seth encouraged me to speak to you quite freely but Jonas told me to make my statement brief and cosmetic. Whether or not the killer is caught interests him only marginally. He just doesn't want bad publicity. Jonas knows you are very well connected so he doesn't want to offend you, but he does hope you'll go away quietly *and* never return."

"And how do you feel?"

Meg Millar sighed and sipped her tea.

"I liked Beau. I want his killer punished. If you can make that happen, then I'm all for you. That's why I'm here. The Rupert brothers do not make moral decisions for me. Nor does anyone else." She smiled for the first time and added, "I'm here, Mr. Tree, because I believe it's the right thing to do. Does that seem old-fashioned?"

"It may sound odd here in the land of let's-make-a-deal, but I believe there are more people in the world than we know, Horatio, who care about morality. Now, let's order lunch before you brief me on the history of *Manor House*, if you will."

"Mr. Tree, despite my moral stance, I'll do just about anything for the tortilla soup."

Pier signaled their waiter. "The lady will have the tortilla soup. I'll have your great hamburger sandwich, heavy on the cholesterol, but first bring me a Scotch and water. Miss Millar, since I've dropped my defenses, revealing my weakness for Scotch, could I persuade you to have a glass of wine or something stronger?"

"If anyone could persuade me, you could, but I'll stay with hot tea, thanks."

"That's it then?" the waiter asked, evidencing mild disappointment.

The moment he left, Pier asked, "May I call you Meg? And will you call me Pier?"

"Yes, Pier."

"Good. Now tell me all about the magazine."

Meg Millar sat up even straighter, squared her shoulders, smiled and said, "It all began on a dark and stormy night when a little old lady who lived in Pasadena decided to start a publication of sorts to promote her husband's furniture stores. At least that was ostensibly the reason. Actually, they both hoped it would keep their son, then in his late twenties, out of the bathhouses. He was interested in decorating so they began publishing a catalog called *Paxton's Manor House.* Beau was the editor.

"*Manor House* was published quarterly with pictures of houses chockablock with furniture from Paxton's Fine Furniture Stores. The advertising manager for the stores suggested they sell ads in *Manor House* to other companies. He urged Beau to put some editorial material in the catalog to make it seem more like a magazine. That worked pretty well and Beau loved the attention that comes with the title of editor, so his parents put up the money to launch *Manor House* as a real magazine. Of course, Beau needed someone to do the real work. Enter Meg Millar."

"Hold it right there, because I'd like to know something about Meg Millar, but . . ." Pier gestured toward the approaching waiter, who served them and moved swiftly to the next table.

"If I can tell you between bites, I will. I'm suddenly very hungry. I've hardly eaten since I first heard about Beau." Meg sampled her soup and buttered a roll.

Before she could resume, Pier asked, "And where were you when you heard about Beau?"

"Ah, a variation on the classic question. I was driving to the office when I heard a news report at eight A.M. And, to anticipate your next question, I was home alone working the night Beau was killed. No alibi. Nevertheless, I didn't put on blackface, a dreadlocks wig and shoot Beau. And I wouldn't know how to hire a hit man unless there's a section in the Yellow Pages. I can tell you about myself just as quickly. Born in Hollywood, although no one believes anyone is actually born there. My parents were bit players in the movies. They adopted me when I was a year old. We always lived nicely but they were never sure they would get another job. If there were no more jobs, we would lose the house. That's what they always said when they had a little too much to drink, which became more frequent as they grew older. Dad actually had a heart attack on a movie set and died right there. After that, Mother never left the house. She looked at their scrapbooks, watched their old movies on television and tippled. Three years ago, she had a stroke and that wrote The End. I inherited their house in Hollywood and I still live there."

"Where in Hollywood?"

"Near Sunset and Laurel Canyon. A lot of old-time movie people have houses there. Mike O'Shea is my next-door neighbor. He's my godfather. I grew up calling him Uncle Mike. He directed a lot of great Westerns."

"What about you, Meg? Didn't you want to be in the movies too? You look enough like Jodie Foster to be her sister."

Meg laughed.

"I wanted a career in something solid and secure, which journalism certainly is not, but I managed to overlook the obvious and was lucky. Do you mind if I smoke? Sorry, but I'm addicted." Pier lighted Meg's cigarette and placed an ashtray in front of her now empty plate.

"To continue, I started right out of school with a small newspaper in the Valley, then I survived a short stint at the *Herald-Express* before becoming managing editor of one of our local magazines, *L.A. Now.* I was only twenty-five when the Paxtons hired me as Beau's ghost editor. That's it."

"Beau didn't resent you?"

"No. Well, maybe at first. But he was five years older than I was in years and fifty years older in social experience. He knew everyone and had been everywhere. On top of that, he was the son and heir. It didn't take him long to realize I was going to do the work and shut up, so he decided he liked me. The arrangement suited me just fine. I love the actual work of putting out a magazine. Not all the socializing Beau loved."

"Was it a monthly publication then?"

"Oh, no. That came much later. It began as a quarterly. We couldn't increase the frequency until I could build a staff. That's not easy in Los Angeles because there are so few magazines here. We lack the editorial talent pool you find in New York. But we managed to make our deadlines and get through the first year. Circulation was pathetic, advertising was anemic. However, the Paxtons spared no expense for Beau. *Manor House* paper was the best they could buy. Lots of color photographs, fine reproduction, the best printing. The physical package was opulent. But it wasn't going anywhere until I decided to try a By Invitation Only subscription offer. Quite a few actually R.S.V.P.'d. Then a few more. Slowly, it became sort of chic to subscribe to *Manor House.*"

"What happened next?"

"Poor old Mr. Paxton died. Mrs. Paxton kept the magazine going because of Beau. When *Home World* changed their format to an imitation of *Architectural Digest,* a lot of media attention focused on the entire field and the press started writing about *Manor House,* too. One newspaper said that of all the *A.D.* look-alikes, we were not only the best, we were better than the original. The *New York Times* called us a house organ for the very rich. Subscriptions poured in. Everything looked good. Then Mrs. Paxton learned she had cancer. She died a few months later. Afterward, the attorney told Beau his mother had gone through most of the money and mortgaged the stores so heavily there was practically nothing left."

Pier finished his sandwich and his Scotch almost simultaneously before asking, "How did Beau react to all of this?"

"He ran away. When I didn't hear from him for several months, it seemed pretty clear he wasn't coming back. I tried to keep the magazine afloat until I could find a buyer or another job, whichever came first. Then the Rupert brothers surfaced. They told our attorney they wanted to buy the magazine, so we hired a private detective to find Beau . . . Was it you?"

"Not me. Missing persons work is highly specialized."

"You specialize in murder?"

"It seems to work out that way. Where did they find Beau?"

"Tangier. Jonas and the attorney flew over to talk Beau into selling the magazine. It was easy. Beau had discovered kef. He would have agreed to anything. They brought him back to Los Angeles, put him in a drug rehab clinic. When he came out, he was told he could play editor of *Manor House* as long as he stayed clean and let me run things. They gave me a huge raise and promised an equity position if I made it a success. I did but they didn't. Perhaps that's not quite fair. Jonas didn't. Beau could have made it happen if he had stood up for me. But he didn't."

"Did Beau have stock?"

"He retained ten percent of the stock when he sold the magazine to the Ruperts. His attorney insisted, because if the company ever went public it would mean a lot of money."

"Then Seth and Jonas each hold forty-five percent of the stock?"

"Correct."

"Meg, the magazine must be very costly to produce. Is it profitable?"

"Very. The actual figures are confidential."

"Of course. Will you become the editor now?"

"Yes. Actually, the Ruperts told me this morning. I wasn't going to tell you because it makes me such an obvious suspect, but it will be announced early next week anyway."

"Congratulations. Shall I order champagne?"

"No, thanks. But I will have more tea."

"I want you to know I appreciate your candor and I don't want to take advantage of your forthrightness *but.* There's always a but, isn't there? But I really need to know whatever you can tell me about the Rupert brothers, too. Seth, as well as Jonas." Pier nodded to their waiter and ordered more tea and coffee without seeming to take his eyes from Meg.

"Seth is your client. What if you discover that he's guilty?"

"If I uncover evidence implicating Seth I'll turn it over to the

District Attorney. Seth knows that. Would he have a reason to want Beau Paxton dead?"

"No. I can't imagine any reason. Nor can I imagine Seth killing anyone. Jonas has a mean streak. But he's smart. Smarter than Seth and much more complicated. He resented Beau's owning stock in the magazine but, good heavens, not enough to kill him."

Meg squeezed a splash of lemon in her tea, surreptitiously looking at her watch. Pier looked openly at his and assured her, "We'll just be another minute. I know you want to get back to the office. By the way, I'm meeting Seth there later. Would you have time to give me a tour and show me how the magazine is put together?"

"Delighted."

"Last question. Probably. What about the Ruperts' personal lives? Are they married? Divorced? Children?"

"That was four questions, if I were counting." Meg laughed. "Both married while they were still in college. Seth and his wife had a daughter. His wife was crazy, really crazy. They divorced several years ago. He's had several affairs but there's no one currently. At least no one I know about. Jonas and his wife didn't have any children. They divorced about ten years ago."

Meg was sliding out of the booth when Pier asked one more question. "And you, Meg? No ring. Have you ever married?"

"No. I was involved with someone for a long time but we never married. I'm still on my own."

"And liking it?"

"And liking it. Now, before we go, let me ask what you think of me as a suspect, Detective Tree. Am I the one whodunit?"

"Did you?"

Meg laughed again.

"No. But then it hadn't occurred to me."

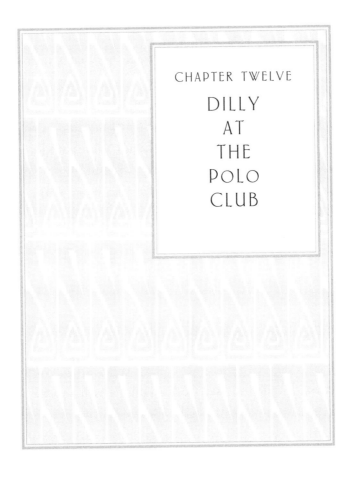

CHAPTER TWELVE

DILLY
AT
THE
POLO
CLUB

The metal-shod hooves of the ponies dug into the ground like small, sharp spades, scooping up divots of moist black earth. The polo field, freshly sodded, thick and trim, cushioned the pounding as the ponies raced, wheeled, stopped, turned on invisible dimes, while mallets whacked balls at killing speed.

Pier left his car and stood at the whitewashed fence for a moment, watching men and ponies practice. He liked the frantic pace, the clopping sound of many hooves galloping on turf. As a boy, he came with his father to the Polo Club matches, watching each chukker, sipping his lemonade. He loved the wide-eyed courage of the ponies, their riders sharing the constant danger. But the men had two advantages: helmets and choice.

Pier could hear the ponies breathing hard, tiring of the relentless pace, racing up and down the field, mallets and balls narrowly missing their heads. Like gladiators, they were forced into battle. Pier could see their sweat, smell their fear. Unlike gladiators, they were not urged on by emperors. Their masters were attorneys, actors, wholesale distributors of plumbing equipment and, often, South American pros for hire to any team for the right price.

Pier turned from the huge green fields paralleling the ocean and walked toward the white paddocks. Dilly had told him she would be there or in the clubhouse. It had been five years since he attended her wedding to Jon Gower at St. Alban's Episcopal Church-by-the-Sea. Those who cried at the wedding had had good reason to weep. Jon Gower was a legendary ladies' man, a worldly forty-four years old to Dilly's naive twenty-one. A stockbroker, his advice was uniformly disastrous, but he romanced one wealthy widow after another, leaving each with a considerable dent in her fortune. Dilly's youth and adoration fueled love in the afternoon, but it was the great fortune she would inherit when her ailing father died that inspired a swift proposal. Dilly's father reluctantly gave her hand in marriage, then changed his will, structuring her future inheritance in a way that would limit her annual income and preserve her capital from his son-in-law.

When he learned the terms of the will, Gower had taken up with an older woman, holder of a lesser, but unencumbered, fortune. He told Dilly he wanted an immediate divorce. And the best polo ponies, not just the ones Dilly had bought for him, but the best of her father's string, too. Old Mr. Dillingham considered the trade of a few horses for the return of his adored daughter the best deal he ever made.

Pier noticed a ponytailed blonde on a paint stallion trotting off the practice field. It was Dilly.

Her mount snorted and pranced. She waved to Pier, kicked the pony into a gallop and rode straight at him. Inches from where he stood, she reined to an abrupt halt. "Hi, Pier. This is Gordo. Isn't he great! Wasn't that the cleanest stop you've ever seen? Did you think I was going to ride you down?"

Still talking, Dilly dismounted, reached up and kissed Pier on the cheek. Close up Pier could see the faint freckles on Dilly's nose. Her big blue eyes made her look as innocent as an eight-year-old. Pier suspected that even as an old woman, Dilly would still play Daddy's little girl. Her voice was breathless, with a slight whine. "It's been a long time. Haven't seen you since my wedding. Was going to invite you to my next but the groom got himself killed. Come on, let's go to the clubhouse. We'll have a drink and catch up."

As Dilly tied Gordo's reins to the rail fence under a shade tree, Pier spoke for the first time. "I want to talk to you about Beau Paxton."

"Guess he wasn't really my true love because I just made a date with that Latin riding the bay over there. No mourning period at all. I must be crazy to even think of going out with one of those guys from the Argentine. They treat women like they treat their ponies."

"Not so good?"

"They break their spirit. Those ponies will do whatever they're asked without hesitation. They'll jump through fire if the rider gives the signal."

"How do they break their spirit, Dilly? The ponies, that is."

"Blindfold them and shoot guns near their heads. Hobble their legs, then make them fall over. They have lots of cute tricks. Polo used to be a gentleman's sport. Amateur riders. But now lots of those guys who've been rich for about five minutes think it's macho to have their own teams. They only care about winning, so they bring in pros. Oh, spit, I'm not going out with that Argentine. That's just going to the other extreme after Beau, isn't it? Beau was so gentle and, well, I guess artistic is the word, don't you think?"

"Dilly, I never knew Beau Paxton. Seth Rupert of *Manor House* asked me to look into his murder."

"Oh, Seth. I only met him a couple of times. He hired you, huh? Pier, why not let Beau rest in peace? I don't know anything anyway." Dilly's muddy boots scuffed the damp grass as they walked to the clubhouse entrance.

"Nothing's changed, I see." Pier glanced at the white clapboard cottage that was the Polo Club's social headquarters before opening the door for Dilly. The interior still looked like a dowdy private residence. A cozy bar with a few stools and nearby a few comfortable wing chairs. Round tables of old oak, scarred by years of cigarette burns, were set up for lunch on the far side of the room. Rays of morning sun made their way feebly through unwashed windows. Mismatched table lamps gave hope of light to come.

"Floyd, give us a couple of Bloodies, will you?" Dilly dropped into a wing chair and put her boots on a tree stump pressed into service as a table. "Alright with you, Pier?"

"Why not? After all, it's only three or four hours until lunchtime."

"Was that sarcasm? I don't remember you being that way. Probably what life with that movie star's done to you." Dilly brushed her ponytail away from one shoulder and pouted. "You should have looked my way before you took up with her. You know how much Daddy's always liked you."

"Always liked him, too." Pier picked up their drinks from the bar. Floyd was busy watching a baseball game on a small black and white television set. Pier called out to Floyd, "Who's ahead?"

"Giants, seven to three."

"Pier, if you're gonna talk baseball, I'm going back out and take Gordo to his paddock. Come on, now. I never see you. Pay attention to me."

"I am. You still look about sixteen years old, Dilly. And you're still a brat. You probably got involved with Beau Paxton because it would bother your father."

"Oh, spit. You know me too well, Pier. But, you know, that was really humiliating when Jon left me for an older woman. Older! Course everybody knows he was just after her money. Even though Daddy's sick, he's probably gonna outlive us all and Jon didn't want to wait to get rich. They're honeymooning in Europe now. I hope they both fall off an Alp or something. What am I gonna do when they come back, Pier? This is a small town. We'll be running into each other at the Valley Club, the Coral Casino and right here at Polo. Spit. I just couldn't afford him. Daddy taught me to live off the interest from the interest. Jon would've even invaded my trust if he could. Anyway, it's gonna be awkward when they come back here, you know?"

Pier changed the subject. "Tell me about Beau Paxton. How did you meet?"

"Do you really have to ask me all that stuff? Listen, let's have another Bloody. I'll tell you what I know and that's that." Dilly bobbed her head as exclamation point and swung her boots down, stamping the floor. "Floyd," she yelled at the barman, but, game over, he was already on his way with two more. "Oh, thanks." She lifted her glass. "Here's to us, Pier. Get rid of that movie star, why don't you? Daddy wouldn't even care that you're still married to Hilary. Techni- cally, that is. Why don't we have dinner tonight? Not a date. Just to talk about how it was before all those new people came up here from Beverly Hills and polluted everything. That's what Daddy says they do. Pollute everything." When she put her glass on the table, it was only half full.

"Dilly, are you trying to avoid talking about Beau?"

"No. Why should I? I just think you should let sleeping dogs lie. Or whatever. I don't mean that Beau was a dog. I'd never speak ill of the dead. Well, what do you want to know, Pier?"

"How did you meet Beau? Let's start there." Pier watched Dilly closely as she tossed her head and sighed with exasperation. She has the mannerisms of a pony, he thought, glancing at his untouched drink. He waited for Dilly's answer.

"Beau came to Montecito looking for places to put in *Manor House.* There was a dinner for him and Beau told funny stories about the people who owned the houses he put in the magazine. He knew everyone in the world, all kinds of fascinating people. He was really sophisticated. Well, I was kind of flattered when he asked me to go with him the next day to see the old Manning house. Some Beverly Hills couple bought it. You remember the story? Old Mrs. Manning built it back in the early thirties, then decided it was too big so she just cut off the second floor. Sliced it right off, just like that." Dilly made an abrupt slicing motion that ended with a wave to Floyd for another drink. Pier looked at Floyd and shook his head, declining another.

Dilly sank back into the wing chair, swung her boots back up on the tree stump and addressed herself to her drink. Pier urged, "Go on, Dilly. Beau was taking you to see the old Manning place."

Dilly looked up at Pier as if somewhat surprised to see he was still there. "What was I saying? Oh, I know. Those people who bought it just built the second floor right back on, only they added a few turrets and some cupolas. No one we know had been inside but I was dying to see it. Well, we went there the very next day. It was awful. Full of fake antiques. Then we had lunch and Beau asked if I would have dinner with him the next weekend. That's how it started. We were going to be married next month."

Pier thought he saw a tear slip down Dilly's round cheek but in the dim light he couldn't be sure. "Did it occur to you, Dilly, that he might be another fortune hunter?"

"Oh, sure. But that was the good part. He didn't need my money. He owned the magazine. Well, he did have those two partners, the Rupert brothers, but he was very well off and he lived with his old uncle who had even more money and Beau was his sole heir. We could have had a real fun time, Pier, going all over the world looking at houses." Dilly sighed and sipped again before continuing. "Daddy didn't want me to marry Beau. He said he'd asked friends in L.A. about him and they said he was a pansy. Well, I said to Daddy, then why does he want to marry me? Daddy just said, we'll see about that. I did take up with Beau for a reason but it wasn't to annoy Daddy. I just wanted to show everyone around here, including my rat ex-husband, that this man everybody was so impressed with chose *me*. And not for my money. Then he was gone. I'm really sorry. You don't have any idea how sorry I am." This time, Pier thought she meant it.

Dilly pulled a handkerchief from her jodhpurs and blew her nose. She signaled Floyd for another drink. Pier spoke to her very gently. "Dilly, who do you think had Beau killed? Do you have any idea?"

"I don't know. Everyone was just crazy about Beau. Well, we did run into people sometimes whose houses he'd rejected. I mean, he wouldn't put their house in the magazine and they were pretty angry about it but not enough to *kill* him!"

"Dilly, you know how much I like your father. But I have to ask you this. Do you think he might have hired someone to kill Beau Paxton?"

"Daddy? Pier, you can't mean that! Daddy would never do anything like that. If he wanted Beau dead, he would have shot him himself, like a gentleman." Dilly's blue eyes were wide with outrage. Her freckles seemed to redden with her anger. "How can you ask that? How can you even think such a thing?"

"Because the police will ask that and a lot more. They'll question you and your father. It's better to hear the questions from me first."

"Why would the police question me? Or Daddy? You do all that detective stuff. Just tell them you've already questioned us." Dilly gulped the rest of her drink.

"Dilly," Pier took her hand, "it doesn't work that way. The police have specific procedures, routines, that have to be followed very precisely. They question everyone close to the victim. No exceptions. Several people have already told the police that you were engaged to Beau and they've probably heard your father was against the marriage."

"Pier, come with me right now. You can tell us what to say. We've never been questioned by policemen. I don't think we've ever even met one. If you won't do it for me, do it for Daddy."

"I can't, Dilly. I've been retained by Seth Rupert to investigate Beau's murder. I can't coach you. Just tell the truth."

"Seth Rupert. What about him? He probably had Beau killed so his girlfriend could have Beau's job. Daddy will give you more money than Seth Rupert ever could."

"What's this about Seth's girlfriend, Dilly?"

"That awful woman who worked for Beau at *Manor House*. I don't remember her name, but she was always pushing herself forward, trying to take credit for Beau's work. Come on, Pier. Talk to Daddy. He'll give you a check this minute. Fifty thousand? A hundred thousand? Whatever you say."

"Not ethical, Dilly. I've already accepted a retainer."

"For God's sake, Pier, just give it back."

"It's not the money, Dilly. This is what I *do.* It's my work. I have my own rules and I won't break them for anyone."

"I'll bet you'd break them for that movie star but you won't do it for us." Dilly threw her empty glass at the stone fireplace with amazing force.

Floyd looked up from the ball game, shrugged his shoulders, came out from behind the bar with dustpan and broom. He handed them to Dilly. "You clean up your mess, Dilly."

"And you go straight to hell!" Dilly's boots pounded as she ran out of the clubhouse, slamming the door.

Floyd looked at Pier and shook his head. "Her daddy spoiled her rotten." He swept the broken glass into the dustpan.

"Did Dilly ever bring her new boyfriend here, Floyd?"

"Nope. Not that I ever saw. But she and old man Dillingham had a big fight about him. They came in one day after she gave one of her ponies a workout. Mr. Dillingham told her he'd give her a million dollars if she'd break up with that fellow. She got real mad. Mr. Dillingham said she'd better take the money because he'd see to it she never married no pansy, was what he said." Floyd bent down to look for stray shards of glass, found none and trudged back to his post behind the bar.

"What happened then, Floyd?"

"Same thing. I swept up the broken glass after she ran out the door. Slammed it too, just like she did today. That little lady gets mad when she can't have her way, I can tell you that."

Pier thanked Floyd and walked outside. He could see Dilly driving her sports car off the polo grounds to the frontage road. She drove faster than she should and clouds of dust trailed her wheels. Was it true, what she'd said, that Meg Millar was Seth Rupert's girlfriend, or was Dilly trying to protect herself, giving him a false lead? Pier realized he didn't really know Dilly at all. He wondered if she could become angry enough to kill. Or use her fortune to get whatever she wanted, even if it meant murder.

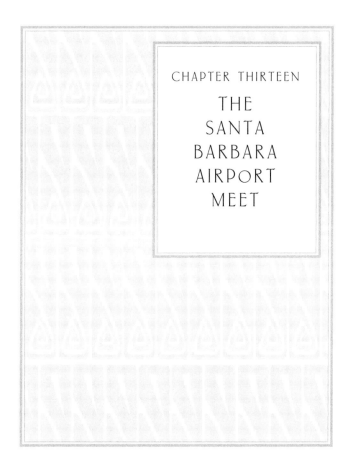

CHAPTER THIRTEEN

THE SANTA BARBARA AIRPORT MEET

Pier headed his old Rover toward the gates of the Polo Club, turned right when he hit the frontage road, then right again onto the Pacific Coast Highway. In the rearview mirror he could see part of the Moorish mansion built smack on the sand many years ago, now hidden by a strip of stores and snack shops along 101. It was called Santa Claus Lane. An eyesore for years, new owners had added a unifying facade and a coat of paint. Santa, permanently stuck in a chimney, still loomed like a Macy's parade balloon. Looking to his right, Pier wondered for the hundredth time why the builders of the Polo Club condominiums hadn't painted them white with green trim instead of brown on beige.

Rolling north on 101, Pier was headed for the Santa Barbara Airport, which was actually in Goleta, the town that was also home to the University of California at Santa Barbara. The airport terminal, built in 1941 by Edwards and Plunkett, the architects who had influenced so much of Santa Barbara's post-earthquake construction, had been designed on the residential scale of a Spanish Revival hacienda.

Pier looked at his watch and estimated the timing would be just right if the traffic kept moving along at a reasonable pace. He would meet Max Steiner's chopper in about thirty minutes. They would have a cup of coffee and compare notes. Since Pier had left the Polo Club, he'd been wondering about Meg Millar. Had she been Seth's girlfriend?

Pier parked in the short-term lot and crossed the narrow road in front of the airport. They had agreed to meet inside the terminal. Remembering his morning *New York Times* crossword, he tried to work "alit" into a sentence but lost the thought when he saw Max Steiner, already waiting, pacing impatiently. He had always been impatient, Pier recalled. But, he reminded himself, if Max had been patient, he might be running his late father's drugstore.

Pier had always liked Max. He knew it hadn't been easy to be the only Jewish kid in a private prep school in the heart of Wasp-land— and a scholarship student, at that. But Max had winning ways even then. He was voted most popular in his senior year. Pier thought it might well be the victory that meant more to Max than any other.

Max was pacing with the concentration that had won him scholarships all the way from prep school to Stanford Law. He saw Pier and walked toward him, smiling the smile that helped him win a landslide victory. After Max won the upcoming election and served his second term, Pier expected he would take dead aim on Washington, D.C.

The two tall men matched strides through the lobby, then up the stairs to the airport restaurant, Pier an inch or so taller, Max a few pounds heavier. Pier's hair was the color of sunburned wheat, Max's almost black.

"Pier, is this place as bad as it used to be?"

"Toast is safe. If you like coffee, you'd better have tea. Come on, let's take that corner booth."

They slid on the Naugahyde until they were close enough to talk without being overheard. Pier opened. "Max, what do the police have at this point?"

"Nothing that means anything. The Rupert brothers are suspects because they had insured Paxton's life with one of those key man policies corporations take out on their executives. Five million. In their bracket, that's not worth a killing. You said Seth Rupert is your client?"

Pier nodded.

Max Steiner took a paper pad from his pocket and made a couple of notes while continuing to talk to Pier. "Then we have Norton Birdwell. He also took out a life insurance policy on Beau Paxton a couple of years ago. Also pays five million. On the surface, Birdwell's financial picture sounds good, but Southern California's biggest crop is funny money. And when you throw in the lovers' quarrel overheard in Le Club, bingo, Birdwell might be the lucky winner."

"China thinks the quarrel proves that Birdwell couldn't have done it. She refuses to believe that Birdwell would have threatened Beau if he knew that in the next hour he was having him killed," said Pier.

"That's because China's so direct herself. She doesn't understand deceit. And so far I'm told that Birdwell is off the charts, *down* off," said Max.

"What about . . ." Pier was interrupted by the slow-motion appearance of a waitress. He quickly ordered. "Two coffees, two Danish and the check." She lost interest before he finished speaking.

Max offered consolation. "Maybe she'll just bring the check and not bother us with the rest."

"Could save our lives."

"Pier, what were you asking before Mildred Pierce interrupted?"

"Any leads on the shooter?"

"Not yet. Nothing beyond the original statement of the waiter who witnessed the shooting. He said the guy was black, wearing a motorcycle jacket, his hair in dreadlocks. He heard him say, 'Which one's the editor?', and he gave us a fair description of both shooter and car but says he couldn't positively I.D. either one. Now, what have you got?"

"Eddie's digging into the financials. *Manor House* is a privately held company so he can't just scan the annual report to the stockholders. He'll come up with something. He's doing background checks on the principal players in our little drama."

Max Steiner's blue eyes narrowed. "Christ, did I fly up here on that metal-fatigued whirlybird just to hear that? Is that it? Pier, I've got the goddamn press all over me. They won't leave me alone. The press gets orgasmic about murder among the rich and famous. KNBC is interviewing decorators around the clock like a Jerry Lewis marathon. Come on, Pier, this is your meat. Murder among the rich. You're one of them. We're grubby public servants intruding in their world of privilege and position. You . . ."

The waitress sauntered to their table, burdened with two coffee mugs. "We got three Danish left. Prune, cheese and apple. Whaddya want?"

Pier pushed one of the mugs across the table to Max Steiner. "Give the cheese to the grubby public servant. I'll take the apple."

"Within our lifetime, miss, if you please," Max said, flashing the vote-getting grin.

"Hey, you guys, gimme a break." The waitress pouted before moving away. Then she turned back and looked closely at Max. "Are you Mel Gibson?"

"No. Sorry."

"I didn't think you were."

"God help us every one. What was I talking about?"

"You were complaining. But never mind, I've got something else for you. A decorator was hurt in a hit-and-run night before last. It was reported in yesterday's *Times* . . ."

"That's the other thing you've got for me? A decorator was hurt? He'll never hang another drape again?"

"More than hurt. Almost killed. I talked to him a couple of nights ago at a party in Beverly Hills. Only for the rich, of course, Max. We all had to show our net worth statements at the door. Now, here comes the good part. The decorator, one Lars Eklund, told me he was going to be, in his words, thrillingly bicoastal, and live with none other than Beau Paxton."

"Better. Getting better. But still not worth the rancid coffee and stale Danish I'm so looking forward to."

"There's more. Beau Paxton was also engaged to be married to a Santa Barbara girl. *Girl.* Dilly Dillingham. Very rich. Lars Eklund told me he thought she hired the hit because Beau was going to leave her for him. Lars, that is. How am I doing?"

"Pretty good. There were a couple of references to a possible fiancée in the *Manor House* staff interviews. We didn't take it too seriously, considering the late Mr. Paxton's sexual preference. No mention of the name Lars Eklund has surfaced but we still have a lot of people to see. That song, 'We Are the World,' must have been about Beau Paxton's friends. Shit, the guy knew everyone and they all want to talk about how well they knew dear Beau. That's what they call him. Dear Beau. It's become chic to be involved in this case. But, okay, Pier, you saved us some time, I'll give you that."

"And I'll give you this." Pier slid an envelope across the table. Max opened it, looked first at the check, then at Pier.

"This is a very generous campaign contribution, my friend. My stomach almost forgives you, but I wouldn't want the taxpayers to think I used the chopper to come up here for political purposes."

"That's why it's postdated for a week from today."

"You demonstrate a sound grasp of political reality, my friend. Thank you. I really want a second term."

"Piece of cake for the most popular boy in the sixth form."

"Have anything more?"

"A couple of things you probably know already. Meg Millar wanted Beau Paxton's job. Doesn't seem enough reason to have him offed but . . ." Pier shrugged and broke off. He'd been going to mention Dilly's accusation that Seth Rupert and Meg were involved. But he didn't. He wasn't sure why he didn't, but he hadn't and he wouldn't. Not now anyway. "Who knows about people?" said Pier. "If we can figure out the why of a crime, the who is usually right there. That's what's starting to bother me about this case. Everybody has a motive. Even our hit-and-run victim might have done it. Maybe Lars knew Beau was leaving him for Dilly Dillingham and *he* hired the shooter. You holding any other cards, Max?"

"One or two. We may have the getaway car. We found one stolen and abandoned a couple of days ago. Had some bloodstains. The lab will have the results tomorrow but we expect the car was decorated with Beau Paxton's blood. Probably splashed on the killer's clothes, then smeared all over the driver's seat of the getaway car."

"Max, congratulations. You may have an actual fact. So far this case is all gossip. The owner of the car? Does he check out?"

"Him?" You surprise me, Pier. Women are committing some of our better crimes today. Equal rights apply to murder, too."

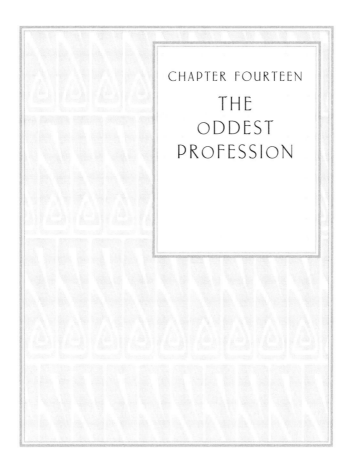

CHAPTER FOURTEEN

THE ODDEST PROFESSION

"There isn't a parking space anywhere. I'll go around again." Pier made a right turn on Robertson. "China, will you tell me how Minnie stays in business? Do her customers all live within walking distance?"

China patted his knee. "Pull up in front, drop me off like the laundry, as Rita Hayworth said to Glenn Ford in *Gilda*. Just don't forget to come back for me later."

"Forget you?" Pier took China's hand.

She looked at him quizzically and asked, "Should I have worn black? More intimidating? Blue inspires confidence. What do you think?"

"Just smile. He'll tell you everything. Who did Minnie line up for you?"

"Jesse something-or-other. She said he's the decorator I should interview because he loves to talk. Well, here goes." China opened the car door and stepped out.

Pier watched as she walked up the sidewalk toward the antique shop, the sun key-lighted on the titian hair brushing her shoulders. Although just a couple of inches shy of six feet, China wore high heels. Her sincere blue suit was softly tailored. A short wrap skirt revealed the legendary legs that had danced an electrifying tango with Barishnykov in *Paris Red.* China blew a kiss to Pier and waved as she disappeared through the open gates into a courtyard.

Pier moved the Rover forward, still thinking of China as he drove along the tree-lined street of antique shops. Then he accelerated, realizing he wanted to have done with the *Manor House* interviews so he could come back quickly and claim China. They might drive up the Coast Highway, home to the ranch and early to bed. China's bed.

China stepped along a curving path bordered by a tangle of roses and ancient marble columns lying about in seemingly random disarray. China knew the antiquities had been shipped from Mallet's in London to be placed as though toppled by the fall of a once great civilization. Before she could ring the entrance bell, a buzzer released the lock and she walked inside, into another world.

Once an undistinguished cottage, the structure had been transformed, the roof raised to soaring heights. Paned, floor-to-ceiling windows exposed the entire width of the shop. Eight antique rock crystal chandeliers, a dazzling mix of English, Swedish, Russian and Italian, hung from the beamed ceiling. The fronds of a dozen Kentia palms in huge African baskets almost touched the rafters. French mirrors magnified and reflected flames from lighted candles in antique holders. China made her way through a mélange of Italian tables, country Chinese consoles, log furniture and Japanese bronzes.

The shop was open "To the Trade Only." Decorators and their clients walked on Bessarabian rugs, sisal matting, and seated themselves comfortably in down-filled chairs.

In an alcove, almost out of sight behind an antique architect's table, a tall brunette dressed in jeans, silk blouse and Western boots looked up from the floor plans she was studying and called out, "China, come on back. Try my new sofa. It just came from the upholsterer this morning. You're the first to see it, let alone sit on it."

China considered Minnie. Great bone structure, high cheekbones, posture that could have won the gold in Olympic competition. She moved with model grace and, in fact, had modeled in New York and Paris before she began designing furniture. Circuitously, her personal interests led her to open a showroom. Minnie greeted China without a kiss on the cheek. She only kissed her horses. "You haven't come into town for a long time."

"You know how we are in Santa Barbara; we never leave home."

China took a pack of cigarettes from her handbag and looked around for an ashtray. Minnie pointed to a small eighteenth-century creamware plate. "Want an espresso to go with that?"

"Please."

"Tino will get it." Minnie pushed a buzzer.

"You still send that poor boy across the street so much?" China leaned toward a French art deco table next to the sofa, looked at the price tag and gasped. "My God. Seventy thousand dollars! Add three hundred dollars to the price and you can buy your own espresso machine! Minnie, who actually sits down and writes a seventy-thou-sand-dollar check for a table?"

"You do, when you're not acting poverty-stricken. But don't for-get, I sell less expensive, reproduction antiques, too." Minnie moved to an Oriental desk. Pounding it with the flat of her hand, she turned to China. "Wait till you hear this. It's to die. Oh, God, I've been around decorators too long. Anyway, Phil Mandell was in here last week and he . . ."

China exhaled and, through the smoke, asked, "Who is Phil Mandell?"

"I thought you'd know him. But I forget, you're a recluse. He's a decorator from back East. He moved to Santa Barbara last year and pretended he was straight. Even got married. I can't stand him, he's so arrogant. He came in here, went right over to this chinoiserie table and said, *Minnie, your reproductions are perfectly adequate but you'll never be able to make anything like this superb antique.* So I said, very quietly, 'That *is* a reproduction, Phil.' "

"And what did *he* say?"

"He was stunned. *Stunned.* Then he just pretended he hadn't heard me and walked out with his nose in the air. I loved it. Oh, here's Tino with our coffee." Minnie took cups from the tray Tino held and handed one to China. "Now, before he gets here, I should tell you, this decorator is so thrilled that he's actually going to meet the famous China Carlyle, he may faint before he answers your questions. You'll have to talk fast. Listen, tell me quickly, does Pier have any clues?"

"You know I can't tell you that."

"Yes, but I always hope you'll forget and blab. Why doesn't Pier come and question me? I knew Beau Paxton. My house was published in *Manor House.*"

"I'll ask you a question Pier might ask if he were here. Did Beau Paxton ever expect decorators to go to bed with him in exchange for publishing their work?"

Minnie laughed. "He never asked me!" She stopped laughing long enough to answer. "But, yes, I've heard that about Beau."

"Minnie, who do you think might have killed him?"

The reply came instantly. "Any decorator who couldn't get his work in the magazine! If a decorator's work isn't published in *Manor House* after a client has spent millions, the decorator might as well commit suicide. Messy. Instead, why not kill the editor who rejected the work?"

"That sounds like a lengthy list of suspects. It will take what's left of the twentieth century to narrow it down. By the way, what is this decorator's name again?"

"Jesse Bartholomew. His work has been shown in *Manor House* three or four times. His clients are old money. At least as old as money gets in Los Angeles. He's managed to convince them he's one of their own. Actually, fifteen years ago he was a street kid in the barrio. His name was Jesus Brazos. Chumley Wales, an old-time decorator, found him hustling on the streets, took him home and spent the next few years polishing him up. Jesse became Chumley's assistant, then took over the business when he retired. One day he'll inherit everything and he can hardly wait. Maybe he won't! How's that for a movie?"

"Great concept. I'll play Chumley."

"China, why don't you do another movie? Would Pier be upset? You've never really told me why you gave it all up."

"Simple. It's important not to stay too long at the fair. In the movie business, when a woman hits her mid-forties, she has to develop her own projects and then find the financing. I didn't want to spend my time doing that. Pier is more important to me." China sighed and stubbed out her cigarette. Her expression darkened. "After my baby died, I was so lost. The booze blotted out the memory. Made it unreal. If I hadn't met Pier when I did, I would probably have drowned in a sea of vodka. And one day I read a quote that seemed meant for me. It was in a script based on a biography of Lola Montez. A reporter asked for her philosophy of life. She said, 'Courage and shuffle the cards.' If I ever needlepoint a pillow, that's what it will say."

"I'll *never* let you needlepoint a pillow." A buzzer sounded. Minnie glanced toward the front of the shop, then lowered her voice and cautioned, "Oh, oh. Jesse Bartholomew just came in. He's pretending he hasn't seen us. You know, if he didn't look like a ferret, he'd be almost attractive."

As Bartholomew intently inspected the underside of an eighteenth-century trestle table, Minnie whispered in China's ear. "He looks at everything like that because he copies everything. He has no talent and no taste. Also, he's a dimwit. Well, ready or not, here we go." Minnie stood and waved to Jesse Bartholomew. "Jesse, come and meet China Carlyle. Do you want some coffee?"

The decorator's eyes shifted from one piece of furniture to another as he threaded his way toward the two women. "Not for me. I can't bear to see the way you work that boy. But I *do* want to meet the legendary China Carlyle."

China held out her hand. For a moment, she thought Jesse might kiss it. Instead, he squeezed her fingers gingerly. "You exaggerate, Mr. Bartholomew, but I don't object. Please make yourself comfortable right there where Minnie was sitting. She tactfully decided to work in the front while we chat."

Jesse Bartholomew seated himself and made a stab at insouciance. "Miss Carlyle, is your pin by Verdura? It's heaven."

"Yes, it is. My first husband gave it to me." China took a pad and pencil from her handbag, and tried to remember how Rosalind Russell talked taking notes as a reporter in *His Girl Friday* opposite Cary Grant. "You mentioned on the telephone that you knew Beau Paxton. Did you know him well? Was he your friend?"

"Oh, no. Chumley Wales is my friend."

China tried again. "Isn't it possible to have *two* friends?"

"I'm not promiscuous, Miss Carlyle. Do you think I could have a cigarette? I quit but it looks so good the way you do it."

China gave him the package. "Please call me China and I'll call you Jesse, if I may."

"Of course."

"Now, Jesse, had you known Beau long?"

"Oh, forever and ever. At least four years. He was the most important person in my life. After Chumley, that is. He taught me everything."

"Who did? Beau Paxton or Mr. Wales?"

"Both, really. Chumley taught me everything about decorating and Beau taught me about the importance of publicity. The right kind, of course."

"What *is* the right kind of publicity for a decorator?"

"Interior designer . . ."

"What's the difference?"

"Well, we interior designers do *everything*. The total concept, space, backgrounds, designing all the furniture, *everything*. A decorator just furnishes." His tone made *furnishes* an obscenity.

"Doesn't an interior designer furnish, too?"

"Yes, but what we do goes *way* beyond that."

"So Beau was helpful about the kind of publicity you should have. Did that mean appearing in his magazine?"

"Well, that was part of it."

"What else?"

"He thought I should be in *Manor House* three times a year."

"What else?"

"That my work should always be photographed at night."

"Shot in the dark?"

"It's much more dramatic that way."

"Did you like Beau?"

"Like him? Oh, yes, he made me a star!"

"But did you like him?"

"Yes, I just said so."

"You said you liked what he did for you. Did you like *him?*"

"Well, sure, Beau was really attractive. Sort of English-looking. Very Savile Row. Whenever the weather was even the least bit cool, he wore a vest. So chic. He had dark brown hair with a natural wave and his eyes were brown too. He looked a little like that old-time movie star Sean Connery."

"Old-time movie star? I did two pictures with him! Of course," China added quickly, "he played my father."

Jesse seemed distressed.

"Oh, I didn't mean that *you're* old-time. Why, I'm your biggest fan." He considered for an instant, then, by way of apology, continued. "I'll even tell you something I've never told anyone." Jesse moved closer to China and lowered his voice.

"Do you think I could have another one of your cigarettes, Miss Car— China?"

China leaned over to pick up the pack, hoping to conceal her irritation.

Jesse took his time lighting the cigarette and China wondered if he actually had anything to tell.

"I had just taken over Chumley's business and I needed publicity. Everyone knew Chumley but no one knew me. I didn't even tell Chum about it but, after all, he must have known because his work has been in the magazine more than almost anyone's, don't you think? Does that help?"

"You haven't told me anything yet."

"Oh. Well. Promise you won't tell?"

"I have to tell Pierpont Tree. This is all background for his investigation."

"He won't tell, will he?"

"Not unless he has to."

Jesse Bartholomew looked at China's Verdura pin and made up his mind. "I paid Beau Paxton."

"You paid him? I don't understand."

"Well, he said lots of young interior designers would kill to get their work in *Manor House,* so why should he show mine? I didn't know what to say. I thought—you know. But that wasn't what he wanted. He told me that new designers pay him five thousand dollars the first three times their work appears. Each time. Beau said it had to be absolutely confidential or he would make sure that no magazine *ever* published my work. So I paid him."

"Did you ever ask any other designers if they paid him too?"

"Never! What if they said no and I was the only one paying? I'd never live it down. I didn't even tell Chum because he might think I was paying, well, some other way. He's so jealous."

"Jesse, we may have to continue this another time. Minnie is coming this way followed by Tino with more coffee."

"Oh, good. Now I can relax. I hate talking about myself. Did you like the house I did in the new issue of *Manor House?"*

China lowered her eyes and smiled her too sweet smile. "It's always more interesting to talk about other people, isn't it?"

"You're so right. You know, China, I never expected an actress to be so intelligent."

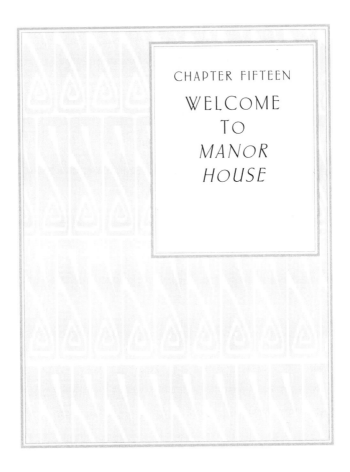

CHAPTER FIFTEEN

WELCOME TO *MANOR HOUSE*

L ike an old madam whose fortunes have dwindled, the Sunset Strip has lost its glamour. Its heyday was in the thirties and forties, when Lana Turner danced at the Mocambo, stars wined at The Player's Club, dined at LaRue and romanced at Ciro's.

Nestled at the eastern end of the Strip was the Garden of Allah, a complex of cottages favored by writers. At the western end, hard by the Beverly Hills border, the same writers drank Pimm's Cups in the

Cock 'n Bull, unanimously considered by serious drinkers to be the best bar in Hollywood. A sumptuous buffet of all-American food was served in the back rooms, but some of the regulars drank there for years without knowing the place was a restaurant, too.

At the top of La Cienega on the Strip was the mob-run Clover Club with gambling behind locked doors and a glass dance floor covering a pool filled with water and colorful fish. Fish and stars swayed rhythmically as a band played on until dawn.

The schizophrenic Strip had a daytime side, too. You might have a Nut Burger at Sunset and Doheny or a hot fudge sundae at Wil Wright's Ice Cream Parlor. Glamour photographer Paul Hesse shot the stars in his own building and always displayed one portrait in a showcase outside. Ruth St. Denis' studio overlooked Los Angeles on the south side of Sunset where her dancers could be seen practicing in the rectangular glass box that was her building. Motion picture agencies conducted business behind the ivied walls of pseudo-Tudors. William Haines' Decorating Studio was on the south side of Sunset too, in a small, classical building often visited by his first client, Joan Crawford.

The *Manor House* offices, two blocks from the old Haines studio, can be identified only by the discreet initials MH. Architect-to-the-stars Wallace Neff had designed the three-story Spanish-style structure for a motion picture producer in the early forties.

When the Ruperts bought *Manor House,* they moved it to the Neff building. Business, circulation, production and advertising occupied the first two floors, with editorial and executive offices on the third. The Ruperts also bought a small piece of property in back of the building and built a two-story parking garage. Pier left his car there and entered the lobby through the rear entrance.

An attractive receptionist announced Pier's arrival to Meg Millar, then gave him directions. Pier found Meg on the top floor, next to a corner office with Beau Paxton's name lettered on the door. Meg was on the telephone but waved for Pier to come in. She handed a telephone message to him, then pointed to another telephone on a table between a pair of Spanish Colonial chairs. Pier punched the digits of the number Eddie Navarro had left just ten minutes before. "It's Pier. I'm at the *Manor House* offices with Meg Millar." That told Eddie he could be overheard. "Really? Interesting. Okay. Meet me at Minnie Houston's shop in an hour. China's there now. See you."

Meg Millar completed her telephone conversation at the same time and walked around her desk to greet Pier. "Welcome to *Manor House.* I rang for coffee, in case you'd like a cup. I'm going to have tea and maybe a cookie. You're not a cookie man, are you?"

"By the pound." A gentle tap on the door and an "Excuse me" preceded a uniformed maid pushing a tea cart laden with silver coffee- and teapots, creamer, sugar bowl and a hand-hammered silver plate piled high with cookies. The maid placed everything on a leather-covered Stickley coffee table and filled their cups. She left the room as silently as she had arrived.

"Now, before we begin our tour, what else can I tell you about the magazine?"

Pier looked around Meg's office. The afternoon sun slanted through wood shutters revealing a well-worn leather sofa, Arts and Crafts lamps and Early California paintings. "Isn't that a Jessie Arms Botke?" He indicated a painting of shadowed cranes on a gold leaf background.

Meg smiled. "I thought you'd recognize it."

"My mother knew her in the late thirties. We have some of her paintings at the ranch. Somehow it's surprising to find one here."

"Perfectly logical, really. We're a California-based company and this building was constructed in the thirties, when the *plein air* artists were flourishing." She hesitated for a moment, then proceeded. "I've heard you have a wonderful collection at Casa Arbol. Pier, let me ask you straight out, will you let *Manor House* present your ranch to our readers?"

"I don't mean to be rude, but why would I want to do that?"

"Think about those artists. Most of them couldn't support themselves by painting. A few had some recognition, most had none. Think how they would have felt to know their paintings would one day be seen by people all over the world. You could give them the fame most never achieved in their lifetime. The collection should be documented and the ranch is part of California history. Why not?"

"Meg, that was good. Really good. And fast. In a few seconds you came up with the only reason that might persuade me."

"I never really try to persuade. That would be presumptuous. But I will ask you to give it some thought and maybe we could talk again. Fair?"

"Fair."

"Now, what can I tell you about the magazine?"

Pier helped himself to a cookie. "Is it always so quiet around here? I thought magazine offices would be noisy to the point of hysteria. Everyone frantic about making deadlines, running around yelling at each other."

"We work six months ahead and we do just fine without getting hysterical." Meg refilled their cups and settled comfortably on the sofa, closer to Pier. "Next question?"

"You told me at lunch that the magazine won't be affected editorially by Beau Paxton's death. What about the advertisers? Are they concerned?"

"Some are. Jonas is busily reassuring them."

Pier took aim and shot his next question. "Why didn't you tell me Beau Paxton had a brother?"

Meg started slightly before she replied, "It didn't seem pertinent. Beau's half brother, Guy, wasn't involved with *Manor House*. He was only around for a couple of years in the beginning. For that matter, since you knew, why didn't you ask me about him before?"

"I just found out. The call I returned was from an associate who passed on that bit of information, although it wasn't his reason for calling." Eddie had called because he was about to stake out Norton Birdwell's house. Pier hadn't given Eddie a chance to tell him exactly what he was going to do because he didn't want to know, but he was sure Eddie was going to search Birdwell's house. Eddie's methods were often illegal but they sure as hell moved things along.

"Tell me about Guy," he said.

Meg shook her head frowning. "He was Beau's half brother by Mrs. Paxton's first marriage. When I began to turn *Manor House* around, Guy decided he wanted to play too. But he just got in the way. Mrs. Paxton gave him the money to start his own magazine, which he did. It was called *homes*, all lower case. He ran his friends' houses. Not surprisingly, it failed. He tried to save it by turning it into an interview magazine, but the only people who'd talk to him were people no one wanted to read about. Guy wasn't like Beau. Everything he did lost money.

"He was jealous of me because what I do looked easy to him. Guy never had the least idea how to do a magazine, but he was sure he knew more than anyone. At one point he even hired a publicity firm to tell the world *he* was responsible for *Manor House*. He went too far. Mrs. Paxton was furious. Beau was her favorite and *no one* was going to take the credit away from him. Guy was more or less pushed out of the family nest with a fat trust fund. He started a magazine, *Inside Palm*

Springs. It may still be going, or it may have failed like his other ventures. And that's all I know about Guy."

Meg was probably telling the truth. Eddie had checked it out and learned that Meg was not Seth Rupert's girlfriend. Dilly had been lying. At best, misinformed.

Eddie had said, "Seth may seem to be the conservative, buttoned-down type, but it's bimbos he likes, not brains. Meg Millar is no bimbo."

While Pier had been thinking, Meg had been sipping her tea, studying him with her steel gray eyes. "I'm not holding anything back," she said. "I'll tell you whatever you want to know, just as I did with the police."

"Have you had an affair with either Seth or Jonas Rupert?"

Meg spat out her answer. "I've worked hard for years to get where I am. I didn't get it by sleeping with anyone. The answer is no." She looked at her watch and stood. "I'm afraid I don't have much time before my next meeting."

"Meg, don't be offended. I'm just asking questions the police will ask, if they haven't already. Here's another one. Do either of the Ruperts have a drug habit?" Pier was thinking of Jonas at the Sultan's party.

Meg relaxed. Slightly. "Not that I know of, but with Jonas anything is possible."

"That's true of humanity in general."

Meg drummed her fingers nervously on a console table. She sighed before speaking. "I might as well tell you. It will come out later, I suppose. Beau had a serious cocaine habit. He left an envelope at the reception desk once a week. A young man would pick it up and, at the same time, leave a small package for Beau. Once someone opened it by mistake. It was white powder."

"How did Beau react when he discovered the package had been opened?"

"He didn't. The art department sealed it up again, so skillfully he never knew. Now, shall we begin?" Pier followed her down a long hallway, its length punctuated by open doors. "As you can see, a tour isn't too interesting. Just people working at their desks, editing galleys, talking on telephones or working at a word processor. Not very entertaining. In the art department it's much the same except heads are bent over drawing boards as well as computers."

"Where and how does it all begin, Meg?"

"It begins with finding a house we want to feature in the magazine. Then we send a photographer to shoot and, later, a writer to do the story."

Meg slowed her pace, leading Pier into an unoccupied room. Color transparencies were spread out on high, boxy tables, topped by frosted glass. She reached under one of the tables, pushed a button and lights underneath illuminated the glass. Four-by-five-inch color transparencies yielded glowing images of chintz-filled rooms, spartan, art-filled lofts, book-lined studies, dining tables laden with settings of silver and gold, bedrooms swathed in silk, a garden aglow with wild-flowers and reflections from a lily pond.

Pier indicated the photographs on the light table. "Do you look for anything in particular?"

"Not in terms of period or style. The houses must photograph beautifully. After all, that's what our readers will see. Interiors are like people. Some are photogenic, some not. Each year I turn down hundreds of interiors that are quite properly done but nothing special. No magic."

Meg turned off the viewing table lights and smiled at Pier. He liked her smile. He liked the straightforward way she looked up at him. And she no longer seemed upset with him. Meg led the way into a much larger, windowless office. "All the photographs and records are here. The screens and charts on the walls display schedules of what's going to be shot, where and by which photographer."

"Are you the computer expert?" Pier asked her.

"No. A programmer feeds all the information into the computer. We can call up anything we want to see on one of the big screens. The first one on the left is for homes recently submitted. They'll be reviewed tomorrow. After I see them, they're filed in Accept or Regrets."

"Regrets?"

"If a house isn't right for us, we send regrets. It sounds kinder than rejection."

"And the next screen?"

"Interiors we've accepted, name of decorator, resident and a date for photography. The next screen displays a shooting schedule for each issue. Name of writer assigned. Basic info. Name of photographer, start date, how many days allotted for the shooting and so forth."

"How long does it usually take to photograph an interior?"

"Two days on the average. But those may be twelve- or fourteen-hour days. Or nights. Each photographer works a bit differently."

"And the chart over there? The one with the black border. When you really hate an interior, do you take drastic measures?"

"You mean murder?" She beamed at Pier with exaggerated innocence. "Look closely at the heading." Pier walked over to the chart as Meg continued, "That's a list of features we've decided not to use for various reasons. We bury them in the Dead File, hence the black border. When we decide not to do a story, we pay the writer and the photographer a kill fee. I guess you'd call it our hit list."

A man's voice behind them startled Meg and Pier. "What are you talking about, Meg?"

"Oh, Seth, I'm showing Pier how we put out the magazine. I was explaining the kill fee."

"Oh. Well, Pier, I won't be able to keep our appointment today. The D.A.'s office just called. They want me downtown for further questioning. Just routine, they say. We'll have to reschedule."

"What about Jonas?" Meg asked pointedly. "Don't they want to question him, too?"

"He isn't here. It looks like you're in charge now, Meg."

Meg smiled. "Fine."

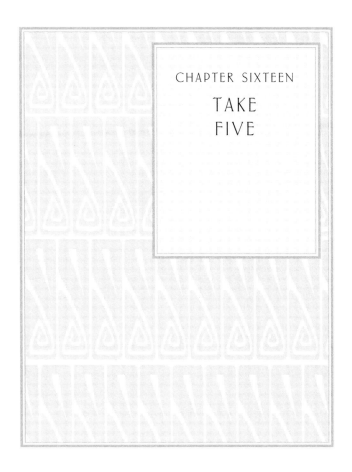

CHAPTER SIXTEEN
TAKE FIVE

Minnie and China were recovering from their lunch with Jesse Bartholomew.

"Godalmighty, Minnie, you should have a sign over your door, 'Abandon Hope All Ye Who Enter.' How can you talk to people like Jesse Bartholomew all day and keep your sanity? He actually asked me what Jack Nicholson is really like." China kicked off her shoes and swung her feet onto an ottoman. "I'm going to smoke myself silly."

"Well, the last customer's gone so we can relax until Pier gets here. China, you're sure you won't stay in town for dinner?"

"Thanks, but we have to get back."

"What is it that . . ." Minnie stopped suddenly and stood up. "Don't move! Don't look around. I think we're about to be robbed. Oh, damnit, I let the staff leave early. Don't worry. The panic button's by the phone. The police will be here in five minutes flat." Minnie ran to her desk, boots clicking. China jumped up and looked out.

"Stop! Don't push the button. I know him."

Minnie looked at China with disbelief. "You *know* him? He looks like a bum."

"He works for Pier. His name is Eddie Navarro."

Minnie looked through the window again. Eddie's hair was long and straight, jacket shapeless, a two-day growth of beard. On a case, Eddie wore what he called his invisible man clothes. His eyes were large, brown and sad. He looked at Minnie for a minute and then turned and walked back toward the street.

"China, where's he going? Does he really work for Pier? Does he shadow criminals?"

"If Pier wanted someone shadowed, I suppose Eddie would do it. He was probably passing by and saw me. He would have come in if you hadn't glared at him."

"China, I'd love to go along sometime on a stakeout."

"I don't know if he does that. It would take more than one man, wouldn't it? Oh, damn, I did it again. Why did I say man? Women can stake out too. If you really want to do something like that, I'll give you Eddie's phone number and you can ask him yourself."

Eddie Navarro stood quietly behind the two women for a moment before he whispered, "You can ask me right now."

Both women screamed, spun around and spoke simultaneously. "How did you get in?"

"Are you two imitating the McGuire Sisters?"

Eddie gave them the slow, lazy half smile that had melted women up and down the West Coast, the East Coast and in that vast flyover in between. "The back door was unlocked."

"That's not possible," Minnie protested. "The door locks automatically and stays locked until it's released from inside. Oh, oh. You unlocked it! How? How did you do it?"

"Easy. You should have a dead bolt. And a couple of Dobermans wouldn't hurt. I'll come back and give you a security check, but right now I've got to talk to China."

"Go ahead."

China intervened. "I think he means privately. We don't want you to get shot because you know too much, girlie."

"I'll go check the useless locks."

When Minnie was out of hearing, China asked Eddie, "How did you know I would be here?"

"Pier told me. I called him at *Manor House*. Told him I was going to sort of see Norton Birdwell and . . ."

"Sort of see him? Do you mean at his house? Or when he's not . . . Oh!" China had figured out what Eddie meant.

"Where else? The guy has no office. He does nothing, so I can't sort of see him there. Where else would I go? Want to try it again?" Eddie loved it when China went ditsy on him. He knew it was because he made her nervous. She associated him with danger. "Do the reaction shot," he commanded, grinning. "Wide eyes straight into the camera for your close-up; *at his house?*"

"I hope Norton Birdwell isn't fleeing the country while you redirect my movies."

"That's the problem. I don't know where the hell he is. Birdwell's missing. I was tossing his house when a black-and-white pulled up, so I . . ."

"Tossing? Does that mean searching? On top of breaking and entering like you just did here?" China sank into a nearby chair, momentarily diverted by the discreet price tag, written out in a spidery script, which read five thousand dollars. "This day has been too much and it's not over. Pier should be here any minute, then we're going back up to the serenity of Santa Barbara." China leaned forward. "Wait a minute. What makes you think Norton Birdwell is missing? Maybe he just went out for a walk. Or to see his broker. Visit his old auntie. How do you know he's *missing?*"

Eddie eased himself into a chair next to China's. "He left a note. Said he was going away to a place where he could find peace and quiet because the world had become unbearable since Beau died. Sounded like he wanted everyone to think he committed suicide. I don't buy it. He just split. I want to tell Pier right away because the police already know. I should have taken the goddamn note."

"Eddie, that would be illegal!"

"*You're kidding!*"

"Oh, Pier is right. It *is* best if I don't know too much. Why were the police coming to see Birdwell?"

"Could be he had a lot of unpaid parking tickets. Maybe he sold coke or made porno films or killed his bookie. Maybe the cops found out he had Beau Paxton offed. And maybe he ran down that decorator, Lars Eklund."

"I showed Pier the newspaper story about the accident."

"No accident. I dropped in on Lars this morning at the hospital. He said the car hit him on purpose."

"But the story said he was in intensive care."

"Yeah. I became an orderly for my little visit. No one looks at a guy carrying a bedpan. If Pier wants me to go after Birdwell, the sooner I get started, the better." Eddie fiddled with the price tag dangling from his chair. "Jesus Christ, this chair costs four thousand dollars!"

"It's one of Minnie's better bargains." China relished Eddie's astonishment. "The small table over there is ten thousand dollars."

"She gets away with that? People actually pay that kind of money for chairs and tables?"

"The big cabinet on that wall is thirty-five thousand dollars."

"No!"

"Here she comes. Ask her."

Before she was close enough to hear what they were saying, Minnie called out, "Stop talking. I don't want to know anything that will get me in trouble. I'm only interrupting because Pier just called. He'll be here in ten minutes. China, he said you'll stop at Jack Banner's on the way home. He wants Eddie to leave for Santa Barbara now and wait at the house."

"Hey, Minnie, do people really pay thirty-five grand for a piece of old furniture?"

"A Russian desk just sold in New York for seven hundred and fifty thousand, Eddie. The antiques business pays better than crime."

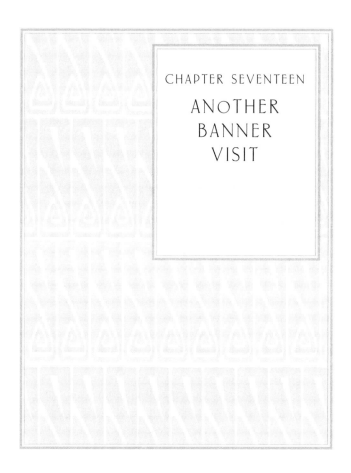

CHAPTER SEVENTEEN

ANOTHER BANNER VISIT

They were well north of Trancas on the Pacific Coast Highway before China asked Pier, "If you were casting an actress to play Meg Millar, who would it be?"

"You're the only actress on my mind."

"Is she a blonde?"

"No. Yes. I guess so."

"No, yes, I guess so," China repeated, studying Pier. "And what about her eyes? Are they blue? Gray? Brown?"

"Yes, definitely." He paused, waiting for China's reaction.

"Yes! Well, which? Are they—" China broke off as she saw Pier grinning. "Stop it! You're not playing fair. What color are her eyes?"

"Gray," said Pier dutifully.

"Name an actress she reminds you of."

"Jodie Foster," he said immediately.

"Jodie Foster!" she exploded. "How old is this Meg?"

"My mother always told me it was rude to ask," he said primly, enjoying China's growing fury.

"Tell me more," said China, narrowing her eyes.

"She's bright. Good at what she does and what she does is interesting."

"Never before have you shown the slightest interest in slipcovers."

"*Manor House* isn't about slipcovers. You told Seth you've subscribed for years."

"I'm canceling first thing in the morning."

"Actually, you'd like Meg."

"Ha! You said that about Edwina Forsyte when she moved to Montecito and declared herself the reigning intellectual. Then we found out she plagiarized huge chunks of her books. The books her so-called researchers really wrote. And that she was the chief recruiter for a cult of devil worshipers."

"Don't exaggerate, China. She wasn't the *chief* recruiter," said Pier. "I just thought you might have enjoyed lunch with Edwina, that's all."

"Pier, I might have *been* lunch."

"Dinner. Dilly would be lunch."

"Have I met Dilly?"

"Yes. At Polo a couple of times. And I've never suggested you have lunch with Dilly."

"Do you suspect her?"

"I even suspect you. That's why I'm holding your hand so you can't get away."

"Let it go and I'll put it on your knee."

"Deal."

China tapped Pier's knee and pointed to a gas station and cluster of houses on the north side of the highway. "We're passing La Conchita. Jack's turnoff is next." Then she added, casually, "Maybe we should ask Meg Millar up for a weekend? What do you think?"

Pier pulled the car over at the foot of the off-ramp and kissed China. "I think her life would be in danger and I don't want to spend the rest of mine visiting you in the slammer with Mattie's goddamned bread pudding."

"Jack has company. I hear voices."

"No," said China. "That's a tape recorder. He listens to books on tape while he paints."

"Doesn't that distract him?"

"Says he stays at the easel longer. When he listens to a book, he forgets about time."

"Forgets about time? Quite a trick. Well, here goes." Pier rang the Burmese bronze bell.

Jack Banner opened the door immediately. "Perfect timing. Come in, come in. I was just going to fix myself a drink. What will you have?"

"Coke, please."

"Scotch, splash of water, no ice."

China placed herself in a bar-height director's chair, crossed her legs and lighted a cigarette. It was like her old movie set chair. She felt completely at home. Pier stood next to her, watching Jack fill their glasses, then lift his.

"Cheers. I asked you to stop by because Dilly called me about a letter she found in a briefcase Beau Paxton left at her house. Godalmighty, I wasn't ready for an hysterical Dilly today. Or any day for that matter." Jack took a slug of vodka before he continued. "Dilly wanted to know if she should call the police or burn the letter. I told her to do nothing until I talked to you. I'm hardly an authority on what to do with murder evidence."

"Did she read the letter to you?"

"Good God, no. She started to but I wouldn't let her. I didn't want to know what it said. Pier, this involves *murder!*"

Pier took the other director's chair. "Jack, do you think Dilly could kill?"

"Absolutely. Her father taught her to shoot. Usually defenseless creatures such as birds, I might add. A man would probably be just a target without feathers. Of course, I never understood why she didn't kill her former husband, the local fortune hunter."

Puffing happily on her cigarette, China asked, "Didn't he marry Leola Abernathy after the divorce?"

"He did indeed, and she settled five million on him the day before the wedding so, as she said, no one could ever say he married her for her money."

"Did he?"

"Of course he did. Leola is a lot older than he, and not attractive, but she doesn't really care if he cheats as long as he's discreet. Now, Dilly was something else. She most definitely did not want her husband straying."

Pier seemed not to have heard. "Dilly didn't tell you any more about the letter she found?"

"Just that it was written by the woman at *Manor House.*"

"Meg Millar?"

"Yes, that's the one."

"Interesting. I'll call Dilly now and ask her to bring the letter to the house." Pier made the call from the small kitchen and returned quickly.

"She'll be there in a few minutes."

China stood, picked up her handbag and tapped a little soft shoe. "They should all be there. Meg, the Rupert brothers, Norton Birdwell, if you can find him, and an assortment of decorators, including Lars. Maybe Julie Warren, too. She wanted Beau's job. Gather them all in one room. Someone will confess just to get out."

"Come on, redhead, let's go home. By the way, Jack, I like that painting of the tiger. The red dot means it's sold?"

"Yes. My maid's buying it."

China stopped at the door.

"Your maid?"

"My maid. And it's almost paid for. I know Pier shields you from the harsh realities of life in Santa Barbara, but maids make a lot of money up here."

As Pier opened the door for China, she looked back at Jack and asked, "Did Leola Abernathy really give Dilly's ex-husband a check for five million dollars the day before they married?"

"Yes. But she postdated it. No good until the day *after* they married."

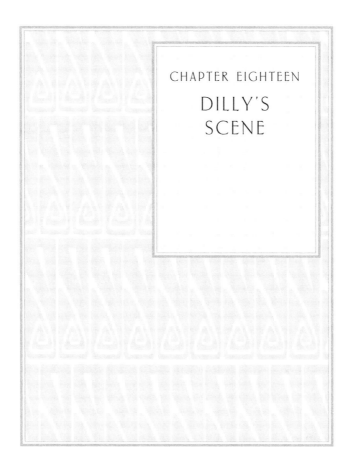

CHAPTER EIGHTEEN
DILLY'S SCENE

China and Pier were walking along the flag-stone path toward the front door of Casa Arbol when Pier stopped and drew China into his arms. "Do we have a date later?"

"My house, ten o'clock." China put her arms around Pier's neck and kissed him. "Be there."

Pier was still holding China when the door opened and Eddie Navarro proclaimed, with a flourish, *"Mi casa es su casa."*

China sighed, "Oh, Eddie, don't you ever wait to be let in? Did you pick the door lock or a window? And don't say Mattie let you in, because she's just pulling into the driveway now."

"I came in the back door," said Eddie, adding righteously, "I wanted to test your alarm system, Pier. It sucks. Needs updating. Besides, I didn't know how late you'd be and I didn't want to sit out on the terrace all night."

"I would never have thought it of you, Eddie," said China, "afraid of the dark. Well, Pier will protect you from the boogeyman. I'm going to see if Mattie wants help with dinner."

"C'mon, Eddie," said Pier. "Let's talk. Dilly Dillingham will be here any minute with a letter she found, written by Meg Millar to Beau Paxton."

"So Meg Millar had Beau whacked?"

"Could be," said Pier, leading the way into his cavernous dining room–office, switching on the lights and motioning Eddie to a chair across the table from his own.

Pier stared at his case cards pinned on the bulletin board. "What have you found out?" he asked Eddie.

"About Meg Millar? Nothing so far. She works long hours, sees decorators for dinner. Always in restaurants. Also visits an old guy in a wheelchair who lives next door. Used to be a director. It's kind of an old movie folks neighborhood." Eddie stood and paced as he continued.

"But I do have information on good old Norton Birdwell. Don't get pissed at me. I was tossing his house when, shit, I had to split just as I found his *makeup*. But as I'm headin' for the back door, I see his closet's pretty empty and there's a note on the bed signed by Birdwell. It said he was going away because he couldn't stand living with reminders of Beau everywhere. Maybe Birdwell is our guy after all.

Maybe he was jealous, sure Beau was going to leave him for Lars, so he had him hit, then ran down Lars. If you want me to trace Birdwell, I should get on it fast."

"Not yet. First let's find out why the police were visiting him. If we want Birdwell later, he'll be easy to track. Anything else?"

"Yeah. I sort of slipped in to see Lars Eklund. He was still in intensive care but he's gonna be okay. Told me he tried to dodge the car that hit him but couldn't. It was deliberate. He couldn't describe the car, didn't see the driver. *Nada.* But he insists it was no accident."

Pier stood. "Hell, there's the doorbell. Dilly's here. Call me later tonight. No, make it tomorrow morning. Early. I'll call you. Come on. You might as well meet Dilly. She's still a suspect."

When they walked into the living room, China and Mattie were standing by the fire looking rather coolly at a distraught Dilly Dillingham. When she saw Pier enter the room, she shook off the two women and ran over to clutch his arm. Instead of her usual boots and jodhpurs, Dilly was wearing high-heeled, open-toed sandals and a silk dress. Her hair, released from its ponytail, fanned out in waves.

Pier detached himself, put his hands on Dilly's shoulders and marched her to a sofa. "What happened?"

"Someone tried to kill me! It was on Mountain Drive. A car came right *at* me. I swerved just in time or I would have gone off the road into the ravine." Dilly noticed Eddie. "Who are you?"

"Eddie Navarro. I work with Pier. Tell me more."

"There isn't any more." Dilly leaned against Pier and dabbed at her eyes with a handkerchief. "Maybe I should hide out? Or stay here with you, Pier."

Ignoring Dilly, Eddie looked thoughtfully at Pier. "Two crazy drivers in this case? Or one? First Lars, now Dilly. Think there's a connection?"

"Somehow I don't, but I couldn't tell you why. Tonight was probably a drunk driver." Pier patted Dilly's shoulder awkwardly. China and Mattie still stood by the fire, watching. They were too quiet. "After all, why would anyone want to kill you, Dilly?"

"No one would. No one at all." She poked nervously in her shoulder bag until she found a piece of paper. "Unless someone knew I was going to give you this letter. Maybe it was Meg Millar. I never did trust her. She probably killed Beau and now she's trying to kill me."

"Why would she try to kill you, Dilly?"

"How would I know? That's your job, Pier. You're the detective." Suddenly Dilly gasped. "Oh, my God, she knows I didn't go into the ravine. She'll try again. Or whoever it was will. What if someone's out there now, waiting for me to leave? What should I do?" She moved closer to Pier and tried to look helpless.

"Don't worry. Eddie will drive you home."

"Eddie? Why can't *you* take me home, Pier? Daddy would be really upset if I came home with a total stranger."

Pier smiled and ignored her comment. "Eddie will drop you and wait to be sure you're safely inside."

"Pier, won't you come? Daddy would just love to see you."

"I'm going to stay here, read this letter and make some calls. Tell your father I'll drop over in a week or so." Dilly swayed against Pier. He motioned to Eddie and together they walked her to the door. Pier looked at Dilly's upturned face and kissed her cheek. "Eddie will take good care of you."

When Pier returned to the living room, reading the letter as he walked, China and Mattie were still by the fire. When he finished reading Pier asked, "What do you two think?"

China spoke first. "She was acting, but *something* was wrong. You could tell by her voice. Maybe she wrote the letter herself? Or maybe she was lying about that other car."

Pier fixed himself a drink. He looked at Mattie. "Out with it."

"If you ask me, that was just Dilly making everything a big melodrama starring Dilly. Just an excuse to come here all upset and throw herself at you. Then she saw us chickens, and it spoiled things for her but she still tried to play clinging vine." Mattie picked up a couple of empty glasses and fluffed a pillow. "I'm leaving. You two figure it out. Your dinner's in the oven. I've got myself a date. See you tomorrow."

When Mattie left the room, China sat next to Pier and put her head on his shoulder. "Right at this moment, I love you very much. Would you like to know why?"

"Absolutely and in great detail."

"Alright then. You really don't like to include anyone in your cases, except for Eddie, of course. But you're including me in this one. You say 'we' and 'us' and make me feel a part of things because you're worried that I might drink again and you want to distract me. And when I said Dilly was acting, you didn't doubt me for a moment. Another man would have written that off as jealousy or a catty female reaction. You took me at my word without a moment of hesitation."

Pier kissed China for a long time before he spoke. "The hell with the telephone calls. Let's go to your house. We can eat dinner later."

"Forget dinner."

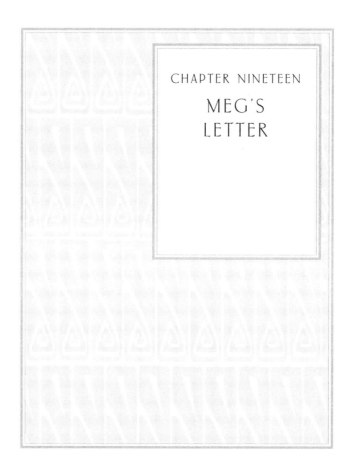

CHAPTER NINETEEN

MEG'S LETTER

Dear Beau:

Our recent discussion became so emotional, this letter seems the best way for us both.

You said I should ask the brothers about the stock they promised to me. I did. Jonas did all the talking, of course, but really said nothing specific. More vague promises.

Beau, you know that soon after your mother hired me, she gave me a letter of agreement stating that I would share in the magazine's ownership and future profits. It's somewhere in the house and I'm going through everything until I find it. Jonas says the letter is worthless. The courts may have to decide one day. However, it shouldn't even be an issue.

The point is that I created *Manor House* as it is today. You once told me you hadn't realized what I was doing with the magazine until after I had done it. When you sold the magazine to the Ruperts you said you'd give me half of your shares and a chunk of cash if they didn't give me stock. They didn't. You didn't.

Beau, you know the small percentage I'm asking for is fair. I want to get on with my work and not be distracted by the necessity to fight for my share. I certainly don't want to leave but I will lose all self-respect if I accept injustice and allow myself to be exploited because of my love for the magazine.

I am pleading with you to face this like a grown-up. Go to Jonas and tell him you insist I be included in the initial stock offering if he gets Seth to agree to go public.

You are my only recourse, short of litigation. I am asking, seeking, requesting, pleading for your help. For years I've looked the other way about certain matters. You know very well what I mean. But you are now on notice that, if I must, I will reveal things you want to conceal. The magazine is my life. And, Beau, your social position, made possible by the magazine, is your life. If I have to give up my life, you will lose yours, too.

Be courageous. Tell the brothers to be fair to me or we will both leave. Your mother wanted me to share in future profits and gave me a letter to that effect. She would want you to do this, Beau. You know that. *Do it.*

With love,
Meg

133

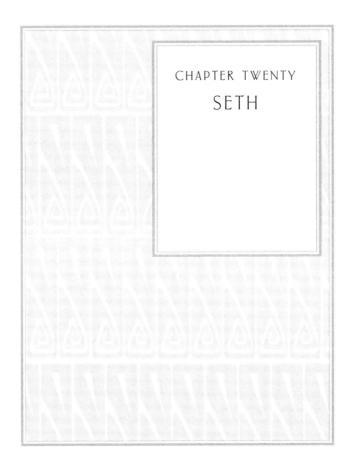

CHAPTER TWENTY

SETH

At three in the morning, most of the windows in the condominium high-rise buildings on Wilshire Boulevard are dark. One building is usually dark well before midnight. Known as a haven for wealthy conservatives who like quiet, good service, and the best security, it affords a wide-angle view of the Los Angeles Country Club golf course. This section of Wilshire between Beverly Hills and Westwood is called the Wilshire Corridor. It is as charmless as it sounds. Phalanxes of tall buildings stand cemented side by side, blocking light, casting shadows. Trees would help a little. Good architecture would help a lot. Neither is evident.

In the dark hours of the morning, cars still speed along the boulevard in puzzling numbers. Where are they going? Where have they been? Seth Rupert heard the motors ten stories below his apartment and wondered as he stared at the computer screen on his desk and tried to concentrate. Usually he could noodle through any problem, but he had been trying to come up with answers since midnight and it just wasn't happening. His brain was out of order.

The key question was, why had Jonas suddenly flown to New York? Even his secretary had been sworn to secrecy. She finally told Seth that Jonas had gone to meet with the world-champion conspicuous spender, Fred Hawkins.

Hawkins, starting with his family's construction business, had built the flashiest fortune in America. His public portfolio included New York skyscrapers, blocks of Manhattan real estate, luxury hotels in ten cities and a major airline. He burnished his image with well-publicized good deeds along the way, restoring an orphanage here, an historic house there, putting police widows on his payroll, funding a program to train inner-city teenagers in a trade. He did not help the homeless. Privately he said, "If they can't afford one of my condos, fuck 'em."

Hawkins wanted to buy *Manor House*. Why not? Everybody wanted to buy *Manor House*. The offers were astounding. *Manor House* was one of the few magazines that hadn't been acquired by the monolithic publishing companies, which over the last two decades had picked up more and more properties. Giants, they steamed along with a whole string of diverse publications scrambling in their wake. Like

135

crack the whip, thought Seth. And like crack the whip, the ones which fell to the end of the line were spun off into oblivion. Until recently, he and Jonas had agreed it was best to remain an independent, privately held company.

One morning Jonas had walked into his office and announced that they had to go public to be competitive. He had already talked to several underwriters who claimed they could reasonably expect a price around three hundred million dollars, if they included the real estate. Jonas said they would use the funds for leveraged acquisitions of other magazines. Seth didn't believe him.

If Jonas were still a high roller, his haste to go public would make some kind of sense. When he had been a compulsive gambler, Jonas was always desperate for money. But he had finally been scared out of the game. Jonas had never told the whole story but Seth knew he must have been heavily in debt to bookies or casinos or both. Maybe loan sharks. Someone had given him a beating and a death threat. He had personally loaned Jonas two million dollars.

Then Jonas had stopped gambling. In time he paid off his loan from Seth. Damnit. Why had Jonas secretly flown to New York? Maybe he shouldn't have concealed Jonas' gambling debts from Pierpont Tree. Well, he might give him a call tomorrow.

Seth was still staring at his computer screen when he heard the knock. At first he thought he was hearing things. Who could be at his door at three in the morning? The doorman invariably called for permission before allowing anyone upstairs. He heard the knock again. Louder this time.

As he walked into the living room, he realized it must be Mrs. Weatherly from the apartment next door. She had given him a key because she occasionally locked herself out. After an evening of "drinkies," she was too embarrassed to ask the doorman to come upstairs with the master key. Seth resolved to tactfully explain that it was really an imposition to interrupt him at such a late hour, though she must have seen the light under his door and known he was still up. Even so, he would say something.

But he said nothing. The shot came too quickly.

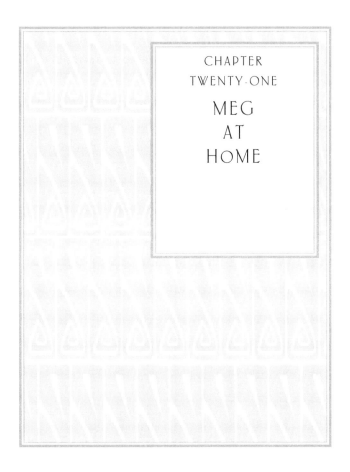

CHAPTER
TWENTY-ONE
MEG
AT
HOME

It was a few minutes after seven when Meg Millar collapsed into the lumpy, chintz-covered chair that had been her mother's favorite and sorted through her mail. The Tiffany lamp offered very little light but Meg kept it because her father had given it to her mother to assuage the pain of her fortieth birthday.

Unable to concentrate, Meg finally put the mail aside, looked around the room and considered how she might describe it if she were writing a caption. Shabby was the first word that came to mind. The upholstery was faded, the rug was faded, the curtains were faded, the soft yellow walls were faded. Even the book jackets were faded.

Meg startled herself with one of those realizations that stun you when you least expect it. After her father died, her mother had faded. Faded gradually until one day she just wasn't there. Meg pondered that for a moment. Maybe she should redecorate before she, too, faded. But she loved the old stone fireplace, the creaking wood floors, the comfortable downy sofa, the old library table and the faint fragrance of rose potpourri.

All the decorators wanted to see her house. But she had never invited one of them into the old bungalow. Even those who had become friends through the years. They would inevitably tell her she should redecorate and she didn't want to do a damned thing.

Whenever Meg even considered redecorating she knew she was avoiding something she didn't want to think about. What was it? What *wasn't* it would be more apt. She didn't want to think about any of it. Beau's murder. Pierpont Tree's investigation. Pierpont Tree. Did he suspect her? And Lars Eklund's accident. Was it really an accident? Then the police questioning Seth. What did they want to know? What had he told them? Jonas Rupert's sudden trip, his secretary refusing to say where he had gone. Why the secrecy?

The only thing to think about now was that, at last, she was editor in chief of *Manor House.* But it had not yet been announced. Both Jonas and Seth agreed the news would be more appropriate after Beau's killer was apprehended. Had there been something odd in their attitude when they told her? Did the Ruperts suspect her too? Did Pierpont Tree suspect them? Did he suspect her? Everything was happening so fast. Too fast. And she still had to keep the magazine going.

Everyone thought editing *Manor House* was so glamorous. So easy. Just travel around, go to black tie dinners, point a well-manicured finger and say, I choose your house. If they only knew. It was like juggling while walking a high wire without a net. No margin for error. And not much energy left at the end of the day for a personal life. What would it be like to come home to a man like Pierpont Tree? The movie star probably gives him full-time attention and overtime adoration.

What, Meg wondered, was China Carlyle really like? At least she hadn't asked Pier that question. If only she had met him first. How could anyone possibly compete with a woman like that? Incredible beauty, fame, intelligence, wealth and everyone said she was nice as well. Hopeless. Well, one day there might be someone again.

But it wouldn't be someone like Pierpont Tree. His brain shot sparks. Even when he leaned back as if he had all the time in the world, you knew he was getting it all, processing it every second. Meg wondered if he had really liked her.

Ridiculous. Swooning like a high school girl. Time to go have a drink with Mike O'Shea.

Meg reached for the telephone and tapped out a number. It rang several times before the familiar, deep voice boomed out, "Hello." Meg smiled at the way the voice rose on the last syllable so that the word became a question rather than a greeting.

"Hi, it's Meg. Would you like some company? Joanie left a lamb stew in the oven, plenty for two. In fact, there's plenty for twenty. If you and that souped-up wheelchair aren't on Neighborhood Watch tonight, I'll bring it over."

It was typical of Mike, thought Meg as she listened to his rumbling response, that he would try to raise the ante. "Okay," she agreed. "Dessert, too, but it'll cost you more than a drink this time. I need help."

Meg took the pot of lamb stew out of the oven, cheese and salad greens from the refrigerator, ice cream from the freezer and rummaged in the cupboard for a jar of fudge sauce. Mike's cleaning woman confiscated sweets on orders from his doctor. Meg sometimes smuggled in something deliciously sugary.

She packed the food in a shopping bag. Before leaving the kitchen, she flicked the porch lights on and off to signal to Mike that she was on her way. From Mike's house next door, the spotlights his pals had rigged came on, mega-wattage, illuminating both houses. That was just the beginning. If Mike heard a suspicious noise, he switched on a tape of the chilling howl from the sound track of *Hound of the Baskervilles.* If the noise persisted, the tape kicked in with the yelps of a pack of frenzied wolves, then Mike wheeled from window to window with a quite illegal sawed-off shotgun at the ready.

He was in the kitchen fixing their drinks by the time Meg unlocked his side door with her key. His resonant baritone voice called to her, "Hello, light of my life. Put that bag down, take your drink. The oven's on."

Meg looked at the big man. Black Irish. Unruly hair, still dark and curly, erect in his motor-driven wheelchair. She remembered him just a few years ago, before his accident, dancing under paper lanterns out by the swimming pool with one of a rapid succession of wives and girlfriends. Mike's attention span was so brief, Meg had long ago stopped trying to remember their names. Even after arthritis crippled his spine, his magnetism was still in full force and an array of ladies visited frequently. When O'Shea cranked up the charm, he was a killer. Gallant, courtly, giving each woman the seductive concentration that made it so easy for her to believe she was special. And she was. For that moment, or a fortnight. His most enduring marriage lasted six months.

When the movies he directed were no longer moneymakers, he had to give up the big house in Beverly Hills with the tennis court and

Olympic-size pool. Never having saved a cent, suddenly bound to a wheelchair, he bought the house next door to Meg's parents and made himself comfortable in his drastically reduced circumstances without a moment of self-pity. "Remember," he had told twelve-year-old Meg when he was teaching her to play poker, "if you can't improve the hand you were dealt, just play the hell out of it. You might win after all."

It was Mike who had made her a journalist, though that certainly had not been his intent. When she had been hurt at not being cast in her eighth-grade play, *The Merchant of Venice*, she had complained to Mike. "Review it," he had barked. He had called a friend at a local weekly and convinced him it would be "cute" to run an eighth grader's review of the school play. That was the beginning.

Meg kissed her uncle of choice, put the stew in his oven and followed his wheelchair as he accelerated down the hallway to his study. The walls were lined with bookshelves spilling over with scripts, an Oscar, stacks of glossy photographs and boxes of love letters as well as books. Meg took her usual place in the wing chair. O'Shea braked when he reached his place behind the desk. "Now, my beautiful Meg, tell me the whole story from the beginning."

He listened carefully for twenty minutes. When Meg concluded with ". . . and that's all I know," he looked at her for a few seconds without speaking and shook his head.

"Meg, don't get interested in Pierpont Tree. I've never met him but I knew China. She's the only woman I'd ever say this about, so listen carefully. No man in his right mind would ever leave China Carlyle. Not even for a glorious creature such as yourself. So don't start spinning a fantasy."

Meg was indignant. "You're way off base!"

"I doubt it. Now, one other thing, Meg." He grinned at her serious expression and laughed. "Did you hire a hit on Beau Paxton?"

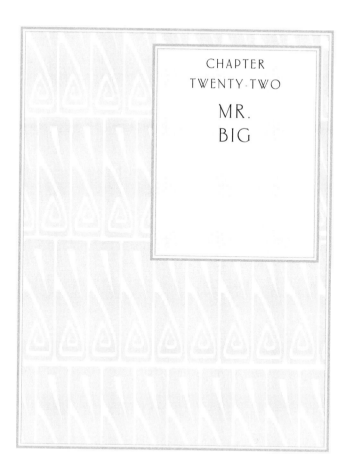

CHAPTER
TWENTY-TWO

MR.
BIG

Jonas Rupert thought of the old movies set in Manhattan. A panoramic view of skyscrapers. The camera sweeps down, down, down to Fifth Avenue. The morning rush hour. The sound track playing the spritely dah-dah-de-dum-dum music that made you want to be there. It was that kind of day. Sunny, crisp, seductively enchanting to a visitor from California.

Even a visitor on his way to a meeting he dreaded. Maybe it wouldn't be as bad as he expected, but the queasy feeling in his stomach told him he had no reason to be optimistic. If he had stopped gambling sooner, he might have escaped their attention. Might have. They didn't miss much. They were everywhere.

The casinos and the bookies told their bosses about any high roller they came across and, if the rolls were high enough and frequent enough, the underbosses reported the information to the overbosses who checked it out. The checking was thorough when the markers were big.

And Jonas' markers were very big. But he knew his luck would change. Two or three major scores would make him well. So he doubled his bets. And lost. And tripled. And lost again.

Then there were meetings with "representatives of the people who hold your markers." It wasn't like the movies. No one threatened him. They just made it very clear that they were very serious and wanted to know exactly when and how he would pay. The last meeting had been with a highly placed partner in a well-known venture capital group. Harvard M.B.A., well-tailored suit, and serpentine language in spirals until you weren't quite sure what he was saying but somehow you got the message. Pay up or they owned you.

Jonas knew his gambling was a compulsion. If he wanted to stay alive, he would have to pay up and give up gambling. He borrowed money from a bank recommended by his personal attorney. They were more than obliging and agreed to accept his share of *Manor House* as collateral. He had paid off most of his debt to the bank, so why should he be worried?

What he was feeling was beyond worry. He was sick with fear. Jonas had first heard the rumors about the bank's mob connections at a charity ball in Palm Springs. That hadn't been too alarming. After all, he wasn't gambling and made his bank loan payments punctually.

When his attorney suggested lunch one day, he had actually looked forward to it. Over coffee, the attorney mentioned that one of his New York clients was interested in buying *Manor House.* Jonas responded reflexively. "Tell them we're not interested." The attorney argued that Jonas should at least listen to the proposal, which would make him a very rich man. He would remain at *Manor House*, of course. Seth, too. Perhaps. When Jonas finally realized what his attorney was really saying, he knew "they" were going to make him an offer he couldn't refuse.

And today was the day.

The uniformed doorman asked for identification, adding, as Jonas reached for his wallet, "Would you mind facing forward, sir? For the video camera."

"The residents here must be the safest in Manhattan."

"This lobby serves only one resident, sir. Mr. Fred Hawkins. The elevator is express to his penthouse."

The doorman walked ahead of Jonas and pressed the elevator button.

The doors slid open and Jonas stepped inside. He remembered the vague rumors which had always attached themselves to Fred Hawkins and he felt his stomach drop as the elevator slid smoothly up to the forty-fourth floor.

The doors opened and Jonas realized he was staring into a foyer covered with mirrors. He saw, infinitely repeated, a round table holding a Lalique vase of orange tiger lilies and a white-faced man who was himself. He dropped his eyes, only to see himself again in the floor. It had been sanded and covered with so many coats of black lacquer that it reflected his face like a darkened mirror.

A young man in a gray jogging suit, with a bristle of beard, stepped over to meet him. "We have to check for weapons, if you don't mind, sir." They both knew Jonas was in no position to mind. Then a second man, wearing a business suit, appeared with an electronic gadget, which he ran over Jonas' clothes. When a low buzz sounded, Jonas jumped.

The businessman said, "It's probably your change, sir. Would you mind emptying your pockets? Step right over here to the table."

Jonas did as he was told. Buzz-free, he faced the massive double doors and noticed a third man, who looked both uncomfortable and incongruous as he perched on a japanned Chippendale hall chair in a corner of the spacious foyer. He was holding an Uzi.

Jonas froze in place until the man motioned with the gun, giving him permission to proceed.

The doors opened before he could knock. A butler greeted him by name, showed him into a dark, richly appointed office and asked if he would like coffee or a drink. Jonas requested coffee although he couldn't remember wanting a drink more than he did at that moment. He waited. He drank coffee. He waited and began to inspect the room, though he was too nervous to leave his chair. He was sitting in front of an old-fashioned mahogany partner's desk. Given Fred Hawkins' ruthless reputation, Jonas doubted he'd ever have let a partner occupy the other side. The wall behind the desk was lined with floor-to-ceiling bookcases. There were no books, just photographs of boxers with their gloves raised, horses taking impossibly high jumps and cars. Jonas had never seen so many photographs of cars. His eyes moved to the marble mantelpiece, which rose to the ceiling, and he noticed for the first time a frieze of stag heads, with magnificent antlers and glassy, dead eyes. The hearth showed no sign of ever having held a fire, but a leather easy chair was pulled up in front of it, the smooth masculine lines broken by an incongruous needlepoint pillow of the same orange tiger lilies which had been on the table in the foyer. There was no computer, no typewriter, no filing cabinet. No sign that Fred

Hawkins ever did anything but sit at the mahogany desk, reach for one of the three telephones, each a different color, and give the order to buy, to sell, or—Jonas felt his throat closing at the thought—to kill?

He scanned *Sports Illustrated,* then *Forbes,* and waited.

At last, he heard footsteps coming toward the office. Three men entered. All were tall. Two were dark, in contrast to Fred Hawkins, who was fair-haired and almost thin. He moved easily in his Armani suit. Hawkins came forward and shook hands with Jonas. "Thanks for coming. I really appreciate it." He seemed sincere. Jonas thought it might not be so bad, after all. One of the two dark men locked the office door, stood aside and stared into space. The other came forward and introduced himself.

"Gene Burdine, Mr. Hawkins' assistant. Please sit down, Mr. Rupert. We'll try not to take up any more of your time than absolutely necessary."

Jonas knew there was no hope.

Fred Hawkins moved behind the desk and sat down facing Jonas. His pale blue eyes didn't look threatening. Nor did his voice portend cement shoes. But Jonas felt chilled as Hawkins began to speak. "I'll come right to the point. My organization wants to buy *Manor House.* Our mutual banker friend in California has already told me you and your brother have no interest in selling. But we thought maybe now, with the tragic loss of your editor— By the way, Jonas, I was sorry to hear about Beau. I met him once or twice." He shook his head and smiled with an expression of mock sadness that seemed to menace Jonas.

Jonas nodded, his throat so constricted he dare not risk speech. Hawkins' smile broadened as his eyes narrowed.

"We sincerely believe you'll change your mind before you leave this room," Hawkins said softly. Too softly.

Doggedly, Jonas continued shaking his head.

Fred Hawkins picked up the gold model of a Ferrari which sat on the corner of his desk and began rolling it back and forth, spinning the wheels, raising it an inch off the desk until they stopped, spinning them again.

"I'm sorry that you've chosen to be difficult, Jonas," he said, not raising his eyes from the car. "You force me to insist that you sell your share of *Manor House* to pay off your bank debt. Oh, by the way, we own the bank."

Hawkins looked up, smiling again. With one hand he continued racing his little car back and forth, knowing that he was about to cross the finish line in first place. "We own your attorney, too, Jonas. We don't want you to go public. We are going to buy *Manor House.*" He held up the car, its wheels still spinning, to silence Jonas' protest. "Don't say anything just yet. Your magazine's cash flow is very attractive. Wash, rinse and spin, if you know what I mean. But there's a secondary reason. Have you met my wife, Maria? She's from Argentina," he said, as though that might explain everything.

"She wants to be the editor of *Manor House.* And if Maria wants it, I want it too. She really loves that magazine. She's got great taste. A terrific decorator. This apartment will be a great feature for the magazine. That Millar girl didn't like it. Big mistake."

Fred Hawkins looked at Jonas Rupert almost affectionately. "Are you alright? Another cup of coffee?" Jonas shook his head and tried to continue breathing. "We're prepared to give you enough to pay your debts and more. At first, say, thirty million each, while we're figuring out how we can do the magazine business our way. Another thirty each in a year or so. Then you and your brother can stay or go." Jonas opened his mouth to protest again but closed it when Hawkins smiled. The last offer for *Manor House* had been well over one hundred and fifty million.

"Now, you're busy and so are we. No point in wasting a lot of time. If the terms aren't right, just say so and perhaps we can make an adjustment."

Jonas opened his mouth again, hoping his voice would follow. "Why should I sell to you? I'm making my payments to the bank. Your bank. And we had an insurance policy on Beau. I can pay the rest as soon as the company settles. If we go public I'll have millions from the sale of the stock and *Manor House,* too."

"But that isn't what you want to do, Jonas. What you want to do is sell to us. In fact, it's the only way. You see, your loan payments weren't recorded by our bank's computers. Isn't that the curse of computers? You come to rely on them, and then they let you down. According to our bank records, you made only a few payments. And there's another problem, Jonas. Your canceled checks are missing from your business manager's office. You have no real proof of how much you've paid on your bank loan. You must have used the money for gambling. We've been very patient. But now we want some action and we're counting on you to convince your brother to cooperate.

"By the way, I was sorry to hear about his accident."

"Accident?" Jonas' voice floated out thin and reedy in the cavernous room. "What's happened to Seth?"

"He was shot in a robbery attempt last night. It was on the news this morning, but don't worry, he's okay," said Hawkins, offering Jonas another version of a smile. "Hey, Jonas, you should see your face. You look . . ." Hawkins looked for a word and failed. "Gene, how does he look?"

"I'd say he looks curdled, Mr. Hawkins."

"That's good, Gene. Jonas, you look *curdled.* But why? I'm just a businessman who wants to make a deal. It's not like the movies. No horses' heads on pillows. We're good to people who are good to us.

It's the Golden Rule. So come on, Jonas, do unto us, so we don't have to do unto you. I can have our mutual attorney in California draw up the papers right away."

Jonas knew he had to agree to whatever Hawkins wanted. Later he would figure a way out of this mess. When he could think.

"Yes. Draw up the papers. I don't want trouble."

"That's great, just great." Fred Hawkins jumped up from his chair and shook Jonas' hand. Then Hawkins added, "You've given me your *word*, Jonas. I take that as seriously as a written contract. *Capisce?* And by the way, you'll like my wife. She's a quick study and she'll do a great job with *Manor House.* Just keep her in California, know what I mean? Well, nice doing business with you."

Hawkins left the room, followed by one of his men. Jonas took a deep breath and tried to summon enough strength to stand. He could remember when his confidence was metallic. When people called him arrogant. He had just been induced into a lifetime of servitude. Or would his bondage actually end with the final sale of *Manor House* to Fred Hawkins? Probably not. He had to think of a way out. It was stuffy in the room. He couldn't breathe. He smelled cigar smoke. Gene Burdine cleared his throat. Jonas had forgotten him.

"I'll bet you're ready for a drink now." The man's wry smile seemed permanently affixed. He moved with feline fluidity as he went to the bar while Jonas tried again for a vertical stance. "What'll it be?"

"Vodka on the rocks."

"You got it. Come on, I'll show you the apartment before you go."

Jonas protested. "Another time."

"Afraid not. Mr. H. wants you to see it today. Then you send the photographer." Burdine led the way. Jonas followed. He was beaten and he knew it. Now all he wanted was to get back to his hotel room,

150

lock the door and get drunk. Tomorrow he would think of something, somehow. Jonas thought he heard a voice. He did hear a voice. Burdine was saying something to him. "Well, how do you like it?"

Jonas looked around. He couldn't believe it. Would this nightmare never end? He gulped the icy vodka before replying, shakily, "It's really something." Except for the walls of glass revealing chunks of Manhattan skyline, the entire room was orange. Mirrors reflected orange lacquered walls, orange wool carpeting, lengthy sectional sofas upholstered in orange velvet. Rows of orange pillows, appliquéd with green suede palm trees, stood at attention against the backs of the sofas, each pillow indented on top so that it looked as though the room had been seized by an army of demented rabbits. In the center of the room a mirrored coffee table, easily twenty feet wide, spelled out the initials MFH. Orange suede poufs, embroidered with the same initials in gold braid, flanked the coffee table. Mirrored lamps shaded with orange satin and emerald green beads lit up the titanic decor.

Burdine smiled as he looked at the room. "Mr. H. really likes orange. It's his favorite color. Maria's, too."

"I thought it might be." The vodka made him feel a little stronger. His edge was returning. "Can I ask you something?"

Burdine nodded cautiously.

"If Maria wants to be editor of a decorating magazine, why doesn't Hawkins just start one? Why go to all this trouble?" asked Jonas, thinking of the records which had vanished. And Seth. Hawkins had made it sound as though Seth's robbery was a coincidence. Was it?

"Well, you know women," said Burdine, who had downed two vodkas to Jonas' one and was fast becoming his buddy. "Mr. Hawkins' first wife was real social. Great in the drawing room, you know? But not so hot in bed. Then he met Maria, who is—well, you'll see when you meet her. Mr. Hawkins tried to work it so that he had Mrs.

Hawkins for show and Maria for fun, but things went wrong and, well, Mrs. Hawkins walked out and then Maria insisted that he marry her. I mean, he wants Maria. She drives him nuts. He only wants her some of the time. If he started a magazine, she'd want it to be in New York. Mr. H. just wants her to *visit* New York.

"Two things about *Manor House*, Jonas. One, the cash flow is incredible. That's important. Very. Two, it will put Maria three thousand miles away."

Jonas felt dizzy, thinking of the way fate had punished him for choosing to live his life in the sun. Or maybe his head was swimming because of the two walls of bronze mirror refracting the cityscape and a blaze of orange. Jonas looked curiously at his reflection. In his dazed state, it seemed to him that a bear was coming up behind him, walking erect on two feet. It moved toward him. Alarmed, he looked over his shoulder. It was still there. It spoke.

"Allo, Meester Rupert."

The bear was a woman. Six feet tall, wrapped in a full-length black mink coat, with the collar turned up so that it partially hid her face. Her mane of black hair was teased to the tips in all directions. Full scarlet lips were drawn back revealing large, strong teeth. Crudely, sensually beautiful, she stared at him from dark eyes beneath arched black brows. Everything about the creature was overscaled. Broad shoulders, huge bosom, burgeoning hips. Only her waist was small. The hand she extended was strong, the nails orange. She shrugged out of the mink, letting it drop on the floor. "I am Maria."

Wincing only a little as her hand crunched his bones, Jonas identified himself. "I am Jonas." My God, all we need is Boy and a chimp, he thought as the spectacular vision of Maria cut through his daze. "Jonas Rupert. I . . ."

Maria moved closer. "I knows all about you, Yonas. My husband,

152

he tell me. We make *Manor House* together, yes? Now eet like flan. We make eet like hot pepper, hokay?"

"Hokay. I mean, yes. But it is very well liked as it is, you know."

"Everyone like better when we get through with eet, no? In California we work on eet. There they not snobs, like New York. Everybody invite me everywhere. Lots of movie stars. You get everything rowed up for me."

"Rowed up?"

Burdine interceded. "Mrs. H. means lined up."

"Oh. Lined up. Yes, I'll get everything lined up." He turned ashen at the thought of Maria rampaging through the *Manor House* offices.

"You know Roberto Redford?"

"No. No, I'm afraid I don't."

"You no know him?"

"Afraid not."

"But you show ees house."

"Oh, yes, that's true. Several years ago. But I didn't meet him. I don't go out on the shoots. I mean, I don't go to the houses when the photographer is there."

"Oh, hoh. Maria be there. Maria go for all photographies. Especial movie stars. My husband say he catch me with movie star he keel me. Oh, hoh. I tell him Yonas send me. Eet is business. Somebody be keel, eet not me." She threw back her head and roared with laughter. "It be *you* he keel, hokay?"

Jonas nodded assent and headed for the door where the only danger was the man with the Uzi. Maria roared again and he stopped, paralyzed. "You row up Mel Gibson, too, hokay?"

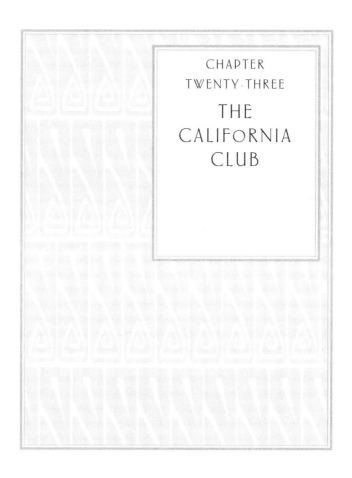

CHAPTER
TWENTY-THREE
THE
CALIFORNIA
CLUB

While Jonas tried to make himself relax, flying at an altitude of thirty thousand feet en route to Los Angeles, Pierpont Tree waved to Max Steiner as he entered the dining room of the California Club in downtown Los Angeles.

Steiner hopped from table to table, shaking a hand here, kissing a cheek there. When he reached Pier, he tapped him on the shoulder. "Sorry, but I want their votes."

Max seated himself, nodding to several constituents. "Pier, I'm glad to see you're still drinking booze at lunch. Somebody has to uphold the old traditions." He looked up at the waiter standing by for his drink order. "I'll have an iced tea and, by the way, I'd appreciate your vote, too."

"Yes, sir, Mr. Steiner." Executing a crisp military turn, he marched away.

"Christ, Max, have you no shame?"

"Shame? Pier, I'm running for office. Shame is for civilians. And solving this case would be a vote-getter. So, let's see the letter. You say Dilly Dillingham found it in Beau Paxton's papers? Is that really her name? How Waspy can you get? And she's the girl Paxton was engaged to as opposed to the *guy* he was engaged to, who is now in the hospital after a hit-and-run probable murder attempt. It's a soap, a goddamned, prime-time soap."

Pier nodded. "And there's another episode. Dilly said a car tried to run her off the road when she was on her way to my house with the letter. Someone could have been watching Dilly's house, waiting for her to drive out. But it was probably just a drunk driver." Pier handed the letter to Max. "You read. I'll drink."

The waiter returned with iced tea. "Here you are, Mr. Steiner."

"Thanks. What's your name, by the way?"

"Bob, sir."

"I'll remember that, Bob."

"Max, you've *got* his vote. Read the goddamned letter so we can order lunch."

Steiner read the letter quickly. "Well, one thing is clear . . ."

"At last."

"This letter confirms that Meg Millar had a double whammy motive to want Beau Paxton dead. He wouldn't help her get stock and she wanted his job. Also, she's smart. She might think she could get away with it. And why not? Everybody else does. Whoever said there was no such thing as a perfect crime was, pardon me, dead wrong. But we can't prove it was a paid hit unless we nail the shooter. If he was imported for the job, we'll never get him. Unless Meg Millar found him through an organized crime connection and *Manor House* starts publishing photographs of weird houses where the owners lounge around the pool wearing shoulder holsters. Then we'll know she did it."

"That makes it easy, Max. All you have to do is subscribe and wait."

"My wife subscribes, which pisses me off. With two kids still in college, we don't need to pay a hundred bucks a year to look at rich people's houses. Hell, Pier, if I get the urge, I'll drive up to Santa Barbara and look at yours."

"What about Seth Rupert? Is he going to make it?"

"Looks like it. Can you believe this cockamamie case? We've already got two suspects in the hospital. It's like *Ten Little Indians*, last one standing is it."

"Any leads?"

"Looks like it's the same guy who did Beau Paxton. Rupert described him in the ambulance. Black, dreadlocks. Not a lot of help and it may be a disguise."

"Did the shooter just duck into a broom closet until he could leave?"

"No broom closet. Everything is locked up tight at night. You can run but you can't hide, and God knows how this guy got in and how he got out. That building houses some of the wealthiest, most influential people in the goddamned city. Some of them are my biggest contributors. I'm already feeling the pressure. Well, we're asking Meg Millar to come in for questioning. I think we'd better ask Dilly Dillingham to drop in for a cup of tea, too, if she isn't too busy playing polo."

"Have you found Norton Birdwell?"

"It's too nutty, even for a soap. Seems he flitted off to the South Pacific. Just an impulsive madcap. Used his own name, his own passport. He's returning to L.A. voluntarily. Said he didn't know we were looking for him."

"Is Birdwell still a suspect?" Pier asked.

"You know me, Pier. I'm just like Santa. Makin' my list and checkin' it twice, gonna find out who's naughty or nice. What have you got?"

"Eddie found out Jonas Rupert was a high roller, a compulsive gambler. Used to go to Vegas every weekend. Never left the crap tables. He also bet big with local bookies on the horses, baseball, basketball, football, pro and college. Croquet is the only game he didn't bet. First he was slow pay, then he was no pay. That kind of fiscal irresponsibility leads directly to a hospital bed and lots of traction. If you're lucky. Supposedly Jonas stopped gambling cold turkey several years ago. He's flying back from New York today. It seems he had a sudden desire to visit Manhattan."

"Another merry madcap. Well, we've already left word for him to come in for questioning tomorrow morning. Maybe Jonas had Beau Paxton and brother Seth shot so he could be sole owner of *Manor House*. If Seth buys the farm, Jonas ends up with the whole crop. Then there's Meg Millar. Maybe she had Seth shot. Maybe she did it herself. Maybe she and Jonas teamed up to do Beau and Seth."

"Max, she's a nice girl . . ."

"Hell, don't go dipshit on me, Pier. Maybe she's so nice she shot them both so she could sell the magazine and build a hospital in Zimbabwe."

"Okay, Max. Who's your best bet?"

"Right now, my money's on Jonas, but, Pier, this case is filled with wondrous possibilities."

"Can you find out what wondrous possibility Jonas was pursuing in New York?"

"We sure plan to ask him. Any ideas?"

"Ephemeral, at best."

"Pier, you'd never make it in politics. You use big words. Elitist words. First thing I was told, you've got to sound like a real guy, one of the people. Listen, let's order. I've got to get back to the office. You got anything else?"

"Lars Eklund told someone in the hospital that he tried to dodge the car but couldn't. It was no accident."

"I don't know, Pier. A hit-and-run isn't the method professionals favor. You risk a lingering operatic aria with the dying victim singing your name loud and clear. Was that 'someone' Lars talked to Eddie?"

"No method's foolproof," Pier pointed out, ignoring Max's question. "Whoever shot Seth Rupert thought he had killed him."

"Big mistake if that was a professional hit."

"Hell, it's hard to get good help. The mafia has problems too. The new generation is really smart, well educated. They're in big business and politics. But finding good street soldiers is almost impossible. Smack, coke, crack. And the elite corps of hit men is just about finished. The mob has to rely pretty much on punks who'll kill for a nickel. You can hire a shooter today for five hundred but it's a K mart job. Real quality work runs at least twenty-five thousand. That gets you an above-suspicion fatal accident. You know, Max, there are rumors about you and the mob."

"There are rumors about everybody and the mob."

"Sounds like you've heard that song before."

158

"An old, familiar score. The opposition party started that rumor during my first campaign. You believe it?"

"No," said Pier. "But I believe it about a lot of folks even you might be surprised to find out about. Back to the case at hand. We've got to move faster."

"Tell me about it. Look, Pier, Beau Paxton knew hundreds of people all over the world. Checking them all out is impossible. And the killer may be way out in left field laughing at us."

"Maybe, but murder is almost always close to home."

"You had to tell me that? What is this, Crime Detection 101? It was Eddie in the hospital, wasn't it?" Max asked. "He got in there somehow and had a little chat with Lars Eklund. Anything else you haven't told me, Pier?"

"No, but as soon as I have something, you'll know it."

"Cross your heart and hope to die?"

"Couldn't take that chance, Max."

"The killer is taking chances. Beau Paxton was a hired hit. Maybe the killer decided to take out Lars and Seth on his own. You know, like building bookshelves. Why pay a pro when you can do it yourself? He follows Lars Eklund until an opportunity presents itself, then runs him down. I admit that makes no sense unless Eklund knew something about Beau's murder. Next, Seth Rupert. He figures it can't be so difficult. Ring doorbell. Bang he's dead. At least the shooter thinks he is. And now he figures it's easy. Who's he going to do next? Come on, Pier, help me. I can't win this election with a conspicuously unsolved murder still on the front page."

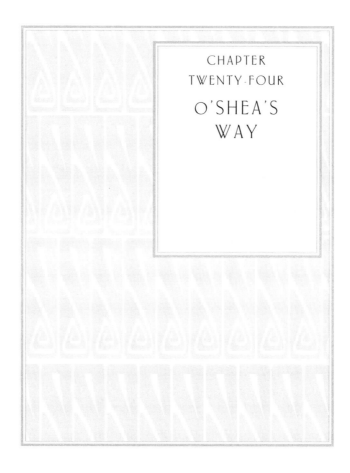

CHAPTER
TWENTY-FOUR

O'SHEA'S
WAY

Meg parked her Jaguar in the driveway because Mike O'Shea insisted she must never drive into the garage after dark. The area had changed since Meg was a little girl and Mike worried that she would forget. "Let them steal the goddamn car," he had growled. "If you drive on in, some guy has plenty of time to duck in before that automatic gadget closes the door behind you."

Meg sounded the car horn twice, quickly, got

out, locked the car and decided to go directly to Mike's house. The door opened before she could knock.

"Hi, Mike." Meg kissed him on the forehead.

He looked up, blue eyes wide, and winked. "I've got a lady coming over for dinner. Come on into the office. I don't have much time." His chair sped along the hall, past walls hung densely with photographs of Mike O'Shea with every celebrity of the last five decades. Movie stars, ball players, politicians, writers, fighters and presidents of the United States. They had all wanted to be photographed with the legendary director of Westerns. When Mike was riding high, film buffs referred to "The O'Shea Way." Many of the celebrities in the photographs were dead now. He rarely heard from any of the others. But Mike O'Shea, now in his early seventies, had always known the rules. Fold and the deal passes to the other players. It was the way of the world.

Meg seated herself and came straight to the point. "The police called me this afternoon. They requested the pleasure of my company in the matter of Beau Paxton's murder and Seth Rupert's shooting. They want me to answer a few questions. I suppose they suspect me too."

O'Shea scowled. "Too? Who else suspects you?"

"You do."

"Me?"

"You. Last time I was here you asked me if I had Beau killed."

"Oh, yeah. Well, why shouldn't you have him blasted? You had good reason. That bastard wouldn't lift his limp wrist to help you. Anyway, you know damn well I'm a day late and a dollar short on all this reverence for human life." O'Shea poured bourbon neatly into a silver shot glass and belted it back.

"Tell me what to do about the police. Obviously I have to answer their questions, but how forthcoming should I be? Especially about that letter."

"Answer their questions but don't volunteer any info. Dummy up. *Of course* you're a suspect. That goddamn letter is going to sound like a death threat. My darlin' girl, you were out of your pretty head to expect Beau to stand up for you. That's the way he was made. A leopard is a leopard and you can't get mad at it for being what it is."

Meg looked at the big man and counted him the blessing of her life. One person who truly loved her. "I should have listened to you, Mike. And you're right. Poor Beau. He avoided me after he received the letter. He was terrified that I might confront him. Mike, who do you think had Beau killed?"

"No idea at all, my darlin'. You told me all about Beau and his casting couch and taking money from decorators and the good Lord only knows who else, but I can't see one of them doing it. Remember, always look for the economic motive. Now that Beau's dead, who gets his share of *Manor House?* Do you know?"

Meg sipped her drink and considered. "Beau's share probably reverts to the Ruperts. Possibly to his half brother, but I doubt it." She put her head in her hands. "Since Seth was shot, it's even more confusing. I wanted to see him or at least call him, but the police won't tell anyone which hospital he's in. His secretary hinted that he's under an assumed name. They told her he's doing fine but she was not to tell anyone anything. Oh, Mike, who would have wanted to shoot Seth?"

O'Shea downed the rest of his bourbon, wondering if he saw tears in Meg's eyes. "What about Jonas? Could he have shot his own brother? Or had it done?"

"Seth didn't want to sell any part of *Manor House,* but Jonas would have persuaded him. He always got his way eventually. He

162

didn't have to kill Seth for that. You told me a couple of years ago you'd heard Jonas was a big gambler. Could that be related to all this somehow? Incidentally, Jonas suddenly flew to New York. I don't know why. His secretary wouldn't say a word. She's more afraid of Jonas than the police."

"Keep after her. We need all the info we can get. Now, this young decorator friend of Beau's, Lars Eklund. That hit-and-run was probably no accident. And let's pay close attention to Norton Birdwell." O'Shea helped himself to another shot of bourbon. "Did he run because they were about to arrest him?"

Meg considered. "Norton was obsessively jealous of Beau. Always afraid Beau would leave him for someone with more money. But would he actually have him killed? I really doubt it."

"There's another possibility. That Dilly girl you said Beau was seeing a lot of . . . the one in Santa Barbara. Would you cast her as a killer? Did she know Beau was gay? Did she care?"

"It's possible she didn't know. He played those games. Maybe when she realized Beau was gay and had no real plans to marry her, she hired a hit man to kill him. It seems awfully far-fetched, doesn't it?"

"Maybe, maybe not. But one thing is certain. When the murderer is discovered, all this will seem absolutely, sure as shootin' obvious and we'll feel like idiots because we couldn't figure it out."

Meg hesitated for a moment, then asked the question she had been holding back. "Will the police arrest me because of that letter?"

"That's not enough to make an arrest. Just enough to make you a prime suspect."

Meg saw Mike glance at the clock on his desk. The one the crew had given him at the wrap party for *Stallion Run.* "I have to go home and get to work." She left the study, headed for the kitchen. Mike followed. At the door, she reminded him, "Don't be so eager for your next visitor that you forget to watch for my signal."

Mike braked his wheelchair abruptly. "Listen, my girl, be extra careful."

He saw Meg's face pale. "Why? What is it?"

Mike paused for a split second. "Nothing in particular, but this is a murder case. Cranks and nuts can always turn up when you least expect it. Don't answer the door unless you *know* who it is."

Meg blew a good night kiss. "I'm always careful."

Mike O'Shea stayed at the door watching for her signal. He had almost told her why he was worried, then realized he would only frighten her. Anyway, he couldn't be absolutely certain the man who had walked by several times that afternoon had been casing Meg's house. He didn't want to overreact and scare Meg. Maybe it was only somebody looking for an address. Mike made notes on a scratch pad by the telephone. Approximate height, weight, hair in dreadlocks.

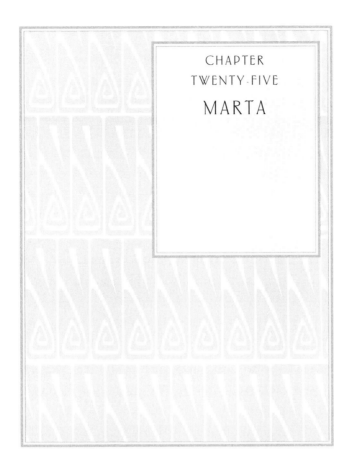

CHAPTER
TWENTY-FIVE
MARTA

Plop. Plop. Eddie Navarro's girlfriend, Marta Parioli, dropped two plastic bags of Lean Cuisine Chicken Fettuccine into a pot of boiling water and silently prayed for her father's forgiveness. Although he had died five years ago, Marta could feel him looking over her shoulder shouting words in Italian so *rapido* she couldn't understand, but his meaning needed no translation. *Plastic pasta!* How could she eat food like that? She, the daughter of Giuseppe Parioli, the best cook in Little Italy.

The men who came to his restaurant ate his food in huge quantities. They always went into the back room where Papa served them himself. When Marta was old enough, she and her older brother, Gino, helped out in the restaurant, but her mother told her they must never have anything to do with those men. Years later, Marta was passing the back room when the door suddenly opened and she saw her papa kneeling before the oldest of the men, kissing his hand. Gino was standing beside him, his thin face illuminated with a look of awe.

When Papa was clearing the tables, after the men had gone, she asked him about the strange sight she had witnessed. Papa had quickly hushed her. Speaking in Italian so her Spanish mother who sat at the cash register could not understand if she were to overhear, he told Marta the man was his godfather. He had kissed his hand to show respect. She was not to tell her mother.

She asked Gino what had happened in the back room. He told her it was "men's business," and that he would soon be doing important work himself.

The next morning at breakfast, Marta's mother announced that Papa had sold the restaurant and they would move to Los Angeles. Her prayers were answered. Marta would grow up far away from Little Italy and "the kind of men your father has to do business with." They would open a much bigger restaurant in Los Angeles. Marta would grow up like a real American girl, far away from "the people who tell your father what to do."

Marta knew better. She remembered Papa kissing the old man's hand and what her brother had said. She knew it was all somehow connected with the move to Los Angeles. She said nothing to her mother. Mama was so happy that morning. She told Marta there were many Spanish-speaking people in Los Angeles and there she would have friends of her own. In Little Italy she was the one who had tricked Giuseppe Parioli into marrying her when he should have married a nice Italian girl from one of the Families.

Mama was not so happy a year later in Los Angeles when Big Joe's Italia was opened. Men who looked like the ones from Papa's restaurant in New York came almost every night to eat dinner in a private room kept just for them.

Gino, grown now, joined the men sometimes. Marta knew he was out most nights doing their bidding. She wasn't certain but she thought he was using drugs and maybe dealing, too. They owned Gino. Only the location had changed with their move from New York. Everything else was still the same. They hadn't gotten away at all.

But at least she had lost her New York accent. She went to school, did her homework and helped her mother with the bookkeeping. After high school Marta enrolled at City College. She was a whiz with figures and wanted to be a computer programmer. Her father wanted her to marry and have children. Her mother wanted her to find a job away from the restaurant. That was what Marta wanted, too.

Everything changed soon after she graduated. It was a humid July night. She could smell the jacaranda outside and the marinara inside as she helped her mother place flower arrangements on the tables for an engagement party. The man she knew to be the head of one of the Families in New York had taken over the entire restaurant to announce his grandson's forthcoming marriage to a Los Angeles girl. Marta knew the girl must be part of a Family. The old don would never allow his grandson to marry an outsider. Yet things were changing. Anything was possible.

Marta helped keep the wineglasses filled that evening. The music was so loud she had to bend down to hear what one of the guests was saying. Marta was small, softly curved, firm. Her dark hair almost reached her waist. Her olive skin glowed without makeup. The guest—a young man—had reached out and circled her waist. "No one told me Joe had such a gorgeous daughter." The young man's name was Naldo and Marta married him three weeks later. Her mother cried. Gino was impressed. Her father was proud.

Marta knew she was good with computers, but she recognized right away that Naldo was a virtuoso. One of the first hackers, he could program a computer to ride a horse. His genius had not been appreciated by the Family for several years. But once they understood what he and his computer could do for them, he was warmly embraced. They bought a house for the newlyweds with an especially equipped computer room for Naldo. Marta was starting on her master's and everything was fine. And then it wasn't.

Marta's belief in the inevitability of mathematics told her the first tragedy would not be the last. She miscarried and was informed she would never be able to bear children.

At about the same time, Marta's father died and the Family bought the restaurant from her mother at a price she was strongly urged to accept immediately and without question. Six months later her mother died from a stroke. Then Naldo left for Mexico.

It had taken another hacker to catch him. Even then it had been an accident. Naldo had worked out a computer program of breathtaking simplicity. He broke into the Bank of Los Angeles' computer and removed $1.00 from each checking account maintaining a certain balance each month, then transferred the funds into accounts he had opened under various names. No one missed a dollar.

When Naldo didn't ask Marta to join him in Mexico, she figured he had a new computer scam going. Marta knew Naldo's infatuation with her had been replaced by his love for the computer. With no demands on his time, he could devote himself to finding new ways to move the Family money around, laundering it so it came out sparkling fresh and lemon-scented.

Even before he'd fled the country, Naldo had been able to wire-transfer funds around the world with a speed-of-light program so intricate only another mob computer wizard, code name Auditor, could understand the transactions. Naldo knew that for a fact. He had told Marta how he'd broken into Auditor's computer and looked around. Then he invented a program of his own to audit the Auditor program which was auditing his. It was then that Naldo had begun to glimpse the power a computer wizard could wield in the modern Mafia. And it was then that he'd begun to resent his marriage to Marta. A wife took time. And a wife who couldn't bear him children? Naldo had better things to do.

Marta wondered if Naldo knew about Eddie. And if he would care. Naldo could ask the Family to arrange an annulment. They might let her go then. She didn't know anything important. And keeping two sets of books for a few Mafia bars was not what Marta wanted to do with her life. She was good with a computer too. She was studying advanced programming so she could qualify for an important legitimate job if the Family would let her go.

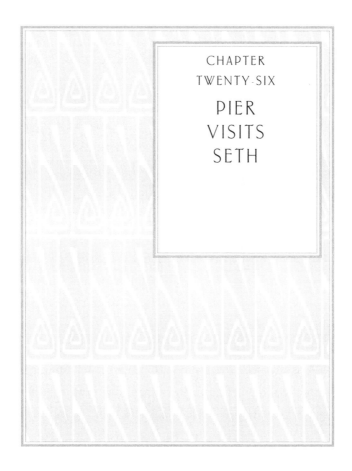

CHAPTER TWENTY-SIX

PIER
VISITS
SETH

Pier waited in the lobby. It looked like the best
hotel in Duluth, Minnesota, but it was a private
wing in Sinai General Hospital in West Los Angeles.
It was a part of the hospital only the rich knew about.
The rooms were spacious and private nurses attended
the needs of each patient. Everything was muted. The
colors, the sounds, the footsteps. Bouquets of fresh
flowers were placed on every table. An attractive young
nurse assured Pier, "You will be able to see Mr. R. in

a few minutes. We don't use his name, by the way, even on his chart. All visitors are cleared by the District Attorney's office." She glided away.

If Seth could be kept safe, he would recover. Who wanted Seth dead? Was the attempt on his life connected to Jonas Rupert's trip? Pier wanted to know more about that sudden visit to New York. Eddie was digging into it. He had his own network of contacts, listening posts in many cities, in many groups, underground as well as above. He could come up with the name of an assistant D.A. in Miami or a beat cop in Spanish Harlem. And they would tell Eddie whatever they could. He would mention the name that would prompt them to reveal information. With a telephone in his hand, Eddie could rule the world.

Pier was pulled from his reverie by the hushed voice of the young nurse. "I'll take you to Mr. R.'s room now." Pier rose and walked with her to the hallway leading to the private rooms. The walls were painted a soothing dove gray and the color of the carpeting was almost identical. "You can only stay a minute or two. Mr. R. is still in serious condition. The police guard must be present when you talk to him. Those are our orders." She smiled at Pier and shrugged as if she wished she could change things but it just wasn't possible.

Seth Rupert seemed to be dozing when the nurse opened his door to admit Pier and the policeman. She touched Seth's shoulder and he opened his eyes slowly. He tried to focus but looked confused. The nurse spoke softly. "It's Pierpont Tree to see you for just a minute or two. If you need me, just ring." She placed a call button in Seth's hand and left the room.

Pier looked at Seth and touched his hand. "I want you to know we'll get the guy who did this. That's a promise. If you can, tell me what you remember about the shooting."

Pier leaned down. He listened closely as Seth whispered hoarsely. "Working on computer. Knock at door. Thought it was neighbor. Opened door. Black guy."

"Did he say anything before he shot?"

Seth closed his eyes for a moment, then opened them long enough to shake his head. When he closed his eyes again, they didn't reopen. He was asleep.

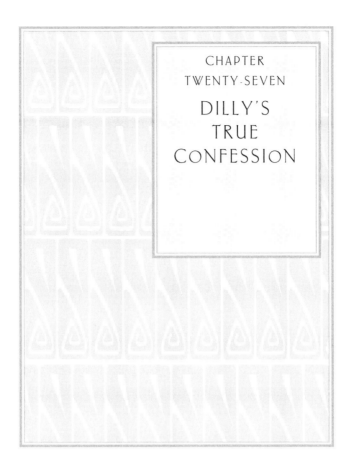

CHAPTER
TWENTY-SEVEN

DILLY'S TRUE CONFESSION

C hina looked at her flooring, wide planks sal-
vaged from an old house in Maine. She sat
curled up in a wing chair near the fireplace. An ex-
panse of wood-paned windows opened onto the wide
front porch punctuated with big tubs of Santa Barbara's indigenous "Freddy" begonias. Beyond, a green
meadow, edged by a stand of eucalyptus, framed the
ocean view. A model boat, *The China*, a present from
her father on her twelfth birthday, rested on a painted
table in front of a bay window.

She considered the comfortable sofa, an eighteenth-century quilt thrown over the back, the *New York Times* on the nearby table. Then, sighing, China returned to the kitchen, faced her old electric typewriter and began again. Hands on the keyboard, she waited for an idea, a thought, a word. Anything at all. Minutes ticked by. Then she remembered something she could write about. She began typing. She was excited. The ribbon broke. She searched her desk for another. Nothing. Went out to her car. It wouldn't start.

China ran up the wide stairs to the terrace of Casa Arbol, on into the huge kitchen. Relieved, she saw Mattie seated at a big worktable making lists, a platter of fresh-baked biscuits at hand. "Mattie, I need to borrow a car. Mine won't start and I have to go into town for a typewriter ribbon. My last one just broke."

Mattie looked at China, put down her pen. "How're you doin' with that book?"

China was surprised. "How did you know?"

"Easy. The girl with that cleaning crew goes to your house, she told me."

"You mean she's read it?"

"She gets tired, sometimes she sits down and reads."

"Mattie, that girl is fired, as of now. I always put the manuscript in my desk when I finish."

"Not always. You leave it out sometimes. The girl was just curious so she read some. I told her not to do it again. So don't fire her. She's got two little fatherless kids to support and she's a hard worker."

China slapped the marble pastry counter hard. "Damnit, Mattie, even Pier doesn't know I'm writing a book. I wanted to surprise him and now the whole world knows."

"You calm down, hear? Sit. Have some iced tea. I just picked fresh mint and crushed it right into the pitcher." Mattie took a crystal glass from one of the cupboards, put it on the marble top in front of China and filled it with tea.

China inhaled deeply, exhaled slowly. "Okay. She's not fired." China swung off the stool, stood erect in white pants and sweater looking at Mattie, head cocked to one side. "Did she like it?"

"Like what?"

"The book. Did she like the book?"

"I didn't ask her."

"Oh. Well. Did you read it?"

"No way. Wanna tell me about it?"

China shrugged. "It's about my life, my career in movies. No tattletale stuff." Calm now, China reclaimed the high stool and drank her tea, slowly. "Mattie, let Pier go on thinking I sleep late, because if I finish the book and it's no good, I'm going to burn it."

"Honey, don't worry. I won't say nothin', no way, nohow."

China was about to run over and hug Mattie when she heard footsteps. Dilly Dillingham's riding boots pounded on the old tile floor of the kitchen. She stopped abruptly when she saw China, then looked at Mattie. "I thought you'd be alone. All the doors were wide open so I . . ."

"Dilly, you haven't come over here for years. Now it's twice in a week. What's in your head, girl?" Mattie stood and walked toward Dilly as if she might check her forehead for fever.

China looked at Dilly and came right to the point.

"Pier isn't here."

Dilly stamped her foot. "Spit. I really have to talk to him. It's important."

Mattie considered for a moment, then poured tea for Dilly. "Sit down, girl. What's so important that you're lathered up like one of your horses?"

Dilly pulled a chair away from Mattie's worktable and straddled it, looking at China with suspicion. "I'd better wait for Pier. I was all set to tell him and now he isn't here. When will he be back?"

China lighted a cigarette with unusual deliberation and winked at Mattie. "Two or three hours."

Dilly stomped the floor in anger. "Spit, spit, spit!"

Mattie stood over Dilly, shaking her finger. "You never were able to wait for anything, girl. You might as well get it out of your system right now."

Dilly again looked warily at China, who offered, "If it will make you more comfortable, I'll leave."

Dilly shook her blond ponytail. "No. You might as well hear. Pier will probably tell you anyway." She turned to Mattie and asked hopefully, "Could I have a brandy?"

"Seems to me you've already had a brandy. But I'm not your mama." Mattie opened another cupboard, took out a bottle, found an old crystal shot glass, filled it almost to the brim and handed it to Dilly. "That'll hold you for a while."

Dilly took the glass, looked out toward the sea and announced, "I killed Beau Paxton."

China stared at Dilly, then turned to Mattie, who shook her head and said, "Come again, girl."

"You heard me. It isn't easy to come right out and say . . . you know."

China looked at the heavy leather shoulder bag Dilly had

dropped on the floor near her chair. "Do you have a gun in your bag, Dilly? This scene is right out of one of my movies, *Blue Lady*. I wasn't actually killed but I was seriously wounded."

Dilly was trying to figure out what China was talking about when Mattie walked over, scooped up Dilly's bag and dropped it in a drawer. "That'll stay right there. Girl, you might just get it in your head to shoot us both."

China attempted a reassuring smile. "Dilly, have you told anyone else that you, ah, killed Beau Paxton?"

"No. I should have told Daddy but I just couldn't. I thought Pier could come over with me and tell him. But you two don't have to worry, for heaven's sake. I wouldn't shoot anyone I *know.*"

China lit another cigarette. The first was still burning unnoticed in a deep ashtray. "You just confessed killing your fiancé."

"I mean I wouldn't kill anyone else. Anyway, I didn't actually shoot Beau. Someone did it for me."

Mattie snapped at her, "Who are you talking about, girl?"

"My hairdresser, Georgie."

China's aquamarine eyes opened wide. "Your *hairdresser?* Dilly, that's silly. Oh. Sorry. But my God, nobody gets their hairdresser to kill someone. And why would he do it?"

"Because he felt— Because I did him a favor, and he wanted to do something for me in return. He knew Beau had been horrible and that I was very upset. So he thought it would be only fair if he—you know."

"Killed him." China finished it for her. "If you can get someone to do it, you really should learn to say the word."

Dilly began pacing, boots clicking on the tile. "You movie people always talk like you think you're in a film. No wonder you're not accepted socially."

China turned on her too sweet smile. Mattie shuddered.

"Dilly, you're going to be *very* social in jail. You can start an all-dyke chapter of the Junior League."

Mattie laughed. She was beginning to have a good time.

Dilly shuddered. "They can't put me in jail, China. I didn't actually do anything except give Georgie some money. He's sick. You know? With AIDS. I gave him the money to help out, and he wanted to do something for me in return."

"How much money did you give him, Dilly?" Mattie asked.

"A hundred thousand." Mattie drew a sharp breath and Dilly turned to her.

"Georgie doesn't have health insurance, and I don't know what I'd do if he died. No one else knows how to cut my hair. I didn't really mean for him to kill Beau, but he came to my house to do my hair before the Emerald Ball. We had some drinks and I gave Georgie the money. He kept saying he wished he could do something to pay me back. So I said he could shoot my rat fink fiancé.

"Then I read that Beau had been murdered. I didn't mean it. It was Georgie who did it, not me." Dilly actually shed a tear. Just one. Then she asked for another brandy.

Mattie filled her glass while China smoked, watching Dilly. Then she spoke. "The night you said someone tried to run you off the road, you thought it was Georgie trying to cover his tracks, didn't you? But what made you say that to Georgie? Why did you want to have Beau Paxton killed?"

"Oh, spit. I wanted to tell Pier about all this first. If you two tell anyone, anyone at all, I'll kill you." Dilly stopped pacing, clapping her hand over her mouth. "That was just a figure of speech. I don't want to say another word."

Mattie cut in sharply. "Open your mouth and answer the question."

Dilly obeyed. "I *didn't* want to have him killed. I just wanted to get back at him for—for making a fool of me. You know what people would have said. 'Poor Dilly. First she loses her husband to an older woman and then she loses her fiancé to an older man.'

"Anyway, it's Georgie's fault. He's the one who told me Beau was gay, or bi, or whatever you call it. I thought Beau just wasn't interested in sex. Or else he wanted to wait until we were married. A lot of people do these days, you know. Sex isn't the same as it used to be."

China groaned. "Dilly, it's not *that* different. And you're a divorced woman, not a trembling virgin."

"Oh, China, you're such a smart-ass. You spent so much time on casting couches you can't even imagine a man and woman waiting to have sex until they're married."

Mattie hushed China with a glance and spoke to Dilly in a low, threatening tone.

"One more word against China and I'll whup your society ass good. Save that sass for those big mutha prison matrons. They're gonna love you to death."

Dilly bridled and stamped her boots again. "I have a right to be upset. I had to do something. You can't just let men walk all over you. Why, Beau might have killed *me*. He had AIDS too."

China lit a third cigarette. The other two still smoldered. "Beau Paxton had AIDS?"

"He told me so himself. Said he got it from a blood transfusion. That was why he had to leave me. He didn't want me to see him die a horrible death. I didn't realize until a couple of days later that he might have given it to me. I don't know how long I have to live!" Dilly pulled a handkerchief from her shirt pocket and sobbed. China and Mattie stared at each other. Mattie spoke first.

"Dilly, listen up. Didn't you just say you never had sex with Beau?"

179

Dilly nodded.

"Then how did he give you AIDS?"

Dilly wailed. "From all that deep kissing. After he told me, I was at the dentist's office and I read an article which said that it's in the saliva. I'm afraid I'm going to die!"

Mattie stared at Dilly and shook her head. "Girl, you're some piece of work."

Dilly straightened up, pleased. "Thank you, Mattie." She shot an angry glance at China. "It's nice to hear something good about yourself at a time like this."

The three women turned at the sound of Pier's footsteps. He walked over to China and kissed her. "What's going on?"

Dilly spoke accusingly before China could answer. "You said Pier wouldn't be back for two or three hours!"

China nodded. "I lied." Then she smiled at Pier. "Dilly has something to tell you." Her tone was sugared. "Tell him, dear."

"Oh, spit. Well. I killed Beau Paxton. Sort of. I mean, my hairdresser actually did it."

Pier looked at Dilly, shook his head and started to leave the kitchen. "I've been on the freeway for two hours. I need a drink and a hot bath."

Mattie intercepted him. "Hey, wait! You've got to hear this. Sit down. I'll fix you a stiff one."

China nodded. "It's true. Dilly has confessed to engineering the murder of Beau Paxton."

Pier walked over to the fireplace, threw in some kindling, a couple of logs. The Mexican tiles covering the floors and the thick adobe walls kept the kitchen cool even on the hottest summer days. He liked a fire. Mattie's mother had once told him, "You'll never be lonely if you have a fire." Pier settled into a big upholstered chair and looked at Dilly. "Okay. You hired your hairdresser to kill Beau Paxton?"

"I didn't really hire him. He did it as a favor because I'd given him some money," said Dilly.

Pier questioned Dilly until she had repeated everything she told China and Mattie and added more. Finally, Pier shook his head in disbelief. "You got your *hairdresser* to kill Beau Paxton?"

"He was the only person I knew who needed money."

Mattie mumbled, "You heard that? I'm taking notes for my new sociology course. You get it? She only knew one person who needed money!"

Pier continued. "Putting aside the revelatory commentary on Montecito economics, there are one or two more questions, Dilly. Did your hairdresser, Georgie, wear a wig and blackface makeup when he shot Beau?"

"How would I know?"

Pier looked at Dilly, then tried again. "Where did you get one hundred thousand dollars in cash?"

Dilly lowered her voice. "Don't tell anyone, but I always keep a hundred thousand and some of those little gold bars in my personal safe with my jewelry because Daddy told me to always keep a little cash on hand for emergencies. I gave it to Georgie that night he came over to do my hair."

"Where can I find Georgie?"

Dilly rolled her eyes toward the ceiling. "Nobody listens to me." She scowled at Pier. "I told you I don't know where he is."

Pier's voice took on an edge. "Did you give Georgie so much because he was supposed to kill three people?"

Dilly's mouth opened but it was a moment before she could speak. "Why would I want him to kill three people? I didn't even want him to kill Beau. And I told you I gave Georgie that money because he was sick and he needed it. It was his idea to do me a favor. So he wouldn't feel guilty about taking the money, I guess. I called him the next day to say I'd changed my mind. There wasn't any answer and he wasn't in his shop. Then I heard about Beau. I didn't really mean for him to do it, Pier, honest. But it doesn't matter what they do to me, I'm going to die anyway." Tears streaked her cheeks.

Pier shook his head and sighed. "Don't cry, Dilly. A good attorney will get you off. And you're not going to die. You probably won't even go to jail."

Dilly brushed her tears away with the back of her hand. "Some detective. You don't even care that Georgie tried to run me off the road. He'll try again, too. And if he doesn't kill me, AIDS will. Beau had it and he gave it to me!" Dilly looked scornfully at China and added, "You can *so* get it from French kissing. The article said you could."

Pier looked puzzled. China swished the ice cubes in her glass. Mattie snorted. "Get on home, girl. We'll explain the kissing thing to him later." Dilly looked doubtfully at Mattie, then beseechingly at Pier.

He waved toward the terrace. "Go home, Dilly."

Pier watched as Dilly ran down the terrace steps to the path where her horse was tethered. She looked over her shoulder, smiled weakly, mounted and trotted down the lane to the front gates. Pier watched, finishing his drink. Then, head down, he turned and walked slowly back inside. China and Mattie said nothing. Finally, he spoke.

"What's for dinner?"

China took careful aim and threw a biscuit at him.

"Come on, Pier, you've got the killer. Case closed."

"Wrong. Dilly's hairdresser didn't kill Beau Paxton. But I know where to find the guy who did."

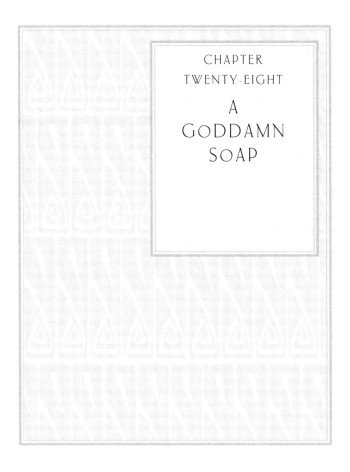

CHAPTER
TWENTY-EIGHT

A
GODDAMN
SOAP

The Learjet turned inland from the Pacific and began its descent, slicing through the thick yellow coils encircling Los Angeles like malignant entrails. Pier sat behind the pilot of the plane he had chartered while they landed at the private Garrick Airfield.

Another Learjet was readying for a takeoff; a Gulfstream taxied into position. The small terminal looked like a motel. Pier could see the District Attorney's car and driver waiting close by. Max would be inside, introducing himself to anyone of voting age.

When Pier walked in, he saw Max helping himself to coffee. He looked up and groused. "Pier, I'm supposed to be the people's candidate. The lounge of a private airport packed with rich folk's toys is not a suitable habitat for such a candidate."

"It's better than being caught on board a boat called the *Monkey Business.*"

"I'll give you that. And it is more or less on my way from Palos Verdes to the Hall of Justice. Did you fly yourself in or charter?"

"Charter. Too rusty to fly anymore. And it worries China." He helped himself to coffee, glancing at his watch.

"None of my business, Pier, but what about you and China? You could get a quiet divorce. No one would blame you."

"Can't do it, Max. China understands. And," Pier added two lumps of sugar to his coffee, "I don't want to talk about it."

Max didn't give up easily. "I'll bet Mattie makes you talk about it. She's a wise old bird."

"Mattie understands too. And she's not such an old bird. Still in her fifties. Sixty is the new middle age, according to the burgeoning numbers of people nearing their fifties. Us among them. How's Barbara?" Pier had clearly changed the subject.

Max acknowledged the change with a resigned smile. "She's fine. Well, let's get to it. What have you got that'll get me elected?"

"Eddie's sure he's found the hit man. He's on his tail now. He's stopping by later with an update on that and a couple of other things. We'll deliver the hitter to you, the media will love you, case closed. Officially."

Max looked closely at Pier. "What else? Unofficially?"

"For now, all you can do is arrest the shooter. But he'll never live to stand trial."

"Somebody big behind it all?"

Pier shrugged.

"Does that eloquent shrug mean I'm not supposed to ask more questions?"

"You won't be able to pin anything on anyone other than the shooter, so take him and get yourself elected."

The District Attorney groaned. For a moment, his shoulders sagged. "Hell, Pier, you don't mean they're making a push into L.A. again, do you?"

"The word on the street is that the hitter works for the mob. He's a freelance. Mostly out of L.A., but he's also connected to a Family in New York."

"For godsake, Pier, why would the mob want to kill the editor of a decorating magazine? It doesn't make sense."

"Eddie's sure he's found the who. Give us a little more time and we'll find the why."

"The way this case is going, I'm not sure I want to know," said Max. "We brought in Norton Birdwell last night, straight from the airport. Took him into the interrogation room. Before we could ask the first question, he broke down, cried and confessed."

"Confessed? He's saying *he* killed Beau Paxton?"

"No. Swears he doesn't know anything about that, and we more or less believe him. He confessed to running down Lars Eklund. Seems Birdwell had a few too many 'martoonis'—he actually used that word—and as he was driving away from Le Club—he still goes there, a slow learner—he saw Lars Eklund about to cross the street. It was after hours. Birdwell was drunk. No one was around. He put the pedal to the metal, aimed his car at Eklund and thud. Eklund is lying in the street, and Birdwell keeps going. Says he 'saw red,' *his words*, 'flew into a jealous rage,' *his words*, and he doesn't really remember much of anything except that he was temporarily insane. But sane enough to leave town. Eklund's going to live, so with a good attorney, Birdwell will be shopping on Rodeo Drive again in two years. If that. Didn't I tell you this case is a goddamn soap?"

"Have you questioned Jonas about his sudden trip to New York?"

"Yeh. It was airport day for us. We met Jonas' plane, too. Thought we'd surprise him. His secretary hadn't been able to get to him before we did. Started out nice and easy. Gave him the good news that his brother Seth was going to be okay. Then we eased into why did he suddenly go to New York. Well, naturally, the trip wasn't sudden. Just very confidential. He finally told us he went to see Fred Hawkins, who wants to buy *Manor House.* Jonas says he's seriously considering selling because it's such a good offer. I'd give you odds it's an offer he can't refuse. What does that do for you, pal?"

"Nice fit. Eddie says word around the bars is that the hitter sometimes works for Fred Hawkins. And I've got something else for you. Another confession. But first I have to ask a favor."

"Why doesn't this surprise me? One of your rich friends needs protection from the insensitive minions of law and order?"

"In the worst way. I promised her father I'd do what I could to help her."

"Her? Ah, Pier, please tell me it's that girl with the funny name. Milly? Tilly? Dilly! That was it. Tell me it's Dilly."

"It's Dilly. She confessed to hiring someone to kill Beau Paxton."

"Listen, I'm taking all the confessions I can get today. Why should I wait for the real McCoy when I've got a rich society girl I can send to the gas chamber?"

"Problem. Her hitter didn't do it."

"You know this for a fact, Pier? Shit, I may cry. You mean, her hit man isn't the one you've got Eddie tracking?"

One or two people in a far corner of the lounge were looking at them warily. Pier lowered his voice. "Right. Her guy isn't the one who shot Beau Paxton. Her guy called me from a phone booth. Someone at her house, maybe a maid, told him Dilly had come to see me. He wanted to know what she'd said. His story is she asked him to knock off Beau Paxton for a ton of money. They were both up to their ears in brandy. Then he heard about Beau Paxton on the news, and he thought Dilly had done it. He didn't want to betray her, so he dropped out of sight. He called me because it occurred to him Dilly might have been setting him up."

"Who the hell is this guy? Who did she hire?"

"Max, put down your coffee mug before I tell you."

"Okay, Pier. I'll play straight man. Who did Dilly hire to shoot Beau Paxton?"

"Her hairdresser."

"Her *hairdresser?*" Max's fist hit the table.

Pier leaned back on the worn leather couch. "Max, you're beautiful when you're angry."

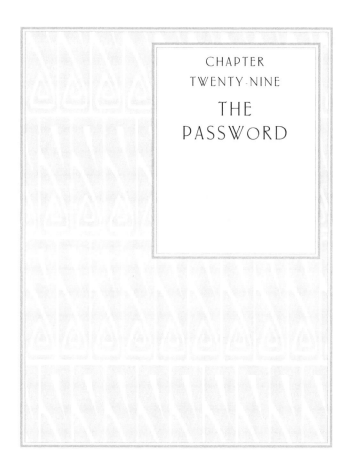

CHAPTER
TWENTY-NINE
THE
PASSWORD

"Mail-order murder."

Eddie had shifted the small pile of folders on the W-X chair to the floor and was sitting listening to Pier let off steam. "Damnit, Eddie. It's difficult enough to prove murder for hire when it's some guy who doesn't want to lose his fortune in a divorce, but how can you nail someone who can call up The Mob's Greatest Hits on a computer and place an order?"

Pier moved the folders off the Y-Z chair and sat down next to Eddie.

Pier's remark reminded Eddie of Marta. Marta had told Eddie a lot about her advanced computer class. And gradually she had told him a lot about Naldo. Before he had fled to Mexico, Naldo had liked to brag to Marta about how good he was on the computer. He hadn't realized how much he was giving away. About his complicated programs. About the mob's computer wizard, the Auditor. And his program to watch the Auditor watching him. Naldo hadn't realized how much Marta understood. When she didn't understand something, she found hackers through her own computer network to explain. She told Eddie that for a while she'd played with the idea of breaking into Naldo's computer. She would secretly watch Naldo while he watched the Auditor. But without Naldo's password, she could do nothing.

Pier sat, hands clasped behind his head, while Eddie talked. Then Pier talked. Eddie grinned and stood up. "What have we got to lose?"

Pier crossed to his desk and punched the number of a friend who had been one of the early pioneers in Silicon Valley. "This guy was a techie when they were still called nerds," he said to Eddie while he waited for his friend to come on the line. "He's way ahead of both Naldo and the Auditor."

Eddie listened while Pier explained what they wanted. "If we can break into Naldo's programs," Pier said into the telephone, "we'll have access to the Auditor's. It may be the only chance we have—a computer court administering computer justice. How about it? Do you want to give it a try?" Eddie saw Pier smile and knew the man on the other end of the line had agreed.

"I'd like to think it was the idea of justice which made him say he'd do it," Pier said after he'd hung up. "But I think it was the challenge. He wants us to try to give him some idea of what Naldo's password might be. Anything we know about Naldo. Will Marta help?"

"Maybe. You scare the hell out of her, Pier," said Eddie.

Pier raised an eyebrow. "What are you talking about? I like Marta."

"Well, intimidate, then. You know she works for the mob. You're law and order. She's crime. You're rich. She's poor. That's the way she feels."

"So you don't think she'd be willing to sit down and talk about Naldo?"

"Oh, she'd be willing. But, like I said, just scared."

"But Marta's the only one who knows Naldo."

"What about China?" Eddie began to pace. "No, I don't mean China knows Naldo," Eddie added, seeing the puzzled look on Pier's face. "What about having China talk to Marta? They only met that once at the house, but Marta talked about China for weeks afterward. Marta loves her movies. She'd do anything to please China."

"I don't know," said Pier. "Wouldn't Marta get nervous and freeze up if China starts asking her about Naldo? Unless— What if China said she wanted the information for a movie role? Mobster's wife."

"I thought China wasn't going to do any more movies."

"Marta doesn't know that," said Pier. "Let me check with China. If she's willing, we'll meet in L.A. tomorrow. Lunch. Then you and I will be called away."

Eddie Navarro eased his old Chevrolet into a parking spot between a Mercedes-Benz and a shiny red 1952 MG. He walked around his own dusty, dented machine and slapped its rear fender affectionately. It was the perfect car for his work. The shabby sedan issued no macho challenges to other drivers. It was completely inconspicuous. Even the color was ambiguous. But there was no ambiguity under the hood which housed enough jumped-up horses to take on a Ferrari.

Eddie opened the passenger door and helped Marta out. She smoothed her hair with one hand, clutching her handbag with the other. She was always nervous around Pier. It wasn't anything he did. It was who he was. The more charming he became, the harder he tried to put her at ease, the more she felt like the little half-Italian, half-Spanish bookkeeper whose late father and brother were minor Mafia minions and whose husband had fled the country.

Eddie put his arm around Marta's waist.

As they walked through the door of the restaurant, her brown eyes seemed very wide. Apprehension? Fear? Marta sighed softly and Eddie knew it was neither. Marta was ecstatic at having lunch with China.

At first Marta was awkward, hiding herself behind the menu. Then the waiter brought a phone to Pier, who spoke tersely. "Yes. Yes. No. Goodbye." After he'd hung up and apologized, he and Eddie left to "follow up on a hot lead. Sorry."

"Usually I hate it when this happens," said China, smiling warmly at Marta. "But now I'm glad. It gives me a chance to ask your advice." Marta looked startled, then awed. "You know I've retired from pictures?"

Marta nodded.

"Well, this is presumptuous, but I do know about Naldo and I hope you won't mind. You see, an old friend is going to direct. I owe him a big favor or I wouldn't even consider doing the movie. It takes place during Prohibition and it's about a gang smuggling booze in from Canada. He wants me to play the alcoholic wife of their secret boss. You know, Mr. Big. It's a great role, but I can't make up my mind."

"Oh, I think you should do it," Marta breathed.

"But I don't know what it would *feel* like. Would I think it was exciting? Glamorous? Would I be drinking because I felt trapped or what?"

Marta picked up her fork and began making patterns on the white tablecloth. "Trapped. And scared sometimes," she said, not looking at China. "Not all the time. Mostly it's just ordinary things. Going to work, shopping, making dinner, watching TV. Then he's late, or he says he's going to be gone for a few days. But Naldo was no Mr. Big."

"What was Naldo like?" China's voice was gentle. She had almost forgotten that she was asking for Pier, that her handbag held a tape recorder.

What was he like when they first met? Any pet names? And did he have pets when he was a kid? Yes, a dog. What was the dog's name? Ringo. And so on.

The waiter brought their lunch. Marta and China ate absentmindedly, China asking questions, Marta answering, telling her all about Naldo, his past and her life with him.

As Marta talked, she revealed the name of Naldo's father, names of the streets he had lived on, cities he had lived in, visited or just liked. The name of his favorite priest and the teacher who had first gotten him interested in computers, along with a list of Naldo's favorite movie stars. Marta apologetically whispered that Naldo didn't have enough class to be a fan of China's. Baseball was Naldo's favorite sport, the Dodgers his team.

China and Marta talked for over an hour. By the time the waiter told the women the check had been taken care of, a long list of possible passwords had been recorded.

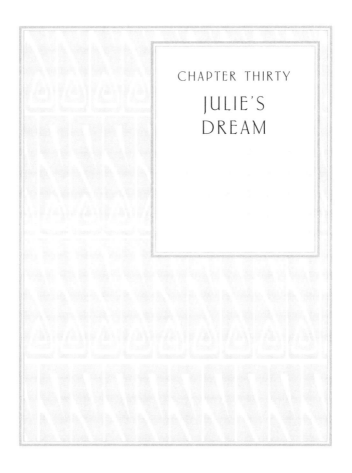

CHAPTER THIRTY
JULIE'S
DREAM

J ulie Warren slalomed skillfully through traffic on
  Sunset Boulevard wondering what the hell was going
on. Why was Maria Hawkins out from New York, invit-
ing her for an "ees secret" dinner at Spago, where everyone in town would see them? Of course, where *could* you
meet for an "ees secret" dinner? The old guard went to
Trader Vic's Sunday evenings. The movie crowd made
Morton's their own. Eclipse moved into the top ten the
minute it opened. At Spago, Wolfgang Puck's reputation brought in foodies as well as celebrities.

But, after all, where could she, Julie Warren, go without being recognized? Nowhere. She checked her lipstick with a glance in the rearview mirror. Everyone knew Julie. Or wanted to. Jody Jacobs had retired from the *Times* a few years ago and a replacement society editor hadn't been named, so Julie's column in the *L.A. Tribune* was the only game in town for those who won't eat dinner unless it's going to be written up.

Without Julie's column they would experience withdrawal pains, their cells craving the adrenaline rush triggered by the sight of their names in print. People assumed she loved her work. Oh, Julie, what fun it must be to go out every night to all those parties!

Hah. Endless food and wine and calories. The militant bores. Then up the next morning to decipher notes from the night before, write the column five days a week, then go to lunch with the ladies. They would tell her how busy they were with their personal trainers, hairdressers, masseuses and manicurists. So little time left for shopping or perhaps a committee meeting before their afternoon naps.

If she could just sell a story idea for a movie or a television series. Or transfer to cityside news or features. Anything to get away from "society." Get away from women yammering on about the insensitive demands of their rich husbands, who didn't understand that shopping was a form of meditation.

Maria Hawkins should have something really good for the column. Julie couldn't imagine why she had been chosen to be the off-the-record recipient of Maria's secret but it was altogether irresistible. Accelerating her old BMW through a yellow light, Julie wondered again what Fred Hawkins' wife had to confide. They had only met a couple of times. Julie tried to remember what she had heard about Fred and Maria Hawkins over the last year, which seemed to be about the length of anyone's history today.

It was rumored that Fred Hawkins was connected in a big way. It was also said that he tried to keep his latest wife, Maria, out of the spotlight because her behavior embarrassed him. Hawkins was supposedly shopping for a deal in L.A. A movie studio, it was rumored. Julie's mood brightened. Maybe that was the reason for this dinner. Perhaps Fred Hawkins had sent Maria to glean inside dish from Julie about the movie industry. Which executives were restive. That was easy. They all were. The town was fueled by fear.

If Fred Hawkins was smart enough to come to her for info about what was really going on, he might be smart enough to succeed in the motion picture business. And if she could put him together with the right people, she might be rewarded with a cushy job in Hawkins' studio and never have to write another newspaper column again. Heaven.

Julie made a sharp right at the light and climbed the hill up to the Spago parking lot. She and Maria would be the first people there. First? At seven o'clock they would be the only people there.

By seven-thirty, a few people had drifted in and Julie was on her second Evian with lime. She decided to give Maria Hawkins another five minutes. Then she would leave. No one kept Julie Warren waiting. At that moment she saw a white stretch limousine speeding up the steep hill. Seconds later Maria Hawkins entered wearing Chanel from the grosgrain bow in her hair to her sling back shoes.

Conservative, for once, though the bow clung like a tremulous butterfly to the teased mountain of hair and the skirt was scarcely longer than a swimsuit. Maria beamed at Julie. "Maria look like a working girl, no?"

"Not many working girls can afford a ten-thousand-dollar outfit, Maria. Of course, that depends on what kind of work the girl does."

Maria roared with laughter. She looked up at the waiter and ordered champagne, ". . . zee best French." Then she turned her attention to Julie. "Theese girls dinner, no? Fred he don't know about. Why tell zem eversing, huh?" She laughed again, leaning forward and whispering confidentially, "He ees so jealous."

A waiter brought Roederer Cristal. When he placed a champagne flute in front of Julie, she waved it away. No booze tonight. She was suspicious now. If Maria Hawkins was in L.A. on her own, maybe Fred Hawkins was not buying a movie studio. Maybe Maria was just trying to soften her up for coverage of—what? Was she going to enter the charity ball wars? Had Maria decided to start a social career in L.A. because she thought of it as off Broadway?

"Maria, let's come to the point. What is the big secret you wanted to tell me about?"

"Hokay." Maria looked around to see if anyone were listening. She made Julie promise to keep her secret off the record until Fred said it was okay to tell. Julie perked up and nodded assent. At least Fred Hawkins had some kind of involvement with the "secret" reason for this dinner, which meant it had to do with business, not charity balls.

"Hokay. I tell you, Julie. Fred want to do beeg L.A. business."

Enraptured, Julie leaned forward. "You can trust me, Maria."

Big smile. Lots of teeth. Maria sipped her champagne, smiling coyly, savoring her secret. It must be good. She would accept Maria's info off the record now in return for an exclusive on the story later.

Maria looked around again. "See, Maria was right . . ." Julie moaned softly. She refers to herself in the third person. ". . . Theez place not a crowd now. Ees early. Nobody who anybody see us. Later, action start, huh?"

"Yes, later. But not too late. We go to work early in this town.

Especially the *studio* people." Might as well see if she takes the bait.

Maria snapped, "I know zat. Fred say if he buy studio, I be in movies."

Julie's heart beat faster. She decided to come right out with it. *"Is he going to buy a studio, Maria? Is that the secret?"*

"Hoh, no."

Julie's heart sank. "No? He's not going to buy a studio?"

"No now."

Julie's heart soared again. At this rate she would go into cardiac arrest before they ordered. She proceeded carefully. "When will he buy a studio, Maria?"

Maria just shrugged. Her eyes roamed, seeking prey. The woman's attention span could be measured in nanoseconds. Julie considered her next move. The waiter returned to refill Maria's glass. He made the inevitable announcement that he would "tell" the menu whenever they were ready. Maria looked puzzled. "Tell?"

"Restaurateurs are convinced we can't read. They insist on talking menus."

"Hoh, good. I don't read, too. Beeg waste of time, you ask me."

"You'll be very happy living here, Maria. Someday."

"Soon, Julie. Ees soon." Teasing smile.

Be still my heart. Julie told the waiter to come back in a few minutes. If Maria were going to live in Los Angeles soon, mischief was afoot. And she would find out about it right now.

"Why are you and Fred moving here, Maria?" Julie's voice was firm this time. No more nonsense. It worked.

"Fred, he buy *Manor House.*"

Julie's heart sank again. Buy a house. Big deal. And how pretentious. A manor house, indeed. Julie responded wanly. "Beverly Hills or Bel Air?"

Maria lowered her head and squinted. "Wha'?"

"Where do you want your manor house? Beverly Hills or Bel Air?" Really, the woman was a bore. Julie decided to plead a headache and leave.

"Hoh! Hoh!" Maria laughed again. The restaurant was starting to fill up and a few people glanced around surreptitiously to see who was so happy. It made them nervous. Not recognizing Maria, they turned back to their goat cheese pizzas.

Maria was triumphant. "My Engleez ees better! I got it! You theenk Fred buy manor *house*. No! He buy *Manor House*. See?"

Julie suddenly did see. "Maria, are you saying Fred is buying *Manor House* magazine?" She had a scoop—and maybe a new job. Not a studio. A magazine. Of course! That was why Maria had asked her to dinner. Fred Hawkins wanted to know if she would be interested in the top spot at *Manor House.* Beau Paxton's job. He wanted a journalism star who knew everyone. Not Meg Millar. Maria was his emissary. An interesting woman. They would be friends.

"You want story?"

Julie looked at her blankly. "Story?"

"Scoop."

"Scoop?" Julie realized she must have missed part of the conversation. What was the dear woman talking about? Then she remembered the thing she had wanted so much just a few minutes before. "Oh, of course. Yes, I want the scoop."

"You not seem interested."

"Oh, I'm very interested. I'll keep this off the record for now, Maria, but then when the time comes, I want to break this story exclusively." She would dangle some bait. "I've always loved *Manor*

House. It's a wonderful magazine. Of course, I've thought for a long time that it needs a new look. A fresh approach. Beau Paxton was a dear man. Ever so sweet. Such a shame he's gone. But *Manor House* needs a woman's touch. After all, the home is still the responsibility of the woman. Feathering the nest, so to speak."

To Julie's delight, Maria bared her teeth. It seemed to be a smile. "Hoh, tha' exactly what I say to Fred. Magazine about decorating needs woman."

Julie's relief was palpable. She would have some champagne after all. The hell with her diet. They would toast her new position. Editor of *Manor House.* "We're going to be great friends, Maria."

Just as Maria was about to speak, Collin Greene appeared at their table. Julie flashed a look at him that signaled "Go away or I'll kill you." He got it. And pulled up a chair from a nearby table. Smiling at Maria, he said, "Will you give a thirsty man a sip of champagne? And tell me what you're doing in L.A.?"

Julie was furious. Collie had interrupted just as Maria was about to bring up the editorship of *Manor House.* And Maria actually seemed pleased that Collie had intruded so rudely. She would have to be sure he didn't learn anything from Maria. Julie took the offense. "More to the point, Collie, why are you here? I thought you went back to New York after the Sultan's party."

Collin Greene was delighted to hear the edge in Julie's voice. She didn't want him to find out something. He instantly decided to abandon the people he had arrived with—low-rent types anyway—and concentrate on Maria. Fred Hawkins kept her on a tight leash in New York but here she was, alone and hungry for attention. He waved to the waiter.

"More champagne, Maria?"

"Hoh, I done know eef I should but, hokay."

The hovering waiter filled their glasses and sprinted away for another bottle.

Collie raised his glass to Maria. "Now, what brings you to Los Angeles, beautiful lady?"

"Hoh, ees big secret." Julie's heart turned to stone.

CHAPTER
THIRTY-ONE

MARIA'S
BIG
SECRET

Two hours and two bottles of champagne later, Julie Warren's heart was still stone, Maria Hawkins' brain was mush and Collie Greene was still digging for Maria's secret with the instincts of a truffle hound. His enunciation was noticeably thicker. He had made the tactical error of leaving the table several times. Julie used his absences to warn Maria against telling Collie anything she didn't want printed for all the world to read. Especially Fred Hawkins. That seemed to get through to Maria. Her bravado had vanished. She was so fearful of her husband's anger, she became uncharacteristically taciturn.

Collie returned to their table and, with a bow and a flourish, kissed Maria's hand. "Why does your husband hide you from the world? You're too beautiful to be concealed, like a mistress. Maria, you could be the queen of New York society. You could be . . ." Collie's laughter began slowly, mounting until rivers of tears flowed from his already watery blue eyes. "You could be . . ." He dabbed at his wet cheeks with a cocktail napkin. ". . . the new Brooke Astor." The moment he said the name, he lost control. He couldn't stop laughing. Julie caught Maria's eye, raised a brow and glanced meaningfully at Collie. Maria frowned at him. She didn't understand why he was laughing. But she knew the joke was on her.

Everyone in Collie's circle knew about Maria. The official story, the one she had given the reporter from "W" who had come to interview her, was that she had been a model in Buenos Aires. She had been disowned by her wealthy family, Maria had said indignantly, because she had insisted on marrying for love.

"But my 'usband, he die," she had told the reporter, dabbing at her eyes with what the interviewer described as "a lace handkerchief designed especially for her by Valentino."

"I work or I starve," Maria had moaned, with one last sob before moving on to the happier story of how she had met Fred Hawkins.

What Maria had told the reporter had a kernel of truth. That was the best way. Then you didn't get too mixed up. She had been a lingerie model until her husband, a small-time drug dealer, got himself shot in a deal gone sour. Then the man who owned the lingerie company set her up in an apartment and kept her very well. When the man's wife caught them together, Maria was forcefully encouraged to leave Buenos Aires for the United States with an extensive wardrobe of lingerie, a mink coat and a few pieces of second-rate jewelry.

She also carried her late husband's address book. She didn't know if the men in New York were dealers or customers but she called them anyway. One of them invited her to a party the next night. Maria dressed very carefully. She wanted to look right for a sophisticated New York party. She didn't look right but she looked so sexy Fred Hawkins didn't care. He made his move. Maria held out. Briefly.

"The new Brooke . . ." This time Collie couldn't get the name out. Julie waited until he finally choked off his laughter, then appointed herself Maria's defender. "What on earth do you find so funny, Collie? We all admire Brooke Astor, and perhaps a few years from now, Maria will be equally revered for her charitable endeavors."

Maria liked that. "Sure. Why not? What so funny, Collie?" She waited for his answer.

Collin Greene sensed danger. He desperately willed himself to a semblance of sobriety. "It's nothing to do with you, Maria. Honestly. It's just that, when I was in the men's room, a fellow told me a joke I didn't get at the time. I just got it and couldn't stop laughing. Delayed reaction, you know. I'd tell the joke," he added, a bit too hastily, "but it's not fit for a lady to hear." His eyes shifted to Julie. "I'll tell *you* another time."

That did it. Julie moved in for the kill. "Collie, are the society ladies you write about in your column still as generous as they were before you lost so much of your syndication?" She continued with mock generosity. "Oh, not your fault, of course. Readers just aren't interested in new-rich society anymore. Paying for publicity was all part of the eighties. Quite passé in this decade." Julie thought her crisp diction contrasted nicely with the slurred words of her . . . What were they? Certainly not friends. Tablemates. Yes, that would do.

Collin Greene shook his head to clear out the muddling effects of the booze. He couldn't deny what Julie had said. The *New York Chronicle* had warned him that if any more newspapers dropped his syndicated column, they would have to replace him. And Collie knew he couldn't afford that. It wasn't the money. His father had left him and his sister trust funds providing each with lifetime incomes most people would consider substantial. But in the Manhattan circles Collie covered and cultivated, the amount was completely inadequate.

His society column, "Collie's Corner," was his only entrée to the world of wealth and its fairy-tale options. Houseguesting in Mustique, jetting to Egypt, yachting trips to the Greek islands, all his for the asking.

Asking? He didn't have to ask. The rich took numbers for their turn to present Collin Greene with offerings. Cashmere robes, jewelry, stock tips, trips, antiques, art, any of three dozen houses throughout the world, his on a moment's notice, fully staffed plus a limo or private jet for transport.

Collie had but to admire a man's suit to hear "Like it? Call my tailor. He'll do one up for you. I'll take care of it." Wink. Translation. Just keep mentioning my wife and her goddamn designer dresses in your column and I'll smother you in custom-tailored suits. Whatever it takes to keep her off my back. Everything was taken care of.

Collie hadn't bought a gift for years. When it was time for the obligatory birthday or wedding present, he checked his "Gifts In Log" and selected something reasonably appropriate to pass along, which he then duly noted in his "Gifts Out Log." Careful records were the key to pass-along success. Flowers and plants were easy. Collie had a deal with the two or three florists used by "his girls." He told the florists to let him know who ordered what but not to send him anything. "Credit me with the amount. Let it accumulate." Using his credits, Collie sent flowers whenever he wanted. No charge, and florists who cooperated were rewarded by lavish mentions in the column.

He played a similar game with jewelry. All the cuff links, 18-carat gold pens, signet rings, key chains and watches were promptly returned for store credits which he noted in a separate record, "Gifts Returned Log," listing the giver, store, time and amount of credit received. Then, when it was birthday time for one of "Collie's girls," he visited one of the jewelry stores where he had amassed credits and selected a pin or bracelet for several thousand dollars. His girls squealed like game show contestants when they opened the small packages. Collie knew there was nothing the rich like so much as an expensive gift or a freebie. Give them airline tickets and they'll go anywhere. Give the wife an expensive present and you owned her.

Not sexually, of course. That was understood. Collie's sexual preferences ran to a tough-cookie dominatrix-for-hire. Spike-heeled boots. A whip. Sometimes a dog collar. His nickname was an inside joke among high-priced hookers. Most of the husbands of his society "girlfriends" assumed he must be gay. At least they were confident he wasn't interested in their wives. They were right for the wrong reason.

If Collie had traded ink for sex, many of "his girls" would have obliged for the instant gratification of seeing their names in print. Or, even better, thinking of all their friends who were not included. That would be well worth a discreet afternoon visit to Collie's apartment. But Collie knew very well he couldn't perform without pain or humiliation. What could he do with those ladies who would carefully hang up their Chanel suits before they tiptoed into bed, closed their eyes and faked. Although some of the former call girls, especially the ones from the golden oldie days of Madam Claude's in Paris, would know exactly what he wanted. They could instantly divine any man's sexual proclivities, along with his approximate net worth, and proceed accordingly.

Had Maria a clue about him, Collie wondered. She certainly hadn't been raised by nuns. At first she had sizzled. Then she fizzled. Too much champagne. Shit. He had thought plenty of bubbly would loosen her tongue, but the opposite had happened. She became silent, almost sullen. No wonder Fred Hawkins kept her locked in the bedroom. And Collie had heard he was even tiring of her there. There was somebody new.

Collie knew he wasn't going to find out Maria's big secret this evening so he decided to return to his hotel and call for a girl to discipline him severely. He had been a very bad boy. Yet he could be worse. Why not? He took aim and returned Julie's fire. "Speaking of passé, as you were a moment ago, your column has been the only game in town for a long time. But I know for a fact the *L.A. Times* has already hired someone to cover parties who they hope will blast you right off your page."

It wasn't true at all but Collie knew Julie would be miserable until she could check it out in the morning. And that Maria. She deserved a parting shot too. "Maria, is it true your husband has a new, shall we say, *interest?*" She didn't seem to have heard him, so Collie heaved himself out of his chair. With a sneered "Good night, ladies," he left without paying the check.

Julie was furious. And sick with fear. She was sure Collie lied just to hurt her. But could she really be certain? She wanted to start checking it out. Right away, no matter how late the hour. Damn him. And her, too. Julie decided to make it clear she wasn't going to pay the enormous check, so she prompted Maria, "I think we'd better call it a night, don't you? Just sign the bill or whatever." Julie refreshed her lipstick and pushed back her chair. Maria was so drunk she seemed paralyzed. Julie decided to try one last time to get Maria to talk. "You wanted to ask me something earlier, Maria. Something about Fred's buying *Manor House* magazine."

Julie stared at Maria, challenging her to respond. To Julie's surprise, she did. "Oh, yes. Secret for now. I weel need help, Julie. You know how to be editor."

Julie gasped audibly. It was going to be alright, after all. Take that, Collin Greene. Die, you worm. I'm going to be editor of *Manor House.* "Yes, I do know how to be an editor, Maria. Is that what Fred wanted you to ask me? About being the editor of *Manor House?*"

"Maria need to know things."

Julie looked at her blankly. "What do *you* need to know?"

"Everything. I going to be editor of *Manor House.*"

Julie stared at Maria. Then she began to laugh. She thought she'd die laughing.

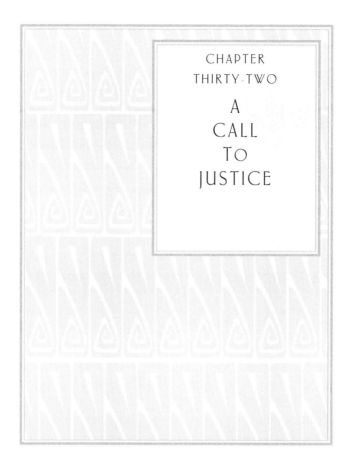

CHAPTER
THIRTY·TWO

A
CALL
TO
JUSTICE

P ier sat with Eddie at the monolithic table which had once been the center of his parents' dinner parties and which now was cluttered with lined yellow legal pads and old coffee cups jammed full of pens. Eddie was silent while Pier stared at the huge cards pinned on the bulletin board opposite the bank of French doors. His hair hung over his collar. Pier was overdue for a trim.

He studied the words printed in big block letters

on each card, trying to focus but thinking instead about the telephone call he would make to a man who could mete out justice swifter than any court in the land. It was a call he couldn't have made without the information that came out of China's lunch with Marta. By trying the names China had gathered, Pier's computer man had gotten the password: Antonia. Naldo's mother.

"Ain't that the way of it," Eddie had mused. "It always comes back to Mom." Antonia had unlocked and let them enter Naldo's programs. Then they had moved right on into the Auditor's. Now there was no doubt that the man behind the murder of Beau Paxton and the attack on Seth was Fred Hawkins.

Pier knew that the law couldn't touch Hawkins. But he knew who could. He had been sitting at the table for several hours, thinking about what he would say—the words that would irrevocably set certain actions in motion.

Realizing Pier's hesitation, Eddie dredged up a quotation learned in some long-ago classroom and bellowed into the quiet, " 'Let justice be done though heaven should fall.' " Pier decided Eddie was right.

He dialed the very private number.

The man he was calling was the head of one of America's best-known conglomerates. He was also in charge of laundering billions annually for organized crime. This was Ivy League–M.B.A. territory. Savile Row suits, rep ties, shoes handmade by Lobb's in London. It was also vast quantities of drugs as international currency and political barter. A network of respectability, charitable causes and trophy wives for a few of the more conspicuous players. This man was neither publicly conspicuous nor famous, but he was well known in the aeries of megabusiness and world governments.

He was also a man who owed his life to Pier's father. In the closing days of the war, amid rumors that Hitler had vowed suicide over surrender, the OSS had sent Pier's father into Germany. His orders were simple: keep Hitler alive for capture and questioning.

The orders were almost naive, so impossible were they. Nevertheless, he set out with his unlikely group. Two of the men were Foreign Service diplomats who had been posted in Germany before the war. Two had recently graduated from Yale. All were discovered before they reached Berlin. Three of the men died. Pier's father was wounded, but he managed to get himself and the other survivor to Switzerland and safety. Every year among the stream of Christmas cards which had flowed into Casa Arbol there had been one signed Dante. Every year it had carried the same message: "I owe you."

The secretary put Pier on hold, but within seconds Dante—now Donald—came on the line. He wasted no time on pleasantries. "What can I do?"

Pier began the story he and Eddie had prepared. He told Dante that the Family's computer wizard, the Auditor, had joined forces with Fred Hawkins to skim millions from the Family. The Auditor sent the money through a complicated web of transactions. At the end of its journey, it was sheltered safely in Fred Hawkins' accounts abroad.

"I can't tell you how I know," Pier said, as Dante began to question him. "But I can tell you how to check it out," and Pier told Dante how to verify the information.

When Pier hung up the phone, he had Dante's assurance. He knew that whatever Dante did, it would be implemented many levels down in his vast organization. Dante would give the order. He would not know, nor would he want to know, how it was carried out.

Maybe Fred Hawkins would have an accident. Maybe he'd disappear. It might even be that nothing would seem to change, but after the telephone call, Pier knew that whether it was a matter of days or of weeks, for Fred Hawkins, things would never be the same. Justice would be served.

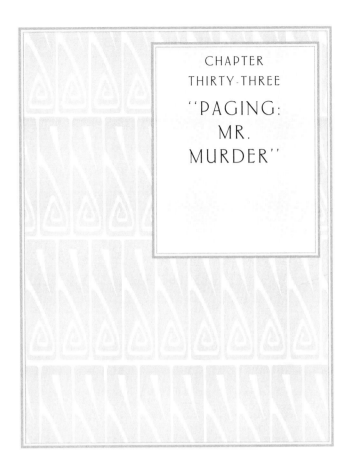

CHAPTER THIRTY-THREE
"PAGING: MR. MURDER"

Meg Millar was not pleased with the August issue of *Manor House*. Worse, she didn't know why. She stood shoeless, arms akimbo, alone long after the offices of the magazine had closed, trying to come up with a solution. As she leaned over the illuminated glass table, looking again at the rows of four-by-five color transparencies, her hair fell over one eye. Annoyed, she pulled it back behind an ear and jammed her fists into the pockets of her jacket. She had thought the answer would come, as it usually did, when she was alone in the office without the distractions of questions, telephone calls, staff problems and meetings.

August would be the first issue on Island Homes. The islands ranged from Bali to Bermuda, Samoa to Catalina. Only Manhattan was excluded. For most magazines, August and February were throw-away issues. January and July were not considered desirable either.

Advertisers didn't want to buy space in those issues. They believed people were on vacation in the summer, presumably too happy to read, and bankrupt after the holidays, dreading income tax time and too depressed to read. Even so, why, during certain months, would people stop reading the magazine they subscribed to? Meg never believed it was true. However, even though *Manor House* was enormously profitable, she still had to keep expenses down and profit margins up. Fewer pages of advertising in the down months meant fewer editorial pages. The ad-edit ratio of *Manor House* was seventy percent editorial to thirty percent advertising. Only the astronomically high *Manor House* advertising page rate made that ratio possible. Most magazines gave their readers half advertising, half editorial. At best. Forty or forty-five percent editorial was more common. Because it was more profitable.

Meg sighed and looked at the pack of cigarettes on the table. Empty. She should quit right now. She recalled Pierpont Tree's flicker of disappointment when he saw her reach into her handbag for a cigarette. Well, she would quit soon, but not tonight. Not while she was trying to figure out what was wrong with this issue. And she had nothing better to do tonight anyway. Even Mike wouldn't be around. It was poker night. He'd be playing with some old movie cronies who lived nearby. Damn. She would not let herself go back to her office to get another pack of cigarettes until she made this issue . . . *splash.*

That was it. Splash! Meg's eye swept the array of color transparencies. Why was it always something obvious that you overlooked? There weren't enough water pictures. Big, full bleed, double truck pages with glorious pictures of ocean views. It wasn't enough to *say* it was an island issue. She had to *show* it.

Now she could fix August. Tomorrow morning she and the art director would drench the pages with oceans of blue. Switching off the lights, Meg padded down the corridor toward her office where she had left her shoes. Then she heard the shouting. The angry, out-of-control sound of Jonas' voice booming from his office. She heard no other voice. He seemed to be shouting at someone on the telephone. Just as Meg was entering her office, she heard words that stopped her cold.

". . . Hawkins, you can't make your wife the editor. You'll destroy the magazine and you know it . . . What? The managing editor? Her name is Meg Millar . . . Are you crazy? Work behind the scenes? She'll walk right out the door the minute she finds out . . . Well, you *should* care, because she may also have an ownership claim on the magazine. Beau Paxton told me Meg has a letter from his late mother promising her ownership in the magazine. It might not hold up in court, but she'd probably end up with a big bucks settlement . . . because I didn't remember the goddamn letter until just now, that's why not . . .

"Settle with her, Hawkins. Meg is reasonable. And Seth will sign the papers. I'll see that he does. You've got your magazine. Just leave us alone.

"What? Wait a minute! Don't threaten me. I tell you Seth will sign. Damnit, Hawkins, I *knew* you were behind the shooting. Were you responsible for Beau, too?"

Meg stood in the doorway to her office, unable to move. So that was why Jonas had gone to New York. Because Fred Hawkins wanted to buy *Manor House.* Wanted it so much that he had gotten rid of Beau and tried to murder Seth. And if he wanted to make his wife editor of *Manor House* and Meg was in the way . . . She had to think. And she had to get out of the office fast, before Jonas realized she'd heard him.

She'd talk to Mike, or maybe she should call Pierpont Tree. The police? Not yet. After all, Jonas didn't know she was in the office. She was safe for a while. So was the letter from old Mrs. Paxton promising her ownership. She'd found it and given it to her attorney. Meg's immediate problem was to get the hell away from the office without being seen.

She could still hear Jonas' angry voice as she picked up her shoes and handbag and ran down the stairs to the lobby. Meg carefully opened the door to the garage, closing it quietly behind her. Without stopping to put on her shoes, she ran to her car. God, she thought, don't let this be like a movie when the girl's life is in danger and the car won't start.

Her hand trembled as she turned the key in the ignition. The motor started instantly. As she drove out of the garage, she saw Ben, the night watchman, waving good night.

Upstairs, Jonas Rupert paced the floor, telephone in hand, still listening to Fred Hawkins' threats, looking out the window at the lights of the city. The carefree city. There were people out there who could have dinner, watch a television show and go to bed without a worry in the world. Something he would never be able to do again. Hawkins ordered so many killings. What difference would one more make?

At that moment, he saw Meg's blue Jaguar leave the garage and turn right on Sunset. "Oh, shit! She must have heard everything!" Jonas had forgotten that Fred Hawkins was on the other end of the line.

Hawkins told Jonas what he must do. When Jonas protested,

216

Hawkins told him how easy it would be to frame *him* for the shootings of both Beau Paxton and Seth.

When Jonas still protested that he couldn't kill Meg, Hawkins said he'd try to have the matter handled by the pro who had done the other jobs. But, "It's not like calling out for pizza. My people have to find him first. We'll try to get him on his beeper . . ."

"His *beeper?* You're going to *page* him for murder?"

"Jonas, shut up! I'll have a gun delivered to you within half an hour. If we can't locate our hitter, you're going to have to do it."

The line went dead.

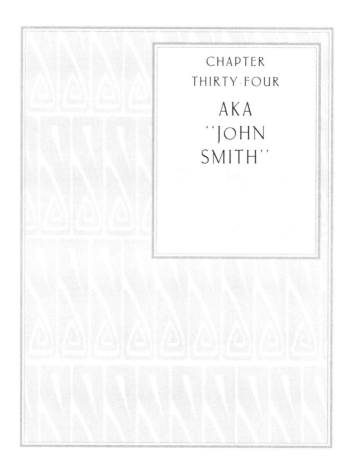

CHAPTER
THIRTY-FOUR
AKA
"JOHN
SMITH"

Eddie Navarro pulled into a vacant parking space a block behind the guy he had christened Marathon Man. The bastard never stopped walking. Eddie had tailed him since dark from Hollywood Boulevard and Vermont to Grauman's Chinese Theater, south of Sunset Boulevard to the *Manor House* offices and a brief tour of the parking garage, then back to San Vicente where he turned north.

He stopped only once, to make a call at a public

phone. Then he walked on. He always looked straight ahead. And kept moving. He was a goddamn nomad. What was that Indian tribe that never stopped running? Taramara or something like that. This guy must be a blood brother.

He hadn't been too hard to locate. Eddie's network of police pals, some retired, Vietnam vets, bartenders and crime beat reporters had soon nailed him. When Eddie had met his contact at Giovanni's Grill, the Marathon Man was sitting in a back booth by himself. He had eaten a pizza and then suddenly leapt to his feet, paid his bill and headed off down the street. Eddie had been following him ever since, taking care not to lose him. His clothes were ordinary enough. Jeans, a black shirt, Nikes and shades. He was thin, height about average, hair dark and curly. The dreadlocks were gone. So was the makeup which had made everyone think that the man who'd murdered Beau Paxton was black.

With a long, unhurried stride and a pace which was measured, steady, the Marathon Man moved on, nearing San Vicente.

Eddie followed in a pattern. Park in any zone with a vacant space; red, white, yellow, green or handicapped. Let the guy walk ahead for two blocks, then drive slowly to the next vacant parking space. Eddie figured he was on his way back to the furnished room he rented in a ramshackle house near Sunset and Vermont. The contact who had first picked up the Marathon Man had followed him home and learned that the name he'd given the landlady was "John Smith." No imagination. Or maybe he saved his imagination for his work.

Eddie was caught at an intersection when a huge moving van, trying to make a turn, had everyone in temporary gridlock. By the time he edged his way around the van, John Smith was gone. Eddie speeded up, looking for his quarry with increasing intensity.

He would continue to look, he would cruise the side streets, double back and check out stores and restaurants. But Eddie knew he'd lost him.

John Smith hadn't evaded Eddie's tail. He never knew he was being followed. He had just decided to zigzag through back alleys for a while, casing the neighborhood for future burglary possibilities. Zapping strangers paid a mint, but it wasn't steady work and a major cocaine habit made moonlighting mandatory. The neighborhood John Smith walked through was middle-income, but he knew most of the houses held easy-to-steal, easy-to-fence merchandise. He didn't hit the streets again until he saw the hospital looming over the cottages and small, shabby apartment buildings populating the surrounding blocks. He would try again.

He knew where Seth Rupert's room was located. He had visited the hospital yesterday, after a junkie orderly, one of his informants, had told him which floor Seth was on. His contact had told him where to find the supply closet. No one noticed a man wearing a white jacket and carrying a mop and a pail. He had worked his way down one corridor and up another, until he saw a policeman sitting on a metal folding chair. It was a reconnaissance visit, though he might have found a way to finish the job if one of the nurses hadn't stopped him as he mopped his way past the nurses' station.

She'd begun asking questions. He pretended he didn't speak English, shrugged and mopped. The policeman watching the exchange had begun to show interest, and so John Smith had picked up his pail and continued down the hall, out of sight. He ditched the jacket, mop and pail and got out of the hospital fast.

Going back so soon was risky, but he had to take a chance. They might move Seth, and his contact was complaining he hadn't finished the job. No body, no money. His cork-tipped ice pick was ready in his pants pocket.

He got off the elevator on the third floor and walked into the room across the hall. The patient, an old woman, stared at him. She showed no curiosity at his presence. Another invasion in a world which held no privacy. He ignored her and picked up the telephone on the table next to her bed. He dialed the nurses' station.

He whispered into the telephone, "I'm in room 301 and a man carrying a gun just went into the room across the hall. Send someone. Please," and he set the phone gently down in the cradle. John Smith waited a few minutes and then he made his way past the deserted nurses' station. The chair outside Seth Rupert's room was empty.

He pushed open the door of room 336.

The officer was inside, standing next to Seth Rupert's bed.

John Smith raced down the corridor, pushing open the steel fire door and racing down the stairs. He had landed on the first floor before the security officer, called by the policeman, came after him. John Smith ran out into the parking lot a full minute ahead of his pursuer.

He threaded through backyards and side streets to the Beverly Center mall, where he mingled with the crowds until he spotted a northbound bus on La Cienega. He boarded with a waiting group of package-laden shoppers. He'd get off at Sunset and take care of his new assignment. The Millar girl.

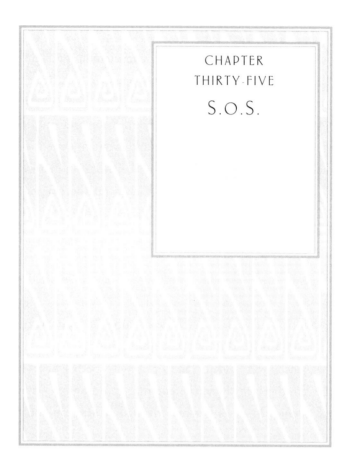

CHAPTER
THIRTY-FIVE
S.O.S.

Meg slammed the front door hard, shot the dead bolt and switched on the lights. She raced to the side door off the kitchen, checked the bolt, then the lock on each window. Cursing herself for not having an alarm system, she returned to the kitchen and switched on the bright yellow exterior light, a signal to Mike that she was in danger.

Next, Meg hurried to the telephone and left an S.O.S. message on O'Shea's answering machine. No

exaggeration there, Meg thought. It's not every day you find out someone wants to kill you.

She hung up and dialed Pierpont Tree. Even the way he said
hello was reassuring, his voice deep, confident, calm. Trying to match
his tone, Meg told Pier about Jonas' telephone conversation with Fred
Hawkins.

"Are you absolutely sure he didn't see you?" Pier asked. His voice
didn't sound quite as calm.

When Meg said she was positive, Pier hesitated and then decided. "You'll be safe tonight. I'll see to that. Don't answer the door.
In the morning, get out of town. Don't even tell your office where you
are."

Pier hung up, then called Eddie Navarro's number. He'd ask him
to watch Meg's house. He'd call Max, too, and get him to send a
patrol car to check on her through the night.

Meg made a pot of coffee. Strong. She wasn't going to sleep
anyway, so why not? Then she poured it down the sink and reached
for decaffeinated. She was already jumping out of her skin at the
slightest noise. She would buy a big dog when this was over. A fero-
cious dog. Maybe two. But when *would* this be over? And, until then,
where would she stay?

"Damnit." Meg's own voice broke the awful silence. She had la-
dled half the can of decaf directly into the glass carafe, bypass-
ing the filter completely. Pouring the coffee back into the can, she
ran water into the top of the coffeemaker and began again. This
time she concentrated and soon the coffee began to drip. Meg
lighted a cigarette and waited, watching the little red "On" light.
The house seemed eerily quiet. No wonder every little sound
made her jump. But she couldn't turn on the radio or television.
If someone tried to break in, she might not hear anything until it

was too late. Meg told herself to stop thinking like that. She was safe for now. If only she could call Seth. He would have helped her. Maybe.

Suddenly, she wondered. If Fred Hawkins had hired someone to shoot Seth, did that mean Seth wasn't involved in whatever was going on, or was Seth involved but they shot him anyway?

Was he going to want her dead, too, when he found out how much she knew? Oh, my God, if only Mike would come home. Meg tried to think where he might be playing poker, but the game moved around and she had lost track of who the players were. She prayed for Mike to lose. He left early when he was losing. Lose, Mike O'Shea, lose. Lose and come home. I'm in danger. I can feel it. Meg's hand shook as she poured from the freshly brewed pot of coffee.

The carafe was almost empty. How long had she been standing in the kitchen, drinking coffee? Almost two hours. It didn't seem possible. She felt paralyzed. Meg wanted to move but thought she might fall down if she tried.

If only she had a gun. But she had refused to listen when Mike tried to talk her into keeping an automatic in the house. If she had taken his advice, she wouldn't be so helpless. So goddamned helpless. Wasn't there anything in the house she could use as a weapon? A butcher knife. But she knew she couldn't actually stab someone. Anyway, she would be shot before she could get close enough to try. Meg kept remembering everything Jonas had said on the telephone. She could hear the blood pounding in her ears. Please, Mike, please come home. Right now. Now, Mike, *now!*

224

There was no answer from Eddie's pager. Pier tried his car telephone. Damn. A recording. "The customer is away from the telephone or out of range at this time." He called Max Steiner's number. The baby-sitter told him Mr. and Mrs. Steiner were out. Yes, she did know where they were. Mr. Steiner was receiving an award at the Century Plaza. The hotel operator told Pier she would connect him with the ballroom. Someone answered and said the District Attorney had just begun his speech. He would try to get a message to Mr. Steiner later. He could promise no more.

Pier looked at his watch again and checked the report Eddie had given him with Meg's address. If he left right away it would be at least an hour and a half before he reached her house. Goddamn it. Well, it was better than sitting around trying to reach Eddie. Pier rang Mattie, told her where he was going and why.

He grabbed his jacket, took an automatic from his desk, checked that it was loaded and grabbed a shotgun from a closet. He stashed the weapons under the Rover's car seat. He would keep trying to reach Eddie.

Pier hoped he was wrong. But his gut told him he had good reason to worry. Jonas could have seen her leaving the office. He'd suspect that she'd heard his telephone conversation with Fred Hawkins. Could Jonas Rupert actually go after Meg with intent to murder? Would he have a gun? He might.

But Pier was more worried about the original hit man. Eddie said he used the name John Smith. If Eddie had a tight tail on John Smith, Meg would be alright. Eddie would never let him get to her. But unexpected things could happen to even the best tracker. He called Eddie again on the car phone. Still no answer.

Pier knew from Meg's voice that she was in a state of shock. When that wore off, she would be in a state of terror. He hoped he could reach her before that happened. Or Eddie could. O'Shea, Meg's friend next door, was in a wheelchair. Not likely he could do much against a professional hit man or a frightened rat like Jonas Rupert. O'Shea may have been a great movie director, but this wasn't make-believe.

Maria Hawkins was still hung over. She pulled down the window shade to block out the glare from the airplane's wing. The first time she went to bed with Fred she told him it was her first orgasm. She had been frigid before him. He was *fantasteek.* Fred bought her a diamond pin the next day. He had bought her more and more jewelry, always telling her that he loved her and wanted to marry her, but that his wife would never give him a divorce.

Then his wife sued *him* for divorce.

Two months after the divorce was final, Maria signed a pre-nuptial agreement and became Mrs. Hawkins. It was a while before she realized her new husband was involved with the mob. Not that she cared. Maria just realized she would have to be very careful.

Maria had been flabbergasted when Fred announced she was going to be the editor of *Manor House.* She would live in Los Angeles. He would fly out to see her as often as he could. Maria knew something was up. That bastard Collie had known something. Fred wanted her out of town because he had another woman. *Sonofa-beetch.*

226

Following his speech, surrounded by well-wishers, Max Steiner accepted congratulations as he moved toward the exit. The manager of the hotel ballroom had given him Pier's message. Max put it in his pocket. He would return the call later. There were still people waiting to talk to him. Most of them were contributors, or potential contributors, to his campaign. A few minutes wouldn't matter that much. They were all voters.

China was looking at the new art auction catalog from New York. She had never found quite the right thing to hang on the wall opposite the fireplace. Maybe she should just leave it as it was. Art was demanding. It compelled you to look at it, exercising a kind of tyranny. But still she kept turning the pages of the catalog, stopping to study one painting, which she thought might be compatible with her folk art and primitive furniture, grimacing and shaking her head at another.

Pier was late for dinner. Actually, China couldn't remember if he were coming to her house or not. Sometimes, when he was working on a case, he might go somewhere in the middle of the night, leaving a message for her with Mattie. She might not hear from him for days. It drove her crazy with worry, though she'd never told Pier. But this time they were working together. She was part of it. China suddenly felt uneasy. Was there danger she didn't know about?

She called Pier's number. Mattie told her where he had gone. "Oh, God, Mattie—a damsel in distress. If he's hurt because of that Millar girl, I'll kill her myself. Do you think I should drive in too? Maybe I could help."

"This is no movie. Forget it. Come on over and eat. I made

chicken pot pie. We'll play double solitaire till we hear from him. But don't walk. You drive yourself over, you hear? There's a full moon. All the crazies are going to come out and howl."

China understood perfectly. She had played the lead in the classic *Creature of the Night.*

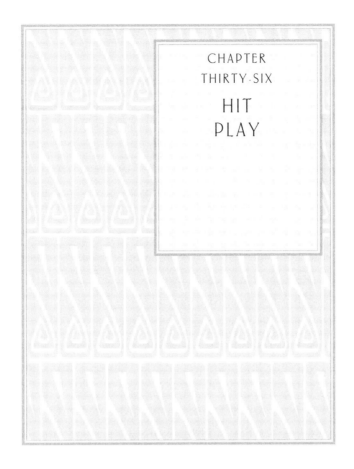

CHAPTER
THIRTY-SIX
HIT
PLAY

Meg screamed when she heard the sound. Loud banging at the front door. Then a male voice. "Open up, it's the police." For a moment, she couldn't move. The release from fear was almost ecstasy. A policeman! She was safe. Pier must have called them. But would they bang on the door like that? Meg remembered Pier's warning. How could she be certain the man knocking was a police officer? She couldn't be sure without opening the door and looking at his badge. But if she opened the door, he could push her back inside or shoot her where she stood. Meg decided.

She tiptoed into the kitchen. She would go out the side door, move along the house to the front corner and see who was there. She unbolted the door and stepped outside.

The door squeaked slightly when she closed it, but Meg knew it couldn't be heard over the renewed banging. Crouching in the shadows, she moved forward steadily. Meg had almost reached the corner of the house when the man's voice again commanded that she open up for the police. She realized he didn't care if the entire neighborhood heard him. So it must be a policeman.

Inches from her goal, Meg saw all the lights go on in the house across the street. The noise had finally attracted the attention of a neighbor. It was the Harrisons' house. They had moved in just a month ago, the first yuppies on the block. Did yuppies have guns?

Meg flattened herself against the stucco wall. Slowly, slowly, she peered around the corner. And froze. It wasn't a policeman. It was a man wearing jeans and a black T-shirt, and he was pointing a gun directly at the front door. If she had opened that door, she would already be dead. Just as she drew back, the man turned his head. He looked directly at Meg.

She lost control. Screaming, she reversed course and ran toward the backyard and the safety of darkness. She heard two thuds. The shots had been close. She kept running, turning abruptly into Mike O'Shea's backyard. If she could circle around his house to the street, she might be able to get to a neighbor or a passing car.

Meg could hear footsteps pounding behind her. He was moving fast. Much faster than she could run. Without thinking, she threw herself into the bushes. Meg held her breath, forced her mind to go blank. Her fear seemed so palpable it might form a beacon leading him directly to her hiding place.

The footsteps passed. He hadn't seen her. But he would surely double back when he realized she wasn't anywhere in sight. He would know she couldn't run fast enough to have gotten far. Meg raised her head slightly and looked through the bushes. She would have to hide somewhere else. But where? He was looking up and down the street, then back to the dark bushes between the two houses where she was hiding. It was too late to move. It was all over.

Meg had only a split second to decide. If she stayed where she was, she would die in hiding like an animal. Maybe someone patrolling for the neighborhood watch would be out on the street. They had piercing police whistles. One blast was a signal for the neighbors to come and help.

Suddenly, Meg heard a male voice shouting. It was Bob Harrison, the blessed yuppie across the street. He called out, "Hey, mister, what are you doing?"

The shooter wheeled around, holding his gun behind him, looked over and answered, almost casually, "Nothing, man. I'm with a private security service. I'll show you my I.D."

"We called the police. You can show it to them."

The shooter let his arm drop back to his side and started to raise the gun. Meg knew she had to act. She couldn't let an innocent man be killed because of her. She stood and walked out of the shadows, toward the street. At first the man seemed not to believe what he was seeing. He paused. Then he turned and aimed the gun at her. The shot nicked her arm.

Two more shots sounded. The rest seemed to happen all at once. A big car, horn blaring, jumped the curb and sideswiped the gunman. Pier jumped out just as Mike O'Shea, whose poker game had been just three houses away, wheeled down the sidewalk, gun in hand. Another car braked hard at the curb and a tough-looking man got out. He had a gun too.

Meg heard Pier yell, "Eddie, he's down but he's armed. Cover me."

Mike O'Shea's voice boomed from his motorized wheelchair, "You're already covered, asshole. I shot the fucker. If he moves an inch, I'll blow his head off." O'Shea called out to Meg without taking his eyes from the still figure lying on the sidewalk. "You okay, darlin'?"

Meg's voice was barely audible. "I'm okay, Mike." Then she fell to the ground, holding her arm.

Another car pulled up and a man called to her through the open window, "Meg, are you alright?"

Meg looked up, dazed, toward the familiar voice. It was Jonas. She could only nod. He revved his motor and raced into the night.

Eddie, gun aimed at the hit man's head, asked Pier, "Want me to go after him?"

"No. We can find him later," Pier replied, moving slowly toward the downed man. Then a spotlight hit him. "Hold it right there, mister! Police!" A black and white patrol car, red lights flashing, came to a stop behind Eddie's car. Two police officers got out, guns pointed at Pier. "Drop it, mister." Pier let his gun fall out of his hand.

"Harry, look out. There's another one." The taller of the two officers turned his gun on Eddie Navarro. "You, too, mister, drop it." Eddie's eyes met Pier's, then he tossed his gun on the lawn. The next voice was Mike O'Shea's. "Hey, don't think I'm invisible because I'm in a wheelchair. I'm the one who shot that bozo. He was shooting at the girl."

Startled, both policemen stared at the angry man who seemed too big for his wheelchair. Then the tall policeman recognized him.

"Is that you, Mike O'Shea? Hey, I was a kid extra in one of your movies. What the hell is going on here?"

"The one flat on the sidewalk was trying to kill the girl over there. The big man who dropped his gun is a private dick. He's working with the D.A. I don't know who the hell the other guy is."

"He works for me," Pier interjected. Hands up, he turned slowly to face the two officers, whose guns were still pointed in his general direction. "Officer, I ran onto the sidewalk because the guy on the ground is a professional hit man. His gun was aiming at the girl. I don't know if he's dead, alive or playing possum."

No one saw the movement. But they heard the shot. The tall policeman went down. His partner hit the ground, screamed, "HALT!" and took aim at the running man. His first shot hit the shoulder. His second tore into the back of the man's head and blood gushed over the sidewalk.

"The sonuvabitch!" The second officer kneeled beside his partner. "Are you okay?"

The wounded man growled, "Yeah. Did you get the bastard?"

"Damn straight. He's had it. I'll radio for an ambulance." He looked around. "Hey, O'Shea, stay with my partner, okay?"

O'Shea looked over at Meg, stricken, staring at the still bleeding figure, one hand on her arm. "Meg, don't look at him. I'll be with you in a minute." When Meg nodded, he pressed a button and wheeled himself toward the fallen officer. Eddie Navarro bent down to get a better look at the dead man. His face was streaked with blood. The Marathon Man at rest.

Pier went to Meg and sat next to her on the lawn. "It's alright now, Meg. You were very brave. But why were you walking toward him?"

"He tried to trick my neighbor across the street. I had to let him see me or he would have killed him. Then shots and your car came from out of nowhere and Mike was there and—" Meg sounded almost apologetic. "My arm."

Pier looked down at Meg and saw her face turn ashen just before she fainted.

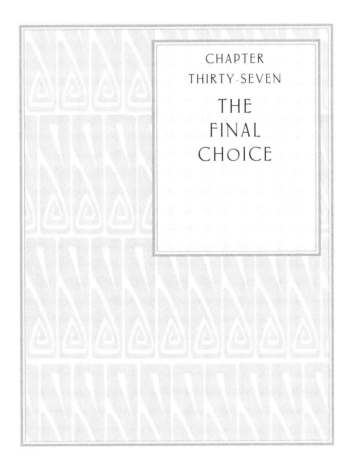

CHAPTER
THIRTY-SEVEN

THE
FINAL
CHOICE

In his room at Casa Arbol, Pier stirred amid the antique linens in the huge four poster bed. Panels of brocade hung from each poster, keeping drafts at bay on chilly nights. As Pier awakened, he reached for China. But the bed was empty. Then he remembered. The gun pointed at Meg, the bloody corpse, the wounded policeman. He stared for a while at the stenciled beams spanning the high ceiling. Pale moonlight seeped through the curtains as Pier gradually became alert.

Groaning softly, he looked at the bedside clock and realized he had slept the day away. No wonder. It had been a long night.

The detectives assigned to the Beau Paxton case had arrived shortly after the ambulance. They had ushered everyone into Meg's living room, where she had told them every word she could recall of Jonas' telephone conversation with Fred Hawkins while they bandaged her arm.

Mike O'Shea was next. The detectives had treated him with deference. O'Shea, vividly angry and drolly amusing in turn, had given them his statement. Back in the spotlight, O'Shea liked the shine.

The detectives had been rougher in their approach to Eddie until he told them he had once been an LAPD cop. By the time he gave them the address where "John Smith" had lived and the bars where he'd hung out, they were best buddies.

Max had been contacted by one of the officers at the scene and had said that he'd handle Pier himself. So the detectives wrote down what Pier told them, that John Smith was a professional hit man, and departed, leaving behind a policeman to guard Meg. It wasn't likely Jonas Rupert would return, but they weren't taking any chances.

One guard wasn't good enough for Mike. He announced his intention of staying on while Meg slept. With both guns resting across his lap, he wheeled his chair over to the couch, where Meg, her nervous energy played out, lay with her eyes closed. Mike made a thumbs-up sign as Pier and Eddie eased themselves out the door.

Pier drove the old Bentley around Meg's neighborhood, looking for a twenty-four-hour coffee shop, while Eddie tried to apologize for losing the tail on John Smith. Now he was John Doe with a tag on his toe, chilling in the county morgue.

"Have you noticed the way life reduces itself to a series of clichés, Eddie?" Pier asked, swinging into a parking spot next to a neon sign

236

whose broken lights promised MEAL- SERV-D 24 HOURS A -AY. "Water under the bridge. Bury the past. What's done is done. They're clichés because they're true."

They ordered from a waitress who didn't bother to conceal her yawns. Too tired to talk, they slumped in the booth until she returned with coffee that had been too long in the pot. The sausages were cold, the eggs overcooked. They ate greedily.

Eddie piled more jam on his toast. Holding it out, he asked Pier, "Who eats grape jam? Answer: no one. So why does every coffee shop have these little packets of grape jam when people only want straw-berry?"

"Ask me something easy."

"Okay. What about Fred Hawkins? He ordered up two murders. Meg would have been the third if everybody hadn't arrived like the Marx Brothers, honking, shooting and running over people. What will your corporate mystery man, Dante, do about Hawkins?"

Pier explained that when Dante's people checked the information Pier had given him, they would find the "evidence" Pier's computer expert had planted in the Auditor's accounts. They would discover that Hawkins had been skimming hundreds of millions of the mob's money and wire-transferring it all over the world. The money, when it came to rest, was in Fred Hawkins' Swiss bank accounts.

Eddie thoughtfully chewed on his toast. "Now all we have to do is stay tuned for reports on Mr. Hawkins' health. Definitely terminal, one way or another."

Pier looked at his watch. It was six A.M. He pushed his chair back. "I'm going to call Max. If he's not up yet, he will be."

Eddie spent the time Pier was gone attempting to get the wait-ress' attention. He thought maybe he could trade two grape jellies for one strawberry jam. He couldn't. They were out of strawberry.

"What's Max got?" Eddie asked as Pier returned.

"Did you ever meet Marta's brother?"

Eddie shook his head, wondering what that had to do with anything.

"Is she close to him?"

Eddie shook his head again. "She hasn't seen him in a long time. He's got—" Eddie stopped. He had been going to say "problems," which badly understated what was wrong with Gino. "Gino's a dope dealer. And a user. He works for the mob. When he was strung out, he'd make Marta give him money. When she stopped, he started stealing from her. As far as she's concerned, he's dead. Why?"

"She's right. Really right. Now he's dead. The man we were calling John Smith? Your Marathon Man? His fingerprints are on file. Eddie, it was Marta's brother, Gino."

Eddie didn't look at Pier. He picked up the triangle of toast which was left on his plate and attempted to fold it in half. When he finally looked up, it was to say, "The sonofabitch. Small world, huh? Guess I've got to tell Marta."

Pier nodded.

Eddie shrugged. "I'm glad he's dead."

Pier, thinking of the lengthy trial that might have been, nodded.

Eddie unfolded his toast and dropped it back on his plate. "What about Naldo?"

"Nothing tied to him, but Dante's people will shut him down and keep a watch on him. The good thing about all this, Eddie, is that Dante thinks that I did *him* a favor. Said thanks, he owes me twice now. Give me a little time. I can probably get Marta out of the Family operation. Then she should have no problem divorcing Naldo."

"Well, that's something," said Eddie. "Maybe I'll make an honest woman of her." And be her family, he thought. Marta might have disowned her brother, but the news of his death would still be a blow. She would feel alone in the world. But he would be there for her. Then Eddie remembered another player. "What about Jonas Rupert?"

Pier conceded, "That's tough. He didn't actually *do* a goddamn thing. All the police have is Meg's statement about what Jonas said to Fred Hawkins. It's hearsay. It wouldn't even justify a warrant for his arrest. But he does have those huge debts the mob planted in the bank's computer. That's one thing we did *not* have our computer guy change.

"We can't get Jonas legally, but he's going to need money to pay off those so-called loans. Can you get to him before the police pick him up? Explain why he should sell out to his brother and move far away." Pier signaled to the waitress for the check.

"I almost forgot, Pier, what the hell happened to Norton Birdwell? There's something about that guy that makes him forgettable."

"He's being held without bail. Mr. Birdwell is not considered trustworthy in law enforcement circles. He's charged with attempted murder. An expensive attorney will get the charge reduced to hit-and-run, then get him off with a stiff fine and a stern reprimand."

"Crime of passion defense?"

"Plus temporary insanity and generally bad night vision."

"And the guy he hit, Lars Eklund?"

"He will live to decorate again. Max Steiner will win the election by a landslide. Seth will recover. Meg will be editor and part owner of *Manor House.* Dilly will dally with someone new. And me, I plan to go home to China and live happily ever after."

And I have, thought Pier, as China came through the bedroom door carrying a tray and wearing a smile that awakened him fully. She placed the tray on the bedside table and dropped her silk robe to the floor. "Maybe I shouldn't. After all, I work for you now. You can't expect me to go to bed with you." China slipped under the covers. "If you fire me in the morning, I'll sue you for sexual harassment."

"You wouldn't do that to your partner, would you, ma'am?"

"You mean it? We're really going to be partners? Like Nick and Nora?"

"We'll even buy a dog."

As you drive north on Stone Canyon Road, turning left just before the Hotel Bel-Air, the narrow road forks. If you were to veer left, driving through the darkness created by the tall trees, you would pass a Tudor mansion, but you wouldn't know it. The high stone wall and solid bronze gates hide the enormous house from the road. Two guards patrol the inner perimeter, attack dogs heeling each step. Few people are allowed to pass the twenty-four-hour guards in the gatehouse and drive the curving half mile up to the house. Even when the gates do open to let a car through, its progress is monitored on a computer screen. The surveillance system is state of the art, and even the FBI has been unable to penetrate it, though they have tried for years.

No newspaper investigation of Sherman Morhaus—and there have been many—has uncovered any concrete link between the reclusive attorney and organized crime. Nevertheless, it is known that Morhaus is the person all the Families turn to when they need major political or legal advice. He can fix anything with a phone call, even a President.

The huge mahogany desk in the traditional book-lined study could have belonged to a banker. In a way, it does. Morhaus has unlimited funds at his disposal. An international drug network sluices money through a series of bank accounts, from Liechtenstein to the offshore islands, before it is considered clean enough to help swing an election. Governors and senators invariably accept his calls, trusting his discretion and his secure telephone line. Fat envelopes of cash, couriered to the appropriate source, have solved prickly problems for more than one Morhaus client.

Sherman Morhaus slouched in his desk chair, leaning his leonine head on one hand, his elbow resting on the desk. His ruddy face was puffy from lack of sleep. Sleep was a waste of time. He wanted to be on the telephone day and night, doing deals, granting favors, gathering useful information, collecting debts. He was a heavyset man, once muscular, now running to fat.

He nursed a brandy and answered one of his private phones. An automatic scrambler clicked on, and no one listening in would have heard him say, "What is it, Dante?"

"I just received a call concerning Fred Hawkins. It will be necessary to deal with a problem he made for us."

Morhaus listened as Dante explained. When Dante finished, he frowned at the betrayal by Hawkins and the Auditor. But he actually smiled when he heard Dante's brilliant solution.

They hung up simultaneously. Everything would be taken care of. Handled the modern way. Fixed in the Morhaus manner.

Paige Rense plotted and executed the rise of *Architectural Digest* to the pinnacle it sits on today, the top of the highly competitive field of international design publications. She has also edited eleven *Architectural Digest* books, including *The Worlds of . . .* series, and she is the author of *Decorating for Celebrities.* A longtime resident of Santa Barbara, Rense now divides her time between Los Angeles, New York and Vermont, where she lives with her husband, the artist Kenneth Noland.